W9-DEK-632

THE
WEAPON

THE WEAPON

BY

HEATHER HOPKINS

VANTAGEPress

Cover design by Molly M. Black

Vantage Press and the Vantage Press colophon
are registered trademarks of Vantage Press, Inc.

FIRST EDITION

All rights reserved, including the right of
reproduction in whole or in part in any form.

Copyright © 2012 by Heather Hopkins

Published by Vantage Press, Inc.
419 Park Ave. South, New York, NY 10016

Manufactured in the United States of America
ISBN: 978-0533-164769

Library of Congress Catalog Card No: 2011909408

0 9 8 7 6 5 4 3 2 1

To my husband Chris and my children

Jackson, Taylor, and Logan.

You are proof dreams do come true!

PROLOGUE

IF NOT FOR his knee, Dr. Dmitri Volkhov might never have become a killer. He enjoyed playing with this idea, spinning off possibilities from that exact moment when he felt his ligaments tear away from his bone. He was a world-class chess player, and, like a chess game, he loved tracing his life and the lives of those he'd come in contact with—through his decision to study science at Leningrad State—to working for the KGB—to designing black-ops radios and televisions—to falling in love with a girl who did not love him—to creating tiny lethal devices—to thirty-five intentional deaths, and thousands of unintentional ones—to being here, in this humid South American jungle, surrounded by the next twenty men he would kill. He imagined his life with forks in the road, forks that might have kept families together, forks that might have saved lives. What if the girl had loved him? What if he had never touched a circuit board? What if he'd been allowed to stay with the Bolshoi as an instructor? What if the KGB had killed him at the moment they realized he was beyond their control? In his mind, the spiderweb of chance stretched deliciously farther into an infinity of possibilities. The African country suddenly without a royal family? The dirty bank without a CEO? The doomed trust fund environmentalists on their sinking boat? For him, the tearing of his knee was a perfect example of the part that fate and chaos play. One bad turn, one split second of pressure against a tiny, overstrained ligament, and—Pow!—his teenage rise at the Bolshoi was over, and something much darker moved into its place. Dr. Volkhov wished he could discuss his ideas with the man standing in front of him. He thought, how interesting, the pre-history of this man's impending death.

"Here is the tower you asked about," said the man. The radio tower stood in front of them, a small concrete box with a large satellite dish on top, all by itself in a tiny clearing in an unnamed jungle. The man called himself El Diablo. Dr. Volkhov had no idea what his real name was. He didn't care. El Diablo was an up-and-coming heroin dealer. The only important thing was that he had power in this lawless, backwater country. He dressed like a child's idea of a pirate, and, in fact, he was still in his teens. A long scar ran from his ear to his Adam's apple, and he wore a clicking necklace made from the bleached spinal bones of his enemies. Dr. Volkhov had helped him acquire the last two—a government judge and the preteen daughter of a drug rival. The necklace was tasteless and stupid—a prop from a horror movie. Even so, El Diablo had proven just as useful as Dr. Volkhov had hoped. He was Dr. Volkhov's hammer—powerful in the hand of his master, too dense to notice his own head was being used to beat down the necessary nail.

"It's perfect. I'm impressed," said Dr. Volkhov.

El Diablo grinned like a child performing in front of his

father. "I told you—this country is mine!" shouted El Diablo. His men were spread out around the clearing, leaning against their jeeps in the hot noon sun. They were young gangsters like El Diablo. Bored and restless, they drank sodas or played with their assault rifles and knives. The potbellied Russian clearly did not scare them at all. Dr. Volkhov also found this interesting.

"You're the only one who knows this is here? I don't want my work to be disturbed," asked Dr. Volkhov.

"Of course! You can use it for whatever you want. Eventually I am going to use it as a relay for my television stations. For now, it's yours. You worry too much—I didn't tell anybody," said El Diablo. His voice was sunny and buoyant. A third enemy was lying in a tub of quicklime back at his hacienda—another gift from Dr. Volkhov.

"Did your men move in all the equipment I asked for? The water? The food? The generators?"

"It was easy! I threw in a few cases of vodka as a gift! You want some girls, too? How about an American movie star for you? A nice one! Maybe that pretty brunette with the long legs, from the cop movie. She looks Russian to me!" El Diablo laughed. His youthful hubris made him easy to manipulate. If Dr. Volkhov had asked for a nuclear bomb, El Diablo would have given it to him just to prove that he could. He never questioned the doctor as to why he wanted the equipment or why he wanted to find an empty relay station to work in far from any village. El Diablo thought the Old Russian was under his control, his own personal Angel of Death. Others much more intelligent and experienced than El Diablo had made the same mistake.

"Well, that's it then," said Dr. Volkhov. He reached into his duffle bag. "This radio is linked to the micro bombs you asked me to set. Make sure you trigger them at a time when the target is within the kill zone, and I would suggest you spread them out over several days. The micro bombs use intense sound waves to kill. When they detonate, there will be a high-pitched whine, but otherwise, they're designed to leave no useable trace. The victims will suffer a nice cerebral hemorrhage and a little bleeding from the ears—but nothing more. A miracle. *Dios mio!*"

El Diablo took the radio from Dr. Volkhov's fingers. He practically petted it like a dog. "I like this. People will be more scared of me than God! I can kill them without them knowing how I do it. I may need you again," said El Diablo.

"You and your men are the only ones who know where to find me," said Dr. Volkhov, smiling cryptically as if he had just made a very good joke.

For a moment, El Diablo seemed to sense something. He hadn't gotten to be the head of the most powerful local drug gang for nothing. But things had been going very well for him since meeting Dr. Volkhov, and he was very young. His ego soon won out over his instinct. "El Diablo will rule this world!" he shouted at the trees. Two parrots spun off into the sky. His men looked over and smiled under their sunglasses. El Diablo's gang was untouchable. They knew they were meant to rule.

"Indeed," answered Dr. Volkhov, his voice flat, with a barely discernible trace of sarcasm.

El Diablo blinked in surprise, his head tilted to the side like a dog unsure of whether he had just heard a far-off bark. "You doubt me?" he asked. His hand rested against the hilt of the knife on his belt.

Dr. Volkhov continued to look at him without concern. "Not at all. But I believe control is one of the many things God chose to withhold from his Creation."

El Diablo leaned back against his jeep and looked at the burning white sky. His necklace clicked through his fingers like a rosary. Finally, he said, "You are a strange man. You're lucky you're under my protection."

"I appreciate your beneficence," said Dr. Volkhov, nodding seriously. He felt around in his coat pockets as if he were looking for something. "Now, if you could excuse me, I must get to work."

El Diablo sized up the small man standing before him one final time. He seemed old and weak—a fugitive from his own country. A bad cold could kill him. Let him have his tough talk. El Diablo laughed and waved his hand—it made him feel good to be so generous. Then he and his men piled into their jeeps. As they turned around in the clearing, Dr. Volkhov carefully slipped two earplugs into his ears and pulled out his own detonator. The jeeps pulled away. Suddenly, several birds and animals dropped from the trees and sky, plummeting to the ground like rocks. The jeeps swerved off the road in half a dozen directions, smashing into the trees or tumbling onto their roofs in the ditch. When it was over, the bodies of several of El Diablo's men lay halfway through the jeeps' smashed windshields, blood gushing from their ears, their dead eyes wide open in disbelief and pain. Nothing moved, except for the steam coming from one of the jeep's smashed radiators.

Dr. Volkhov popped the plugs from his ears. At his feet lay a small blue Chilean plover. It was an extremely rare bird, endangered by the deforestation of the surrounding jungle. Possibly this was one of the last. If it hadn't flown into this clearing, its species might not have ended. Dr. Volkhov considered the possibilities as if he were working a new chess problem.

He'd spent the morning rigging his new killing devices into El Diablo's jeeps instead of planting them in the homes of El Diablo's enemies. The detonator he had given to El Diablo was a fake, nothing more than glued-together pieces of a portable radio. If anyone ever found the wreckage, no one would know what killed El Diablo and his men. But no one would ever find the wreckage. Everyone who knew that Dr. Volkhov was in this jungle—now was dead.

THE

WEAPON

1

VERONICA STONE STOOD behind the podium, looking over the crowd of CEOs and government bureaucrats in front of her. She liked the effect her appearance had on the room. As usual, the conference was ninety-eight percent men, and every one of them was staring at her and fiddling with his wedding ring. As the leading technologist in the world, and because she studiously kept pictures of herself out of trade magazines and newspapers, most people assumed someone as brilliant and successful as she was would look like a female Bill Gates. Veronica was quite the contrary. She was tall, raven-haired, and curvaceous, with startling ice-blue eyes and the classic features of a silent film star. In fact, when people saw her on the street, they assumed she was a model or a movie actress. She kept her picture under wraps. When she was starting StoneCorp, the industry and the stock market would have never taken her seriously if they knew what she looked like. Besides, keeping her appearance mysterious heightened the shock and opened up company wallets. Veronica took a long sip from her water glass, smiling over it to accentuate the suppleness of her lips. She guessed that the pathetic, fidgeting men in the front would make passes at her later at the reception. The conference had been boring, as usual.

She continued reciting her speech from memory, having decided long ago that notes were beneath her. "You might have heard of this. In 1872, near Talcott, West Virginia, John Henry, a black steel driver for the Chesapeake and Ohio Railroad, entered a contest with a steam drill. Stream drills were a new technology, unknown to the men cutting through mountains of shale with their bare hands all the way from where we sit here, in air-conditioned comfort in Washington, D.C., to Cincinnati, Ohio. That morning, John Henry, the strongest man on the line, and his shaker, the man who risked death by placing the bit in front of John Henry's hammer, lined up alongside Charles Burleigh's new drill. Burleigh, a carpet-bagger salesman in a new top hat, had set up the contest. Unless John Henry beat Burleigh's drill, the railroad would buy the new machines, and the infernal technology would make steel drivers and shakers obsolete."

The crowd was rapt, as usual but as Veronica scanned the room in pleasure, she noticed a Japanese gentleman she didn't recognize glance at his wristwatch. The platinum and dia-mond-studded band shot the room's lights back at her in a fan of color. The man was dressed in an extremely expensive suit, older, with a white crew cut and the shrewd gaze of someone who was no longer capable of surprise, or of being put off-guard by Veronica's looks. He leaned back in his chair and held something up to his ear, chatting amiably into it as if he were sitting alone in his back garden. Everyone was so busy staring at her, they failed to notice this man. He was talking into a cell phone the size of a quarter. She'd never seen anything like it.

She took an ice cube from her glass with her lips and let it drop back into the water. The Japanese man was lost in his conversation and failed to see it. The man next to him dropped his fork. Veronica continued. "The gun went off and John Henry hammered, he and his shaker moving faster than wind, their faces sweaty, their muscles tensing and relaxing, faster and faster, their cheeks billowing, their hearts thundering in unison, the two of them turning the shale to dust. The machine followed woefully behind them, spitting smoke and fire, the salesman riding it like a mechanical bull." She looked up again. This was her favorite portion of the speech, the one she practiced on Alex. The men in the crowd were practically drooling over their filet mignon. If they were going to look at her as a sex object, she might as well use it to wrap them up in knots until they were willing to sign over every contract and project they had to StoneCorp. The Japanese man was still on his phone. Veronica fought the urge to throw her water glass. She wasn't used to people ignoring her.

Veronica continued to glare at the man's phone. "Finally, John Henry pounded in his last spike. He'd tunneled through his portion of the mountain. The machine was still far behind, coughing clouds of sparks and black dust. The railroad men around him cheered and clapped, throwing their hammers and spikes in the air, while the salesman stomped on his hat. The machine was beaten. They were saved. Human blood, muscle, and bone had beaten it. It was clear the new technology was no match for a good, strong man. Once again, the human had proved himself unsurpassable and irreplaceable—better than any spiritless hunk of bolts and steel! Nothing could beat a living, breathing man!" exclaimed Veronica. She paused. The crowd glanced around at each other, unclear whether they had missed something. What kind of speech was this for a conference on cutting edge technology? A few of them looked at their list of speakers. Had they made a mistake? Was this some Luddite environmental activist who had broken into the conference? She *had* seemed too beautiful to be the famous Veronica Stone.

Veronica smiled. "Then John Henry looked around him one last time. He nodded sadly at his friends, his shaker, and the tunnel he'd made through the rock, the surrounding mountains, and the rail line at his feet. Then he collapsed. The company doctor ran forward and picked up his thick wrist. There was no pulse. His heart had exploded. John Henry, the Great Steel-Driving Man of the Chesapeake and Ohio, was dead. While the railroad men sobbed and wailed, the machine continued to hammer, breaking through the rock and trundling past John Henry's body to the next mountain. John Henry lay in the dust, his courage and strength amounting to nothing. Ultimately, the steam drill destroyed John Henry . . . And I'm on the side of steam drills."

The crowd cheered. The speech was a classic bait-and-switch. Veronica grinned down at every person in turn as if she had been telling the story solely to them, solely for their benefit—a private joke they could share. But the Japanese gentleman was still not paying attention. He ran his pen over the program. Something like a black eraser stuck out from the end of his pen. Was it a *scanner?*

Veronica finished up her presentation, going into the details of her newest invention—a high-definition, three-dimensional video cell phone. Members of her staff circulated through the crowd, passing out prototypes of the new phone. The clarity of the picture was almost unnerving. The person on the other end of the line looked as if a miniature version of his or herself was literally inside the phone, looking out from the little window like a person sitting on their stoop. Some of the assembled businessmen actually tried to touch the image with their fingers, as if they could pluck the little person straight from the phone and dangle him or her in front of them like Fay Wray and King Kong. The assembled leaders laughed and smiled, showing the phones to each other like children with a new toy.

At the reception afterwards, Veronica strode through the crowd nursing a gin and tonic, glad-handing all of the conference-goers. An assistant followed close behind her, collecting business cards and writing notes, sometimes disappearing for a moment to freshen Veronica's drink or chase down someone Veronica wanted to talk to. The Japanese gentleman was nowhere to be seen.

Finally, Veronica had the chance to step outside for that rare cigarette. She sent her assistant away and stood under the eaves in the hotel's center garden, looking up at the night sky. A light drizzle fell against the flowers. If the initial interest was any indication, her speech tonight had been worth almost one hundred million dollars in contracts to StoneCorp.

"I enjoyed your speech," said a richly baritone voice behind her.

Veronica turned. The Japanese gentlemen stepped out of the shadows, reaching toward her with a silver cigarette lighter. She accepted the flame and smiled at him. "Really? You didn't seem to be paying much attention. I had the impression I was boring you."

"My apologies. It's early in the morning in Japan. I had some things to attend to. That was very rude of me."

"Was that a scanner you were using?"

The gentleman was clearly impressed that she had noticed. "A translator. I wanted to see how it worked on colored type. It's still being beta tested. The signal goes to a small transmitter in the arm of my eyeglasses. Saves the user from embarrassment."

"Interesting. I assume they're yours?"

The gentleman shrugged. "Some of my company's new ideas. We'll see how they do. My name is Hirojia Nakashimi. I am extremely pleased to meet you, Ms. Stone." Veronica tried not to look too impressed. Nakashimi's TechWorks was the only technology company Veronica truly considered a rival. Nakashimi was legendary and, like Veronica, very little was known about him personally. He and his company had been at the forefront of every technological innovation of the last twenty-five years. If TechWorks were a country, it would be one of the wealthiest and most powerful in the world. In fact, that was the major criticism of Nakashimi and his business methods—TechWorks acted as if it were above the law, using the protection of Japan and the other G7 countries interested in having the first chance to bid on its newest inventions for its own ends. It operated from a private island off the coast of Japan. Naval destroyers patrolled at a safe distance. Supposedly, the coast was mined, and there were anti-aircraft cannons in the island's mountains. TechWorks was completely isolated and untouchable. Veronica couldn't help but be jealous. Imagine what she could do without prying eyes or regulators looking over her shoulder! The idea made her head spin. "I've always admired your work," said Veronica.

Mr. Nakashimi bowed—really only a slight bob of his head. "Please accept my pen as an apology for my behavior. I'll have my people send you a receiver—you can place it on a pair of eyeglasses, or maybe a set of earrings. As of now, it is able to translate sixteen major languages back and forth between each other."

"Thank you. I appreciate the gesture, Mr. Nakashimi. It's very kind."

"Call me Hiro," said the gentleman. He took an intricately carved jade cigarette case from his jacket and lit a cigarette for himself, pausing to admire a blossoming hollyhock. Then he turned to Veronica with a big smile. "How long before you take that pen apart to find out how it works?" he asked.

Veronica paused, unsure whether Hiro was joking. Then she grinned with him. "As soon as I get back up to my room. I have a set of tools with me," she said, laughing up at the raindrops.

"I wouldn't have expected any less," he said.

"How about my cell phone?" She asked.

Hiro smiled even broader.

"On a plane to Japan as we speak," he answered.

"So, are you planning on reverse engineering a copy and flooding the Asian market to hold StoneCorp to America and Europe?" asked Veronica, smirking ruefully at the moonlight. Flooding the market with technological knockoffs was one of TechWorks's favorite power ploys. If it wanted to take over a market or destroy another company, there was nothing its victim could do to stop it.

"That depends on you," said Hiro. He inhaled deeply, clearly savoring the smoke. It smelled vaguely of berries.

"What are you talking about?" asked Veronica, her eyebrow arched in suspicion.

"I have a proposition," said Hiro. He smiled again but this time, there was no humor in it.

2

Nineteen-year-old Veronica Stone looked out over the crowd gathered in Harvard's Tercentennial Theater. It was a beautiful blue graduation day, and the sun danced over all of the happy parents and graduates from where Veronica stood in front of Memorial Church all the way to the top of Widener Library's wide steps. Flashbulbs lit up like tiny explosions. People screamed. Some of the undergraduates danced and sang songs. Although this was not Veronica's first speech in front of such a large group, she was still nervous. She couldn't help but feel anxious, even though everyone acted as if she admitted her jitters just to be polite—as if she had been pointing out an odd constellation of freckles on her perfect face. She'd entered Harvard at sixteen, and she'd graduated in three years, picking up a master's in French along the way. She'd won a Hoopes Prize and a Fulbright to Oxford, along with a dozen smaller awards. She was applying for jobs that summer, and her resume was already four pages long without any padding. She was brilliant, gorgeous, and qualified to do anything—but she was still human.

She counted the lines on her fingertips to calm her nerves, surrounded by two Nobel Prize winners, several top CEOs and politicians, and one of the most respected writers in America. She decided to run her Latin address through her mind once more. She was a whiz with languages, and she had decided that morning she wasn't going to use any notes. Several of the older men smiled at her concentration and focus. Their smiles seemed to say that Veronica looked too young and pretty to be graduating first in her class, especially in science. She was determined to show them.

She sailed through her speech. Three boys who considered themselves rivals for Veronica's affection stood to applaud, and the entire Tercentennial Theater burst into a standing ovation. Veronica walked back to her seat. The assembled dignitaries clapped and nodded their congratulations. Several raised their eyes in mock shock. Veronica studied the graduation program. She didn't trust the haughty expression she knew she had on her face.

Afterwards, Veronica made her way through the crowd, hugging friends and being congratulated by her professors. Although she knew better, she kept her eyes out for her parents—maybe they'd come back from Rio or the Costa del Sol or Switzerland, or wherever they were this time, to see her graduate. She hated herself for hoping. This weakness was one of the things she was trying to get over. She knew caring would be a liability in the male world of international technology and business.

Finally, Veronica made it all the way to the back of the Theater. At the top of Widener's steps, her friend Mary O'Donnell jumped and waved and tried to catch Veronica's attention. Mary's family lived in Beacon Hill, in a huge mansion bordering the Common. Everyone in Mary's family was a lawyer, all the way back to the founding of Boston. However, unlike Veronica's family, they were interested in more than money and power.

It looked like every O'Donnell had come to the graduation. Mary was surrounded by her large Irish family—aunts, uncles, cousins, second cousins, third cousins—all of them carrying balloons or flowers or packages. Veronica recognized a few of them from Mary's summer house on Nantucket, and a couple of cousins who were also attending Harvard. Suddenly, Mary's Uncle Ted whistled and waved his hand above his head as if he were rounding up a herd of escaped horses. When he had gotten the attention of everyone, all of the O'Donnells who were not immediate family trooped away toward Harvard Square.

Once Uncle Ted and the rest of the O'Donnell's were far enough away, Veronica climbed up to Mary and her mother. "Hi—congratulations, Mary. Hello, Mrs. O'Donnell," said Veronica.

"Your speech was so great!" exclaimed Mary. And I can't believe Harrison stood up to clap for you. After showing up drunk and naked last week, like some goofball freshman. And that poem he wrote on his butt, so stupid."

Mary's long and lustrous red hair glowed in the sunlight, like fire dancing above her porcelain skin. Then she noticed her mother frowning at her. She gave her mother an annoyed look.

"A lampoon prank, mother. He's probably hoping it will get him a job with Conan O'Brien."

Mrs. O'Donnell rolled her eyes. "Is that the boy I just met two minutes ago? His dad runs the banks in New Jersey?"

"Yes," answered Mary. "That's him."

Mary grabbed Veronica's arm and pulled her to the side, hoping to get just far enough from the ears of her family.

"Thank God we graduated!" Mary exclaimed as she pulled out a little mirror from her handbag and began to check her face. She gave her vibrant red hair a toss and put the mirror back. "We're that much closer to getting out there and making our own money!" She winked at Veronica, who winked back in response. Their friendship was based on the fact that they both wanted to be unbelievably rich and that they wanted it to be money made with their own hands.

Just then, Mary's mother leaned in to interrupt them. "We want to meet your parents! They must be so proud! First in your class! The Latin address! The Fulbright! The master's degree! I wish some of your drive had rubbed off on our Mary!" said Mrs. O'Donnell, grabbing Mary by the shoulders and squeezing her next to her side. Mary cringed.

"Thank you, Mrs. O'Donnell," said Veronica, fighting not to laugh. She knew Mary was a hard worker and just as smart, but she was more interested in partying than awards. She claimed the partying was networking and would actually prove to be more valuable in the long run. Straight A's came as easily for her as they did for Veronica. Mary was convinced she was going to be rich without having to work too hard for it.

The crowd around them was thinning out. Veronica brushed her hair from her eyes and glanced at her wrist watch.

"So, where are your folks? I think your dad deserves a congratulations drink—it's tough work raising a genius. I know the difficulties firsthand," called Mr. O'Donnell, playfully acting as if he were wearied by the very thought of the brainpower trapped inside the skulls of his daughter and her pretty friend. Although he seemed to like hiding the fact, he was a name partner in the most powerful law firm in the Northeast. He stumbled toward them up the Widener stairs, dragging Mary's bored teenage brother, Brendan, along behind him. Two cameras and a pair of binoculars dangled from an intricate tangle of lanyards and banged against each other on Mr. O'Donnell's chest. His free hand held a video camera. A pink sunburn reached across his cheeks from ear to ear. Brendan was carrying a nylon bag somewhere near his ankles. It looked like it might be full of film. Mr. O'Donnell caught his breath and continued. "Ted's getting a bunch of tables for lunch at Mr. Bartley's. I think we beat the rush. We'd love it if you and your family joined us, Veronica."

Mary looked at Veronica and studied her face. "Yes," she said with mock concern. "Where *are* your parents?" She knew as well as Veronica did that her parents were never showing up, but she wanted to hear what Veronica would say.

"Seriously," piped up Mary's little brother. "I'm starving. Can we get out of here now?"

Mary gave her brother a smack on the back of his neck without taking her eyes from Veronica. Veronica knew what Mary was doing, and she liked that Mary kept her on her toes. But she wasn't saying anything. She did care that her parents weren't there, and she knew they weren't coming at all. However, she didn't like that it bothered her. Just tell them they're not coming, she thought to herself. Why do you care what they think? But nothing came out of her mouth.

Mr. O'Donnell shot Brendan a look. Brendan stared at his shoes. Mr. O'Donnell turned back to Veronica. "So can we finally meet the great Mr. and Mrs. Stone? We're beginning to wonder if you're ashamed of us," he joked.

"I think that pink shirt is what's doing it," laughed Mary.

"Even I don't really want to be seen with you." She swatted her father playfully. It was clear he was her favorite, which Veronica couldn't understand at all.

Mr. O'Donnell glanced down at his shirt and laughed. The shirt was so pink it practically glowed like a lamp. "Too much? I thought it was festive. I was in a good mood this morning. Well, what are you going to do?"

"Buy some clothes that weren't made in the 1970s," said Brendan.

"I think you all look wonderful," Mrs. O'Donnell said. "Now, seriously, Veronica, do you and your family have plans for lunch?"

Veronica had been slowly backing down the steps as the O'Donnells kidded and joked with each other. They all seemed so happy, it was too much for her. "Where are you going, Veronica?" asked Mrs. O'Donnell.

"I'm sorry. Mom and Dad are waiting for me at their hotel." She shot Mary a quick, icy glance not to say anything. "I've got to go over and meet them—but I would have really liked to come with you guys. Maybe another time?" asked Veronica.

Mrs. O'Donnell couldn't hide her disappointment. "Of course, honey. We're just so proud of you and Mary. Give my best to your parents," she said.

"I will. See you at the Athena party tonight, Mary," said Veronica, turning down the steps.

Veronica walked out the gate to Harvard Square, checking to see if the O'Donnells were behind her. When she was satisfied they weren't, she took a hard left and headed straight to her apartment.

3

THE GRADUATION PARTY at the Athena Club was going strong. Although Veronica never liked them herself, she secured a new rock band for the Club's private dance. They were hugely popular, and those students who were not Athena members had been begging Veronica for tickets. For the past several weeks, she'd been saying no to most of the campus' rich and powerful. She loved the feeling of power it gave her. For tonight, at least, this band was her favorite band in the world.

After several glasses of merlot, she'd largely dismissed the fact that her parents had failed to show during her graduation that morning. She stood satisfied in the corner and watched her friends dance. The room couldn't hold anyone else. Even though the windows were open, it was so hot that people were starting to lose parts of their suits and dresses. Beer, wine, and champagne flowed everywhere. Several of her Athenian sisters had already come up to tell Veronica that this party was the best one they had ever attended. Veronica smiled and hugged them like a queen doling out favors. She would miss the university, and she would miss the Athena

Club. In many ways, these college years had been the best years of her young life.

A lot of her happiness came from the Club itself. She had founded it with a few other girls as a dining club, but it had quickly become much more than that. In fact, it was a major force on the male-dominated Harvard campus, and it had all of the university's most talented women as members. The Club also hosted classes and programs designed to make the Club's members independent forces of their own, with talks and presentations by some of the most important writers, business people, artists, food connoisseurs, and politicians in the country. Membership was based on talent, background and power—consequently, many of the Club's speakers were the friends and family of the members. Individual members sponsored new girls through a type of invitation-only rush. If the sponsored girl did something embarrassing to the Club (whether it be getting drunk in public, failing a class, or dating "the wrong kind of boy"), both the sponsor and the sponsored were dismissed. Consequently, the members policed themselves. Veronica had had to make an example of two girls in the first year of the Club's existence—the ostracism and shame of being kicked out of the Club was so complete that one dropped out of school and fled to her family in Connecticut (her father subsequently taking back a large endowment he had gifted to the university itself), while the other transferred to a college in Europe. Veronica couldn't even remember what the girls had done. It didn't matter— after that, no one stepped out of line. What some called cruelty, Veronica simply saw as a matter of practicality—there was no point to the Club if it was no different than some third-rank sorority. These young women would grow to be the leaders of their worlds—and Veronica would be the leader of them.

Veronica's date waved at her from the far side of the room. She gave a small wave back with a wink. Her date was incredibly good-looking—a star basketball player, student body president, and a genuinely decent guy. More importantly, his father was a United States senator. Veronica considered him like a nice bracelet—she appeared in public with him because he looked good on her arm. In fact, she thought he was boring and foolish—he was born rich, and he was already planning on inheriting his father's political career. He had no drive, but he had no reason to have one. His life had been handed to him. He would die old, comfortable, and respectable. If not for his pedigree, Veronica wouldn't have gotten within ten feet.

"Veronica! I want you to meet someone!" hissed Mary as she sauntered up with her arm wrapped around a handsome young man's waist. Veronica flipped her hair out of her face. It was a move she had practiced. She knew it was devastating.

"This is my friend Alex. Our families used to summer together on Nantucket. He's going to Oxford, too. And he's British." Mary had a small smile in the corner of her mouth. She was studying Veronica's reaction. It was clear she knew he was gorgeous, but she also knew Veronica would hate the fact that he was from England.

Veronica looked him up and down while resting her cup against her lips. Then she smiled, letting Mary know that Veronica approved. Slowly, Mary stepped away to let them talk and to go find her own date, some son of a Greek shipping magnate who had already proposed to her three times.

"Pleased to meet you—this is really an incredible party!" said Alex, holding out his hand.

"Thanks," said Veronica, shaking his hand. In the dim lights, the only thing Veronica could make out was his thick sandy blonde hair and dazzling white smile. Alex looked like someone who had grown up on a yacht with the wind blowing in his face.

Alex pointed over his shoulder at the stage. "The band—very cool!"

"Thanks!" answered Veronica, a little flustered. "Not really my thing, but everyone else seems to love them!"

"So, what is your thing?"

"My what?"

"Your thing! What kind of music are you into?"

"I'm not really."

"Why are we standing here, screaming?"

"What?"

"Why are we standing here?"

Veronica tapped the side of her head apologetically. "Sorry, I can't hear—"

Alex took Veronica by the hand and led her through the crowd, through the hallways and front dining room, and out onto the Athena House's front steps. The two doormen glanced at them, nodded, and went back to chasing away people trying to crash the party. During the fall, the bouncers were second-string linemen for the New England Patriots. A group of drunken older men were begging for their autographs.

Alex offered Veronica his arm and the two of them sat on the porch railing. "I couldn't hear anything in there," said Alex.

"The band was very loud."

There was a long awkward silence between them. "So, you're going to Oxford? What for?"

"I got a Rhodes. I play water polo at Cal Tech."

"Where do you keep your horse?" asked Veronica.

Alex frowned in confusion. He said, "I don't—wait, you're kidding."

"Yes," smiled Veronica. "I thought Mary said you were from England?"

"I am. Most of my family is still there. My parents moved here when I was fifteen. My father is a bit of the black sheep of the family."

"Was he a jet-setting playboy or something?"

"He told my grandfather he didn't need the family fortune—that if you scratch the surface of old money, you're sure to find the blood underneath," said Alex, glancing off down the street at a passing pack of graduation revelers.

"So, you're a black sheep too?" asked Veronica.

"Me? Oh no. *I* never said *I* didn't want the family fortune," laughed Alex. "I think my family's company does great work. It's a pharmaceutical company—we made our money making malarial medications during the colonial era."

"And the blood would come in from keeping the troops healthy enough to beat the natives into submission?"

Alex rolled his eyes. "You and my father would get along smashingly," he retorted.

"So you're okay with the relatives?"

Alex nodded over his beer cup. "My grandfather blames Cambridge for turning his son into a 'bloody screaming communist.' I'm perfectly all right. I went to a good, sensible American university. No books without a diagram or an equation in it."

"How do you know Mary?"

"I'm friends with Mary from when I was in high school. I'm visiting Boston for a few days before I go on to France. My family used to own the house two doors down from hers in

Nantucket—Dad couldn't stand too much sun. I think Nantucket was suitably dreary for him. Mary said you've been there. Ours was the house with the green trim and the widow's walk on the roof—there's a huge spyglass up there."

"It's been repainted—kind of purplish. The spyglass is still there."

Alex beamed in remembrance of his old toy. "The spyglass was mine. It got left behind when my parents divorced. The house was sold as part of the settlement, and we weren't allowed to take anything that was attached to it. I had actually walled up some of my old sports trophies and medals when I was a kid and my bedroom was being remodeled—I keep thinking I should leave an anonymous treasure map for whatever kids live there now. Or maybe deliver it mysteriously, dressed up like a pirate."

"I don't think they have kids," said Veronica, spinning the ice around in her gin and tonic.

"Oh well, maybe the next family after those folks get divorced and sell it off."

Veronica smiled. "You have a lot of faith in humanity," she said sarcastically.

"You do?" rejoined Alex, smiling himself. "Why would you? What has humanity done to deserve such a thing from me? So, what are you going to be doing at Oxford?"

"Fulbright. I'm a computer engineer. I've got some projects I'm working on. Communications stuff, mostly."

"I wouldn't have guessed you were a scientist."

Veronica's eyes flashed angrily, her entire body winding up as if she were about to throw a punch at him. "Why? Because I'm a woman?" she asked.

Alex waved his hands as if he were warding off an imminent attack. "No. No. No—of course not. It's just that, well, I always kind of picture scientists as being pasty kids with two friends and *Star Trek* addictions. And you don't seem like that. Really—I didn't mean anything by it. I'm a chemist myself. Everybody I've ever been in a lab with is either one hundred years old or one hundred pounds overweight."

"So, by your own admission, you're a geek," said Veronica. She loosened up again, but kept her eyes on Alex's mouth, as if she were waiting for it to trip up and make a mistake.

"I'm a complete and unimpeachable geek. I actually got my dad to wrangle me an audition for Wil Wheaton's part on *Next Generation*. Seriously—they let me stand around in a crowd scene once. I got to wear a prosthetic second head. I'm being serious, this is my childhood you're giggling about," said Alex with a big grin.

Veronica covered her mouth with her hand. "Sorry. Sorry. It sounds really great. Did you get to keep the head?"

"My Halloween costume for six years running," answered Alex. "Next Athena party, invite me, I'll wear it. I've got a real lightsaber from the *Star Wars* movies too."

"Present from your dad?"

Alex nodded. "He missed a lot of birthdays—and stop laughing at me."

"I'm not. I'm sorry. Really."

"At least you don't look like you're going to hit me anymore. So if we're going to be completely honest, I have to let you know that I'm wearing Green Lantern underoos as we speak. It felt wrong to leave you in the dark about that."

Veronica smiled and rocked back and forth. She smirked down into her drink. Despite herself, she was warming up to this lanky English boy in bad need of a haircut. She said, "You shouldn't tell that to people."

"I feel as if a huge weight has been lifted from my shoulders. You've really done me a great service," he said. He finished his beer then looked into the cup as if there might be some left hiding in the bottom. He continued, "So—"

"Veronica—I was looking for you. The band's totally playing my favorite song," said the booming, all-American voice of her date. He stood smiling in the doorway. Before anyone could answer him, he stepped close to Alex. He loomed over him like an oak tree. Alex looked up at him as if he were trying to figure out the most appropriate remark to cut him to the ground.

"Okay—I'd like that," said Veronica, stepping to her date's side. She wasn't in the mood for any silly boyish posturing over her, especially when the one she was most interested in was likely to get flattened. "It was nice to meet you, Alex."

Alex's face twisted in evident disappointment. He put his cup to his lips, frowning as he realized he was out of beer. Just as Veronica started to step through the doorway with her date, he yelled over to her, "So, we're set for that date in Oxford? Don't worry, I'll find you! You're going to love the University Nudists! It's the best club at the college!" He grinned merrily, as if he'd just made a particularly good joke.

Veronica's date glared, but Veronica smiled back. "We'll see," she said. "Good night. Good luck with the malaria." Then she disappeared into the party.

4

THE HELICOPTER SWOOPED low over the ocean, its skids practically slicing the waves below it. Veronica kept her fingers wrapped around the handhold above her head and let the rush of speed crash over her. "Why are we flying so low?" she yelled to the pilot.

"Missile defense," he said flatly, his eyes never turning toward her. "We go any higher, they'll knock us right out of the sky." The helicopter swooped past a gray patrol boat. The men on deck watched them pass. The helicopter was so low Veronica could almost read the name tags on their uniforms.

"Really?" asked Veronica, laughing. Apparently, every rumor she'd heard about Nakashimi's island was true. In the distance, a jagged crown of black mountains rushed to meet them. As they got closer, Veronica could see the island itself. The mountains were surrounded by thick green jungle, with only a few bare spots of rock or sand, and what looked like missile batteries hunched down on thin stone jetties that stuck out into the sea like grasping fingers. A gigantic gray satellite dish hung suspended in the caldera of an extinct volcano in the exact center of the island. There was nothing else but water for as far as the eye could see. The tiny island seemed to float on the ocean as if it had been set adrift from an older, prehistoric world. Veronica half-expected the serpentine head of a brachiosaurus to peek out at her over the trees.

The pilot slowed down and circled the edge of a pristine white beach. A black helicopter pad squatted in the middle of it like a scar. Men with helmets and orange flashlights ran out to meet the helicopter and waved them down to the pad, while others lined the perimeter, with black machine guns ready in their hands. More men holding guns stood near a staircase leading off the pad to a wooden walkway. Nearby, a collection of gray buildings disappeared into the tropical forest, linked by wooden platforms and protected by several evil-looking anti-aircraft guns. As the helicopter touched down, the armed men swarmed to surround the vehicle. They stood motionless, staring at the island's new arrival. Veronica waited, unsure whether she should open the door and get out. After a moment, two brightly dressed geisha came up the stairwell and offered their hands to help her from the helicopter. Their purple and red robes sparkled in the late afternoon sun like gemstones, and the white makeup on their faces made them resemble porcelain dolls. Veronica thought that maybe her idea about the brachiosaurus wasn't as whimsical as she had thought. Next to the helicopter, soldiers, and the monstrous satellite dish, the geisha appeared as archaic as dinosaurs.

The two geisha waited until the rotors stopped, then rushed forward to help Veronica from the helicopter. The two women knelt to the ground in front of Veronica. "Mr. Nakashimi is very honored to have you as his guest. Please excuse the security. We have had problems in the past," said the one on the right. Her voice and manners moved like music. Except for the colors in their clothes, the two women appeared identical.

"I understand. It's no problem at all," answered Veronica. "I'm just happy to be here, and this island looks lovely."

"Thank you. Mr. Nakashimi is waiting for you to join him for dinner on North Beach. May we take you there now, or would you like to freshen up?"

"Now is fine."

"Please follow." Both geisha stood, and the soldiers swung open like a doorway to let them pass. Veronica followed the women down the staircase and onto the wooden path. It branched off into several directions like the top of a tree. They followed one of the branches that led straight out onto the beach. Except for the women in front of her, and the armed men now filing off the helicopter pad behind, Veronica didn't see another living person. Brightly plumed birds fluttered through the sky, and something quick and small swung through the trees. A huge iguana stood just off the path, indolently licking at the air with its tongue. The sand was so perfectly white it looked as if it had been painted there. Veronica felt as if she were walking around in someone's dream of what a tropical island should look like.

The women led her to a dining room on stilts right at the high-water line. Small fish and sea life were trapped in the little pools next to the stilts, swirling around them as if the room were a part of the ocean itself. The room was made of white pine, and open on four sides. When Veronica got to the top of its steps, she was dazzled by its view of the rapidly approaching sunset. Hiro was waiting for her. He stood and bowed. "I hope your journey wasn't too tiring," he said, gesturing for her to sit. In the center of the room was a low table covered in bright blue dishes holding dozens of intricately sculpted pieces of sushi. Delicately embroidered silk pillows covered the floor. Orchids stood in a vase in the center of the table, and two banners covered in beautifully elegant Japanese characters fluttered on the walls. The salt air smelled sweet, like flower petals. The room was absolutely perfect. Hiro continued. "Sometimes Edward likes to fly a little lower and faster than absolutely necessary."

"This island is just beautiful," said Veronica, taking in the view.

"Along with the laboratory, we also run this island as a nature preserve. We are the sole guardians of some key species. I am very proud of the work we do. Every so often, I need to remind our more alarmist politicians and environmentalists of that fact. Now please, sit."

"When I was flying in on the helicopter, I half-expected someone to slip a blindfold over my head," laughed Veronica. She sat on a silk cushion. She couldn't take her eyes from the sunset over the ocean. The entire sea looked like molten gold.

"We'll just erase your memory on the way out," joked Hiro, sitting himself. "Would you like a spider roll?"

"Thank you. Everything looks delicious," answered Veronica. She leaned back on the cushions behind her and let the good sushi flavor dance around on her tongue. The two geisha stood at the top of the ramp as motionless as statues. Periodically, as Hiro and Veronica ate, one of them would touch her ear and disappear down the ramp to remove dishes or return with more wine or food. The dusk was perfect. Along the beach, torches sparked to life and lit the edge of the water. The mountains burned pink in the sun like plump baby fingers. The satellite dish hung over it all like a moon. Veronica sipped her wine and said, "Thank you for flying me out here. Everything is delicious. I look forward to hearing the real reason you've brought me here."

Hiro smiled and ignored the last part of her comment. "It's my pleasure. I don't think I have ever dined with such a beautiful woman. You fit the view perfectly," he said. One of the geisha suddenly walked over to Hiro and leaned down to whisper in his ear. Veronica guessed one of her earrings contained a radio receiver—probably connected to a transmitter in Hiro's kitchen. Even though she was whispering and the waves were crashing on the beach, Veronica could still make out the clear bell tone of her voice. "The new chef burned the tuna. It will be a little longer. The kitchen is very sorry," she said in Japanese.

"It's fine. I'd just like to enjoy the wonderful view for a while," answered Veronica. The geisha looked up at her in surprise. Then she backed away without saying another word.

"You speak Japanese," said Hiro.

"Among other things."

"It's not in your bio."

"I try to keep some things to myself. It comes in handy at times," said Veronica. Hiro glanced at one of the geisha as Veronica finished her wine. She immediately rushed over to refill Veronica's glass. After she had backed away to her post by the door, Veronica continued. "When I was first starting out with StoneCorp, I was trying to sign a deal with LaTech Electronics for a new, cutting edge microchip that would have saved us ten months of research and development time. But while I was in Paris for negotiations, I overheard one of the LaTech executives explain in detail what he would like to do to me later that evening. I guess they never considered the fact that even an American might be fluent in French."

Hiro gestured for the geisha to fill his wine glass as well. "I've never heard of LaTech Electronics."

Veronica smiled wickedly. "Exactly."

"I see it's unwise to anger you."

"Last I heard, LaTech's former CEO was working as a waiter in an Italian restaurant on the rue de Mar."

Hiro laughed. "You're heartless."

"I hear it's a very nice restaurant," responded Veronica, shrugging her shoulders with a sly expression. "But enough about the past. Last time we met, you said you had a proposition."

"So, you're interested?" asked Hiro.

"Yes, I'm interested. I'm interested in protecting StoneCorp's position in the Asian market as well as hearing other ways to prosper."

Hiro made a slight gesture with his fingers. The geisha set two bottles of wine on the table and then backed down the ramp and out of the room. Hiro and Veronica were alone.

Hiro said, "Nakashami has always been involved in the periphery of the weapons business—guidance systems, micro-computers, timers, satellite navigation, some aeronautics—but our specialization in electronics has always hindered our ability to take a bigger share of the market."

"Why don't you just move into hardware? I'm sure you have the capability."

Hiro shook his head. "That's like telling a sushi chef he should cook a nice steak for his patrons. He can probably cook a better steak than ninety-nine percent of the world, but it will still be weaker than his fish. I don't like knowing something

I've created is not the absolute best the world can offer. Otherwise, there is no reason to do it. TechWorks has made its name with electronics."

"Still—you could sell an awful lot of steak."

"I have more money than I even know what to do with. I pay my employees ridiculously high salaries—one, to buy their loyalty, two, just because I like knowing I can pay more than any other employer. I fund thirty different charitable organizations on five continents. None of them know TechWorks is their benefactor. Sometimes I think I might just pile up a few million dollars and burn it on the beach. Money used to be a good indicator of my success—not anymore. I couldn't spend what I have in a thousand years."

"It'd be fun to try," joked Veronica.

"True, true," responded Hiro, smiling as if he knew.

"If it's not about money, what is it about?"

"After you've exhausted money, the only things left are power and perfection. Hence, I don't make steak."

"Don't you already have power?" said Veronica. "Japan protects you. You own this island, don't you?"

Hiro paused awkwardly, his eyes suddenly seemingly unsure. Finally, he answered, "I do own this island and many other things. But power has a very fluid, moveable boundary. The American president has power, but he is at the beck and call of the ones who bought him his office. The Pope has power, but he must abide by two thousand years of Church doctrine. The Chinese emperor had power, but he could never leave the Forbidden City. Even the very powerful can sometimes be controlled by the insignificant and the stupid."

"So, what are you looking for then?"

"I want truly untouchable power—that of a god—that of the earth. You're smiling? You think I'm being foolish? Megalomaniacal?" asked Hiro.

"No—no. Not at all. I'm sorry—I'm more impressed than anything else. I admire your vision. I hope to have enough money to be bored with it one day," said Veronica, swirling the thick wine around her glass. "What does any of this have to do with weapons, or me?"

"I want you to help me make conventional weapons obsolete," said Hiro.

"That was not what I was expecting," answered Veronica. She set her cup down and leaned forward.

Hiro cleared his throat. "Beginning in the early 1930s, Russian scientists started testing the use of radio signals and light as a tool for assassination. They were successful in creating a psychological weapon for torture and whatnot, but they also got close to a device that could disrupt a person's cellular structure, giving them a wasting disease similar to leprosy. Once the victim was exposed, death was quick and inevitable."

"Sounds like something out of James Bond."

"Actually, they'd gotten the idea from one of the early communist science fiction writers—a man named Dr. Anton Illych Volkhov who was purged in the early 1940s. He got the idea from his studies of the mentally ill—at the time, the communist government funded a lot of dystopian literature—propaganda visions of the nightmarish potential futures the communists were avoiding through their rejection of capitalism. Consequently, many of the writers they funded were trained in psychology and psychiatry. In the early days of radio, many schizophrenics complained of people using radio waves to harm them."

"Are you going to tell me this was true?"

"Not at all—but it provided the idea. Fiction is the basis of most of science—someone has an idea for a flying machine, we make one. Someone dreams up a laser gun, we make one. Someone dreams of man walking on the moon, we build a spaceship. As a point of fact, many schizophrenics still complain of radio-wave attack. It's where the stereotype of crazy people guarding themselves with tinfoil hats comes from. There are actually websites selling kits to make your own radio wave-stopping hat. Some are quite handsome."

"Cute," said Veronica. She was smiling and listening very intently, but something was eating at her inside. Could she really get involved with making weapons? All of this sounded ludicrous yet captivating.

"For schizophrenics, the radio fixation probably comes from the fact that they hear unexplainable voices. In the time before radio, people claimed the voices came from God. No matter how ill, people always try to make sense of their world."

"You know a lot about all this."

"I'm interested in everything. I read. I watch films. I listen to people talk."

Veronica nodded. "So, what happened to the weapon?" she asked.

Hiro answered, "It was never completed. The project was halted, and the team was broken up. The lead scientist disappeared. The details are murky. We know he was using Russian prisoners as guinea pigs, and we know he was forced to flee Russia for some reason. There were rumors that he had started to use orphans from the provinces for his tests, and that he had accidentally tested one of his devices on the son of a high-ranking Soviet official—the mother had hidden him in a northern boys' home to keep him away from the government turmoil. The KGB hunted him for years, but they stopped looking for him sometime after the Wall fell. Apparently, they decided he had to be dead. Or they simply ran out of money. No one ever heard from him again."

"And you're going to try to complete the project? Can it even be done?" asked Veronica.

"We've managed to get hold of the lead scientist's old notebooks. They're very interesting. If my people are reading them right, they were very, very close to a large-scale weapon. Surprisingly close. If the Soviets had just stayed out of their way, we might have fought the past half-century of wars very differently."

"You sound angry."

"I don't like small-minded hooligans getting in the way of the truly magnificent," said Hiro.

Veronica nodded. The beach was now dark. Only the torches along the edge of the water provided any light. The waves rolled against the beach, one after another, crashing like a ticking clock. Finally, she said, "A weapon like that would change everything."

Hiro smiled. "You could project an image and kill an army or an entire city without harming one piece of property. You could flash it on a cloud and a fleet of bombers would fall like stones from the sky. You could kill every sailor on a ship and then take the boat for yourself—your own Flying Dutchman," said Hiro.

"What do you need *me* for?" Veronica's heart was racing.

"The visual technology you designed for your new cell phone. Without perfect lifelike clarity, the weapon does not work. The 3D image that you have created on this phone is remarkable. I have never before seen a phone that can produce such clear images of the person or place you are looking at. It is the first of its kind and still exceptionally rare. As of now, our projectors and screens leave the image too flat to do anything but the most minor damage," answered Hiro.

"You could just engineer it yourself. You have one of my phones."

Hiro refilled her wineglass, and topped off his own. "We could. But it would slow the project down. And, whatever we do, it would never be the best—your design is the best. I would just be making steak. Good enough, but not perfect. Plus, we think your phone by itself could be a perfect delivery device for assassinations and whatnot. We want to help you get your phone into the hands of every person on the planet. Then we tell governments we have the power to cull whomever they don't like from the herd—and we start the bidding. Once they get their fingers dirty, they won't be able to get out from under our thumbs. Then we fix things. Save humanity from itself. Put people with intelligence in charge instead of these democratic oafs and despotic dictators. But I'm getting ahead of myself. Right now, I'm interested in the weapon."

"Do you actually think this weapon could work?" asked Veronica.

"I know it will, especially with your good help. We're weeks away."

Veronica ran her forefinger along the top of her glass. "Why should I work for you?"

Hiro laughed, "I can give you whatever you want

in compensation. Would you like your own island? There's several off the coast of California that I could get for you—or perhaps one closer to home on the Atlantic? Your president has offered me whatever I wanted if the United States gets a first look at the weapon—you could name your own island. Isle of Veronica." Hiro smiled at his joke, then continued. "Technology, money, access, whatever you may want—but, that's not much of an incentive for you. We both know you will get all of that on your own. Eventually. What I am really offering you is the chance to be one of the engines behind one of the greatest technological discoveries the world has ever known. Your name would be synonymous with Oppenheimer or Wright or Einstein—you would change the way wars are fought. You would make bullets obsolete. You could change geographical boundaries. You could choose what nations rise or fall. You wouldn't have to live in a country run by fools and imbeciles. You would be in charge. You would stare out from the schoolbooks of every child on the planet—and the caption would read, 'This is the incredible face of the twenty-first century.'"

Veronica looked out over the dark ocean. The salt air was pregnant with possibility. She saw a world where projectors and ray guns shot a mix of radio wave and light. She saw world history with the undeniable stamp of Veronica Stone written across it. She saw herself as the greatest scientist the world had ever known. It was a bigger and better future than she had ever dreamed of. She would be the face of the future. All her hard work would finally pay off. She would be able to prove herself to the world and this time show her face while doing it. It was almost too good to be true. There had to be a catch here. She was determined to find out what it was.

Just off the coast, the lights of one of the Japanese cruisers sailed by. When it was gone, the entire world seemed to turn as black as a blank piece of slate, just waiting to be written on.

5

A WEEK AFTER her graduation from Harvard, Veronica sat alone on the second floor of Algiers Coffee and Tea, nursing a mocha latte. Her father was already an hour late to meet her. Veronica half-read a *Forbes* magazine she'd picked up in Porter Square subway station, but she couldn't lose herself in it. What did her father want? Was he going to apologize for missing graduation? Did he want to try and patch things up between them? Veronica's father told anyone who would listen to him that he didn't believe in apologies. And even if he were planning to apologize, Veronica had already decided it was too late. This time, she was going to make sure that her father understood exactly how she felt, and that he was not going to be let off the hook so easily.

A few people smoked water pipes or ate late lunches, but the majority of the patrons were students working their ways through packets of cigarettes and thick textbooks. Student life never seemed to stop in Harvard Square—even in the summer. Now that all the graduation hoopla had died down, Veronica was happy, and her time was her own—she didn't have to wait for anyone else's approval, or try to conform her schedule to any other person's. Even when she left for her Fulbright later in the month, she'd be allowed to conduct her own research and work on her own projects. Everything was going according to her master plan, and the beginning of StoneCorp was only a few short weeks away.

Veronica read the advertisement on the back of the magazine. She wondered why she had even bothered to come. Her father had called that morning, saying he was in Boston and had some important news for Veronica. For some reason, he was meeting Veronica without her mother.

The brass bells over the Algiers's front door clunked dully. Veronica looked down through the skylight to the first floor. Her father stood just inside Algiers, studying the room. Even in the summer heat, her father was wearing an impeccable charcoal suit. Veronica had never seen him sweat. He seemed to walk in his own rarified cocoon of air. His sunglasses rested on the bridge of his sharp Roman nose, and his gray hair was cropped close to his head. He emanated power. Veronica had always thought his profile looked as if it belonged on an old Roman coin, like an emperor, which, within real estate and stock finance circles, he was. He glanced up and caught his daughter's eye. He nodded slightly, a mannerism Veronica had inherited, and then walked toward the staircase.

Veronica didn't stand when he reached her table, and he sat without greeting or touching his only daughter in any way. He took off his sunglasses and slipped them into his shirt. "I suppose this place is collegiate," he said. "What are you drinking? It looks like a milkshake."

"A latte."

Her father glanced up at the waitress, who had suddenly

appeared at his shoulder. The Algiers waitstaff was famously hard to get the attention of. He said, "A shot of espresso." The waitress smiled and hurried off. Even though the waitress seemed to be about Veronica's age, she still looked at him as if she were flirting.

"I've never understood how you're able to do that. It usually takes me twenty minutes before anyone even notices I'm sitting here," said Veronica.

"It's really never been a problem," he responded. He glanced at his watch.

Veronica crossed her arms and stared flatly at her father. "Are you late for something?"

"Of course not. I'm here to see you."

"So what do you want?" asked Veronica.

He reached into his breast pocket and took out a thick envelope, laying it in the tiny open space left on the table. "Your mother and I are getting a divorce. She's remarrying."

"You're getting a divorce?" asked Veronica, her eyes wide with shock. Then her eyes grew even wider. "What's in the envelope?"

"We've both decided we want to start anew."

"What's in the envelope?" she asked again.

"The envelope is a gift," he answered.

She opened the envelope with a hardly detectable gasp as she thumbed through the thousands of dollars inside. She looked up at her father and paused in shock. "What is this?" she asked, smiling unhappily. "Why are you giving me cash?"

"You're old enough now. You can't expect either your mother or I to keep looking over you. We've done our job. You've gotten a top education, a roof over your head, that horse of yours, and whatever else you needed to get to this point in your life," said Veronica's father. "We've lived up to our obligations. I'm giving you cash so I don't have to see you rip up a check or something else as a dramatic statement. If you don't want it, walk it down to the homeless shelter."

Veronica looked sadly at the envelope. "Since when have I made dramatic statements?" she asked.

Her father shifted in his seat and frowned out the window. "I have no idea. It just seems like something young women do."

"You get that idea from your girlfriends?"

"I'll pretend you didn't say that," he said, nodding at the waitress as she set his drink in front of him. "How come you're not studying?"

"I graduated, Dad," answered Veronica.

"Oh right. Good."

She cringed. Good! She thought to herself: that's all he says to me. No congratulations on a job well done, no words of support or encouragement. She was sickened by the sight of him. She would be powerful and successful and come back and throw this money in his face.

"How is Mom?" asked Veronica, trying to keep her composure. The envelope sat in front of her like an ugly joke.

Veronica's father rolled his eyes. He said, "I haven't seen her in months. She's moved in with some guy in Cabo San Lucas, I think."

"I'm surprised you didn't just mail this," said Veronica, tapping the envelope with her fingernail. She felt as if she were going to throw up. Her father's face was like an unreadable mask. He showed no more connection to her than a stranger sitting next to her on the subway. Veronica had the strange sensation that her father had died when Veronica was very young, and she was simply sitting with an old photograph.

"I wanted to see my daughter," said Veronica's father. "See how she's making out in the world. So how are you making out in the world?"

She looked at him with utter contempt. Did he really want an answer? Did he now want to have some kind of warped father–daughter chat with her? She was disgusted and she had to leave, immediately. She stood up and sighed. "You've fulfilled your responsibilities. No need to worry about me anymore," said Veronica. She picked up the envelope and slowly slipped it into her purse as she stood. "Thanks," she said with a wicked smile. Then she walked down the stairs and out the Algiers's front door without looking back.

6

VERONICA LOVED LABORATORIES. She sat in her chair by her desk in her personal laboratory in StoneCorp's Cambridge office, flipping through the Russian scientist's old notebook. Hiro had given her the original copy—an unprecedented display of trust. If she were Hiro, she would never have handed it over. Of course, he likely had the whole thing photoed and digitized on his computer back in Japan. He knew that she was a scientist just as he was, and that she would protect the ideas no matter what—but it was proof of the respect he held for her. They were working together as equals to change the nature of the world. Veronica appreciated Hiro's gesture. Even so, it hadn't stopped her from scanning the entire thing into her computer notebook as she sat in first class on the flight home from Tokyo. She didn't want to gamble on how long she would have possession of it. As a woman in a man's industry, she knew a lot of men's seemingly polite gestures, such as opening doors or picking up a dropped pen, were really displays of dominance. If men were going to use such things against her, she'd simply flip them into advantages for herself.

She watched a racing scull slice its way up the Charles River outside her window. The lab itself was designed to Veronica's personal specifications. Besides her large oak desk and plush leather chair, there were three industrial black tables in the room, and a wall of electrical outlets powered by an independent generator in the room below. On another wall, cabinets stretched to the ceiling, the top ones only accessible by a rolling library ladder. Above her desk hung a digital flat screen chalkboard flashing a constant stream of information from the Internet; several programs of her own design crawled through cyberspace, snatching e-mails, postings, Web pages, and news articles that might be of interest to her work, all archived into morning reports she read while drinking her coffee. The stream flashed through the room like lightning.

Two of Veronica's assistants kept the tables stocked with the latest available techno-gadgets from all over the world, whether tool, computer, communication device, or even toy. In fact, some of the most interesting ideas came from toy companies, especially Asian ones. More than once, Veronica had based a new circuit or fuse on something she'd first seen in a toy designed to entertain five-year-olds. The Russian scientist whose notebook she was studying was right to begin his ideas with a science fiction filmmaker's. Obviously, he'd recognized the same fact as Veronica had: scientific breakthroughs required a childishly open imagination.

The Russian's notebook was extraordinary. Even though it was written in Cyrillic, Veronica had no problem translating it. The notes began as dry descriptions of machinery, circuits, numbers, algorithms, geometry, and arithmetic. Schematic diagrams of circuits and waveforms followed. There was a notation regarding some imminent tests. Up to that point, the notebook looked no different than the writings of any scientist trying to keep a record of his research—but then the nature of the notebook changed completely.

The strange shift started with a childish drawing of a man with his head exploding, the crown of his skull spinning off to reveal the brain underneath sitting like a hard-boiled egg in a cup. Suddenly, the schematic drawings sprouted wings, or were entwined with fire-breathing serpents, angels, devils, and monstrous tentacles. A large Lenin with fangs strangled the Statue of Liberty. Naked women leered from between the letters. At this point in the notebook, not everything was completely legible—coffee stains covered some of the drawings, and some equations looked intentionally burned out with a cigarette. At first glance, the notebook looked as if it had no rhyme, reason, or scheme, like the intricate doodles of a disturbed child. For those who were intelligent enough to follow it, however, it became increasingly clear that the madness within might actually work.

Veronica slid one of her experimental phones from her pocket. The screen felt like gelatin. In fact, it was a new collection of polymers and electrons held together by a slight magnetic field. If she hadn't designed it and put it together herself, she might have never believed it.

Veronica closed the notebook and set it on her desk. She sat back in her chair and thought long and hard about her meeting with Hiro on his island. She had never thought of using her ability to persuade others with the rich and powerful. She was trying to work her way up and into the hands of those people with hard work and determination. She had never thought of taking her expertise and using it elsewhere. Particularly in the one place where the world was sensitive. Her ideas and creations could prove to be exactly what this world needed. She could sky-rocket to the top of the most powerful humans in history. Only one thing was bothering her: that Hiro could do this himself. He didn't need her. She was sure of that. Everything he had said to her was appealing, but deep down she knew she wasn't the only one who could do this, and she sure as hell wasn't the cheapest. He was testing her. She was sure of that. There was something else he was after; she just hoped she could figure it out before he used it against her.

Even with the proof of its theories sitting in her hand, the notebook made her doubt the scientist's sanity. Like the story of John Henry and the steam engine, the technology within the notebook seemed to require the destruction of a person, and if she had believed in superstition, she might have said the notebook was haunted. For the umpteenth time since Hiro had given her the notebook, she reminded herself she believed in cold, hard fact. She was letting herself get spooked by pen and ink scribbles and cheap Soviet primer paper. Nothing more. There was no ghost locked between its pages. The only thing in the notebook was science.

Outside, cars zipped along Storrow Drive, and she could see the exhaust of an airplane flying high overhead. Hers was a world of science, progress, and technology.

It was not a world of ghosts.

7

THE OXFORD MUSEUM was a favorite of Alex's. It was unlike any museum Veronica had ever seen in America. In fact, she thought it looked as if someone's world-exploring Victorian grandmother had exploded, throwing her collection of Aztec gold against one wall, her African tribal shields against the ceiling, and her Peruvian prayer beads on top of the stairs, a little bit of almost every culture of the world stuck willy-nilly, here and there around the Museum's small square building. It was as organized as the shoes piled in the bottom of her closet.

Alex tapped the glass case protecting one of the displays. He said, "Apparently, this was these people's god. Could you imagine? These tribal people come out onto the beach for the first time and see a shipload of white people. The white people ask some questions. The tribal people describe their lives a little and then say, 'And this—this is our god!' And the white people are like, 'Thanks, mate! Zoink!' And onto the boat it goes, to be stuck under some dusty plexiglass for spotty undergraduates to gape at in merry old England."

"Well, at least it's protected here," said Veronica, studying the case full of shrunken heads, all piled one on top of the other like a pile of billiard balls.

Alex smiled. "Propaganda! How do you know the tribal people wouldn't have protected it?"

"I don't. But what does it really matter anyway? It's all just old junk."

"You don't like old things?"

Veronica answered, "I just don't see the point of venerating something because it's old."

"Because it tells us where we came from."

"You read that from the museum brochure. What does it matter where we came from? Where we're going is the only thing that matters. All this stuff just keeps some old men with spectacles and brushes digging in the sand and ripping off people poorer than themselves. It keeps humanity looking back over its shoulder as if something is going to rush up and bite it."

Alex smiled widely, "Good God, Miss Stone! You're starting to sound as crabby and cynical as I am!"

Veronica leaned forward and kissed him lightly on the lips for a long moment. Then she said, "No one could ever be as cynical as you. Come on, let's go get a drink or something."

Veronica and Alex stepped from the museum and headed down the sidewalk hand-in-hand. They'd been at Oxford for almost six months. Veronica had bumped into Alex in the first week in a small pub outside Magdalene College. Alex had obviously been overjoyed to see her. He invited her to a dinner that night at his college, where, as the only American in the room, she was sat under a large portrait of President Clinton. Where all the other portraits looked as if they had been painted by a less-talented cousin of Rembrandt, Clinton's portrait was a riot of color and whimsy—something closer to Rauschenberg or Warhol. Alex clearly loved the painting and its strangeness in relation to the others. He'd kept her laughing all night with his different, extensive theories on how such a thing had been created, most of them involving stained blue dresses and saxophones.

They spent the night laughing and talking about their futures. Veronica's was clear. She would work hard, be successful, and live happily ever after. Alone. Alex caught onto that fact early on. He, on the other hand, was determined to make sure he became a part of that happily ever after. He could feel Veronica's cold hard exterior, but was certain that underneath there was room for him.

After that night, they started dating regularly. Although she studied and tried to learn as much as she could from her professors, Veronica found the work astonishingly easy. She knew she was smarter than her colleagues, but she collected what useful information and contacts she could. She got the top marks in all of her classes, and even those few professors misogynistic enough to believe there was no place for women in science had to admit that she was one of their best students. After a week, no other boy was brave enough to try and ask her out. They scattered like birds whenever she approached, apparently too disconcerted by Veronica's beauty and brains to even try to talk to her.

Many of her professors contacted their colleagues in the public sector about their new discovery, and soon Veronica was being invited to dinners with this or that European technology superpower, all of them vying to hire her once she left Oxford. She brought Alex along as her constant companion, and on the way home in the taxi they would invariably dissect the pitches being thrown at Veronica and have contests over who could do the most wicked impression of the important man they'd just met. Most of the pitches involved enormous amounts of money, but very little else to tempt Veronica away from the dream of creating her own company. As it got closer and closer to the end of her program, the companies became desperate. In fact, one French CEO had practically accosted Alex in the bathroom, challenging Alex's control over his girlfriend and trying to get Alex to commit to moving Veronica and himself to Southern France.

"Apparently, he was under the impression we were going to get married," said Alex on the drive home that night. He smiled at her.

Veronica burst into laughter. "Why would he think that?"

"We are dating," Alex reminded her, his voice dejected and smarting.

"We are," said Veronica, leaning forward and rubbing Alex's arm. "And sleeping together. And two pairs of my shoes and a chemistry book are currently in your apartment. But that does not mean I'm marrying anyone."

"But we could, you know. It's not like we're that young." As they passed under the flashes of streetlights, Veronica caught the look in Alex's eyes. It was as if the usually arch and funny Alex had been replaced with a desperate and weak man. She didn't like it.

Veronica sat back in the taxi, moving herself as far away from Alex as possible. "Look, I am not interested in getting married right now. Marriage is not an institution I'm fond of," she said.

"I understand, but don't you want kids? Security? A family?"

"No," responded Veronica soundly.

Alex laughed coldly and looked out the taxi window. It was starting to drizzle outside. It always seemed to be raining in England. Finally, he said, "You don't mean that. I don't believe your 'Veronica-only-needs-Veronica' act for a second."

"I do mean it."

"Then what do you keep me around for?"

"The sex," responded Veronica, her eyes sparking with mirth.

"Be serious."

"I am being serious," she said again, smiling.

"How could you not want a family and kids and a house and a normal life? It's unnatural!" exclaimed Alex, turning to face her with a wild look in his eyes.

Veronica stopped smiling. She wasn't going to deflect Alex's questions with jokes. She asked, "What? Because I'm a woman I'm supposed to be waiting to find myself a man and settle down and start popping out babies and changing diapers and waiting for said man to come home from the office while wearing a little French maid outfit and holding out his dinner for him?"

"Well, that's a romantic spin on having a family," said Alex sourly.

"There's nothing romantic about having a family. Getting married and having a family is just strapping an albatross to your neck and trying to convince yourself it's a gold necklace. Now, what we have is romantic." Veronica inched back across the seat and put her hand back on Alex's thigh. She put her lips very close to his. He could smell the wine on her breath— sweet and pungent as a promise.

"What we have won't last," said Alex.

Veronica kissed Alex's neck and the top of his chest. "Yes it will. As long as you never ask me to marry you again. It can last as long as we want," she said, before kissing him hard and sliding onto his lap. She put her lips right against his ear. "Isn't this a lot more romantic?" she whispered.

They pulled up in front her flat and she leaned forward, paying the cab driver before stepping out of the car. Alex didn't follow. She leaned back down and looked him right in the eye.

"You can stay in this car and go home, alone, or you can come upstairs with me and have an unforgettable night. I'm telling you right now though, this is me." She raised her eyebrows and studied his face. She smiled and brushed his lips with hers. Then whispered in his ear, "We have a wonderful thing here, don't screw it up." She looked at him and laughed for effect. He cocked his head and looked into her eyes. Staring at her. She looked away, uncomfortable by his stare, and cleared her throat. That made him happy. For now he knew that she did have a weakness. He got out of the car and followed her upstairs, smiling all the way.

Okay, he thought to himself. I can play this game for a while. For the rest of their time at Oxford, Alex never brought up the subject of marriage again.

8

It was a long flight to Japan. Veronica spent the entire flight reading and rereading her notes in hopes of finding something new and exciting to tell Hiro when they met. She was looking forward to seeing him again. She was elated over the promises he had made to her when she accepted his proposal.

By the time Veronica's taxicab made it to the restaurant in Kyoto, it was raining steadily. Before her foot was even out of the cab, Hiro was standing over her with a wide black umbrella, reaching down to give her a hand over the gutter. They hurried inside the restaurant. It was a traditional Japanese establishment in the very center of the city. The walls and floor were made of yellow pine, with a few beautifully colorful tapestries scattered throughout the main entranceway. A geisha took their wet coats and shoes, and then floated away down a side hall as an officious man in a Western-style suit led them through a rabbit warren of passageways. Muffled voices, music, and laughter whispered from the other rooms. By the time the man pulled back a paper screen to show them to their table, Veronica was completely lost—if something were to happen, she wasn't sure she'd ever find her way out again. She loved when Hiro took her to these traditional places. His life was based in technology—and yet he insisted on discussing research in places that looked ripped from Imperial history books.

Veronica hadn't seen Hiro in several months. After visiting him on his island, she had taken some time to mull over his proposal. Once she had decided to take the job, they met again to discuss their plans to work together on the new weapon. After that, she had told him it would be months before she would see him again. Veronica knew that she would need some time to review the information and begin her work. She also knew that the last thing she wanted was someone checking in on her with deadlines and watching over her shoulder as she worked. She promised Hiro that she would send him progress reports as she went along, and then when she was ready she would contact him. He was not to contact her unless it was a dire emergency.

He waited until she sat down before situating himself on a cushion and ordering sake and appetizers for the both of them. He looked tired—his face seemed to have more lines in it than before—and his manner was slightly more hurried. Something was on his mind, and whatever it was, it was obvious that he couldn't help worrying over it like an old diseased tooth. What was bothering him? Did it have anything to do with the project?

"I read through your last report. It's all moving much faster than I even hoped," said Hiro. He didn't necessarily sound happy about Veronica's rapid progress.

"Did you think I couldn't do it?" asked Veronica, trying to gauge what it was that was troubling him.

"No. No. I knew I had picked well, I just didn't know how

well I had picked. Frankly, I'm beginning to realize you're much more than just the technical genius I thought you were."

"I appreciate the flattery."

Hiro waved his hand dismissively. He said, "It's not flattery. I'm simply stating a fact. If I pointed out how beautiful you look in that dress, it would be as if I was pointing out how beautiful a flower or the sky is. Simple fact, nothing more."

"Well, I thank you anyway," said Veronica, flattered despite, and perhaps because of, Hiro's explanation. "And I'm glad you like my work."

"It's exquisite. You and the mad doctor seem to be on the same wavelength, if you don't mind me saying so."

Veronica accepted a cup of sake from one of the geishas serving them. She answered, "He wasn't crazy. Eccentric. Brilliant. Disturbed. But not crazy. Not at all."

"How did the latest test go?" asked Hiro. Even with all their pleasant small talk, he still seemed distracted, as if he were waiting for something to happen. He seemed to want to hurry things along, as if by doing so he might be able to avoid whatever it was he was worrying about.

Veronica frowned. She wished she had nothing but good news to report. She said, "While we've further improved the digital picture and sound of the screen and speakers, we haven't been able to figure out how the Russians intended the weapon to work. We've run some preliminary tests on rats. While their death rate has gone up, it hasn't been enough to attribute it to the weapon. Right now, it could just be a bad virus or a problem with the feed we're giving them."

Hiro didn't seem to register the test's failure. Instead, his mood seemed to brighten. "The new prototype phone you sent me was even more incredible than the last one. If nothing else, we'll have something with astonishing commercial potential," he said.

Veronica sucked the sweet beans from a single edamame into her mouth. She licked the salt from her lips. "You'll have your weapon—believe me," she said decisively. Maybe the worry she was sensing was his fear that the project would never be completed. She was slightly angry. She almost wanted to bolt from the room and go straight to her laboratory in Boston to prove him wrong this very second. He knew that she knew he wasn't interested in the project for any "commercial" reasons.

"I don't doubt you in the slightest. Forgive me if I gave you that impression. I spoke foolishly," said Hiro, gesturing for another cup of sake. His brightening mood seemed to dissipate in an instant.

Suddenly, the paper screen slid open. An enormously broad man stood in the doorway. He was wearing a finely tailored suit and a short, cropped haircut, but he looked more like some type of medieval warlord. "Hello Hiro, Miss Stone. I hope I am not too late," he said, his voice growling with a soft Russian burr. The man made Veronica think of a large grizzly bear—as if he were some animal who had come to the restaurant disguised as a man and was only barely keeping himself civilized. At any moment, he might rip the room apart.

"Hello, Sergei. I hope you found your way here without too much trouble," said Hiro. His spine had stiffened noticeably. He seemed as wary of the man as Veronica was.

Sergei strode over to Veronica and brushed her hand with his lips. His lips were as cool and dry as a snake's. "I'm happy to finally meet the engine who will bring forth another moment of Russian genius," he said. It sounded like he was growling in her ear.

Veronica's eyes narrowed. The man sent out a palpable aura of menace that floated around him like an unpleasant smell even his expensive cologne couldn't cover. "Thank you, although you forgot to mention the American and Japanese genius involved," she said.

Sergei cocked his head to the side, clearly taken aback. He seemed unused to anyone questioning his assertions, no matter how trivial. His smile slid from his face like a greasy piece of bacon. "Of course," he said, flatly. He walked over to the other side of the table and sat elegantly. The geisha brought him a cup for his wine, but he didn't even look at her. His eyes remained locked on Veronica's throat as if he were considering ripping it out.

"Russian genius?" Hiro muttered before raising his voice louder. "Despite anything others bring to it? You sound like the communists." His voice was bitter and angry, as if he already knew he would dislike the answer and was able to do nothing about it. Hiro seemed out of sorts, as if he hadn't been in a position like this since he was a child. Veronica guessed he hadn't.

"You don't think us Russians have a special type of genius?" asked Sergei, leaning forward, his palms flat. He turned to address Hiro. "Even with hundreds of years of serfdom, followed by seventy years of the world's most grossly stupid government, we managed to produce Olympic stars, chess champions, rocket scientists, writers, poets—I would say that is a special kind of genius. A genius that rises up from the shit and the dirt! And never call me a communist again. But I didn't come here so we could quibble like schoolchildren. In fact, I can't believe you're acting like that in front of our guest, Hiro." His voice started to lilt into a

singsong, as if he were enjoying toying with Hiro. Hiro was
visibly fuming, but he contained himself by studying the
plate in front of him.

Veronica watched both men as the geisha placed steaming
bowls of miso soup in front of each of them. What did he mean
by *our* guest? And why was Hiro seemingly too scared to do
anything about Sergei? Why didn't he just put him in his place
and order him to leave? Who was he?

"I don't believe we've been introduced yet," said Veronica,
smiling innocuously and holding out her hand. He took it and
stroked it with his other hand, not saying anything.

Sergei shifted his weight so he could look at her more easily.
There was a bulge under his jacket on the right side. "It's not
important who I am. I hear the project is coming along. Tell
me what you have been up to."

"And why should I tell you?" Veronica was still unclear as to
his part in all of this.

Sergei cracked the bottom knuckle of his forefinger. His fingers were covered with rings. "You can consider me an
investor," he said finally.

"I wasn't aware we had any investors," said Veronica. A
shiver rolled down her spine. "And you still haven't told me
who you are."

"My name is Sergei Dmitrivich Nostov. I am involved in the
Russian communications industry. Like yourself."

"Really? What do you do?"

"I own things. How do you think you got the notebook? It's
not something you can go pick up at one of your shopping
malls, is it? Or one of your Walmarts? But in Russia, if you
know what you are doing, anything is available."

Veronica glanced over at Hiro. He was stirring his soup in

thought. Why was he cowed by this man? Hiro owned an island. Governments and nations bowed to his will. Hiro was untouchable. Who was Nostov? Was he somehow more dangerous than a nation? "So that makes you an investor?" asked Veronica, trying to keep her voice even.

"Of course it does."

"And what is your interest in the project?"

"Like I said, I own many wondrous things," said Sergei, smiling from behind his sake cup as if he might enjoy owning Veronica herself. His smile was full of lead-capped fake teeth, as if he were something very dangerous and old brought up from the bottom of the ocean.

"If you're not honest with me, I'm not working on the project," said Veronica.

"Feisty. I like that about American women. They think they're men. It makes things so much more interesting in bed."

"Good-bye," said Veronica, standing and bowing to Hiro. That was the last straw for her. She had to admit before that last comment that this man intrigued her. His power was illuminating and she was fascinated by the way he seemed to make Hiro slither back into his own shell. She had dealt with many chauvinists over the years, and just like them, she preferred to get up and leave before she would lose all control. She had no patience for chauvinism. She kept her back to Sergei, pointedly not addressing him. "I'm sorry, this was lovely, but I have other things to do than be insulted. I'll continue to send you my progress reports."

Sergei cleared his throat to get her attention. "Please," he hissed. "Sit down. Tell me how're you're doing with the project."

"Why would I do that?"

"Miss Stone," he leaned closer to her. "I don't think you really want to ask that."

"Is that a threat?" asked Veronica.

"It could be," said Sergei, staring pointedly. Hiro remained silent.

"You can't touch me," replied Veronica. "I'm not someone who's going to be cowed by some common gangster."

Sergei ran his finger across the rim of his sake cup. "But your family on the other hand—"

Veronica laughed loudly, clearly shocking Hiro. Her cheeks were flush with fury. "My family? I'll send them over to you myself. Save you the trouble of tracking them down," said Veronica. She started to walk to the door, the frightened geisha servers scattering from the room like windblown leaves in front of her.

"Your work then," growled Sergei after her. "What would happen if StoneCorp ceased to exist?"

Veronica spun on her heel and froze in the doorway. "What do you mean?"

Sergei shrugged his shoulders, almost as if he were bored with the conversation. "When I was a child, there was this government inspector who used to extort money from my father. It was his clever business, like your StoneCorp. No one in the village could do anything about it. This man would take the last of any shop's earnings, the bread from children's hands, the egg money from the old women, anything he could get his grimy fingers on. He took so much money, my family had to skip meals to make sure my father's payments were made on time. Otherwise, the police would show up on your doorstep, and someone in your family would 'disappear' to a labor camp, and people would keep disappearing until you paid up. He rode over us all like a devil. In many ways, he controlled us just as StoneCorp controls electronics—a monopoly created from sheer power." Sergei popped another piece of sushi into his mouth before continuing. "Now, one payment day after I had become a man, the government inspector didn't come. Everyone in the village wondered what had happened. He didn't come the next day, or the next. His family had disappeared as well, along with the government henchmen that helped him, and the village police who took away people's families, and their families, women, children, old people, everybody. Suddenly, every other house in the village seemed empty, as if everyone connected with the central government had simply got up and left. No one could figure out the mystery. People said it was aliens, or vengeful ghosts, or a purge, but no one really knew. It was as if the government inspector's entire business had just closed up shop and fell off the planet."

"I don't see the point of this," said Hiro angrily. "Just let her go and be done with it. This is completely unnecessary." Unlike Hiro, who was obviously nervous, Veronica was simply annoyed. She stood in the doorway with one hand on her hip. She was neither impressed nor scared, and she wanted Sergei to know it.

"Wait," said Sergei, holding up his hand to cut Hiro off. "This is when the story gets really interesting. Now, at the same time the government inspector disappeared, people started to notice how fat the village dogs were getting. A pack of them held reign over the center of the village, and we village children used to play with them sometimes. They were good dogs—skinny and neglected, but good to keep away vermin and wolves. Sometimes they would even chase a ball, or walk in the woods with you. Someone was leaving big piles of meat for them at night. But the strange thing was, no one could tell where it was coming from. No cattle or goats or sheep were disappearing—it just seemed like meat was dropping out of the sky. The dogs ate so much, some of us worried they might get sick with this unexpected food. They sat on their haunches in the center of the village, drunk with meat, their jowls covered in blood, like mangy sultans dazed stupid by their good fortune. Some villagers said it was a shame someone was wasting so much meat on dogs—they even tried to get some of it away, but the dogs would have none of it. Eventually, the stacks of steak stopped appearing and the dogs returned to normal, carrying sad memories of their former wealth. They never seemed as happy after that, as if they'd suddenly been shown the poverty of their actual lives. I felt bad for them. There was never another government inspector in the village again." Sergei sat back on the cushions. His expression was inscrutable.

"I hope you understood my meaning. Anything, no matter how important or special, can be dismantled, as long as someone has the will to do so." He paused for effect. "Now, please, sit down and tell me about the project," said Sergei, popping another piece of sushi into his mouth.

"That's a disgusting story," groused Hiro.

"Business and commerce are disgusting. No more than dogs fighting over meat. The only question is who gets to be a dog and who gets to be the meat," answered Sergei.

Veronica continued to waver in the doorway. Whoever this man was, Hiro obviously didn't feel powerful enough to challenge him. Hiro had an island, gunboats, missiles—StoneCorp had ten acres next to Storrow Drive and four security guards. If Hiro couldn't handle him, StoneCorp had no chance. She didn't want to see her junior research scientists turning up as corpses and fed to the town dogs, especially now that she was so close to completing what she was sure would be her life's work. She'd have to be careful and bide her time, at least until she knew what she was dealing with.

Veronica sat back on the cushions.

9

VERONICA SAT IN her office, staring at her computer screens. She'd found little information about Nostov. He seemed to have come from nowhere, appearing in Moscow in the early nineties like some kind of ghost. Soon, he was the owner of dozens of large television and radio stations. It was as if he'd just walked into town one day with nothing, and the next day he was worth close to sixty billion dollars. There was nothing in the Russian or international newspapers—like Veronica, he seemed to avoid publicity. From their meeting, it was clear he was dirty, but it was just as clear that no one in the press seemed willing to write anything about it, like Nostov was a genie and saying his name aloud would invoke some type of curse.

"Ms. Stone, a woman is on line one. She says she's your mother," said her secretary, her voice speaking clearly from the computer. At the same time, the secretary's words were typed out across the flat screen above Veronica's head (something Veronica had designed in case she was lost in thought or on a conference call). Veronica hadn't said a word to her mother in several years.

"Are you sure it's not *The Globe* trying to pull a fast one? Or another MIT student with a resume?" Veronica asked.

Her secretary paused. "She seemed pretty convincing. She called me a 'low class secretary' when I asked her to hold."

"That sounds like mother. Put her through. And bring me a double espresso when you have the chance," said Veronica.

"Yes, Ms. Stone. Here she is."

"Hello?"

"Hello, honey. How's the new phone going?" asked Veronica's mother. Her voice was cloyingly sweet, like some kind of parody of a good parent–daughter relationship. "I've read about your work in all of the papers. I was surprised they didn't use your picture. Don't you think that would help sell your little techie things? You're older, but you still look good."

Veronica switched off the overhead transcription of her mother's voice. Otherwise, it seemed uncomfortably like her mother was actually in the room with her.

"What do you want?" Veronica asked. This was only the second time she'd heard from her mother since she graduated college.

"That's some greeting."

"What do you want, Mom?" asked Veronica sarcastically.

"Now you're just making fun of me. You sound like a snotty fifteen-year-old."

"I apologize," she said in a voice that was not apologetic at all. "What do you want?"

Her mother paused for several moments. "Fine, if you're going to be that way. Your sister, Carrie, is pledging the Athena Club."

Veronica smiled as her secretary came in with her coffee and a handful of printed-out e-mails. Veronica guarded her personal e-mail address fiercely—she changed it every six weeks, and used a different address on her business cards so her secretary could filter out the crackpots and the curious. "Good for her." Veronica started to scan through the papers. They were mostly invitations to dine or to meet from CEOs and government officials. Several of them slipped in the fact that they were unmarried. It was clear more people were interested in the phone project than in anything else StoneCorp had ever done.

"That's all you have to say about your sister?" her mother asked.

"I don't even know her. While I was still naive enough to send them, all my Christmas and birthday gifts came back to me unopened," said Veronica. She paused. In her hand was an e-mail from Hiro asking for a meeting. She studied the paper, as if the spaces between the words could provide some clue to what he wanted. Was it something about Nostov? He knew not to contact her unless it was an emergency.

"That was my fault. Henry didn't like the intrusion, and he thought you were spoiling her," said her mother. Henry was Carrie's father, and her mother's third husband, one of the unlucky men scattered through Veronica's mother's string of lovers and bad boyfriends. Veronica had only met him once for about ten minutes when her mother wanted her to sign some papers regarding her inheritance. Tall, imperious, with an expression of permanent disgust etched into his mouth—he reminded Veronica of her father. Her mother coughed. It was obvious the necessity to apologize was making her angry, and she was doing her best to cover it. She was bad at apologizing, and clearly uncomfortable, as if she were trying to force her body into a dress that was five sizes too small.

"And how is Henry?" asked Veronica sarcastically.

There was another long pause. "If you must know, we've separated. We're taking some time apart."

Veronica snickered. "Trouble in paradise? I can't believe it! Is it the pool guy again?"

"Laugh if you want. You don't understand anything about marriage. How could you?" asked her mother.

"What's that supposed to mean?" asked Veronica coldly.

"Look, I didn't call you to fight. The Athena Club has become a major force on Harvard's campus—"

"I know, Mother. It always was. From the beginning, when I started it. You really should have come and seen it while I was still in school."

"I should have, but I guess I can't do anything about it now. I'm just calling to ask if you would be willing to be a little unselfish for a change and help your sister."

"Half sister." Veronica turned over the e-mail in her hand as if there were some hint of Hiro's intentions on the backside of the paper, or some secret message that would tell her who Nostov was.

"Fine. Half sister. Carrie has become very good friends with President Monroe's daughter, and the two of them want to pledge together."

"Good for them. I'm sure they'll do fine." Veronica was impressed her half sister was friends with such a powerful girl, but she wasn't going to let her mother know it. Despite herself, wheels of possibility started spinning in her head. "What do you need me for? I don't think the two of them will have any problems at all."

Veronica's mother knew that mentioning the president's daughter might help her case. "Look, you know as well as I do how girls can be. Some of those privileged tarts might decide to blackball both of them because of some misguided liberal principles or something. I've heard some rumors, and Carrie's worried they might lump her in with some statement against the administration."

"They might. You never know."

"A call from you could stop that from happening," said her mother flatly.

Veronica spun Hiro's e-mail message in her fingers. She couldn't blame Carrie for their mother. Periodically, she made computer inquiries, and from what she could tell, Carrie was a nice, well-adjusted Exeter graduate with a love for horses, field hockey, and Sylvia Plath. She wasn't sure how Carrie and the president's daughter had become friends. The president's daughter had a reputation for partying and mingling with Hollywood's A-List. There'd been a couple of incidents involving drinking. She was a pretty girl. She was constantly in the pages of women's and entertainment magazines, usually on the arm of some hot young actor or singer. Veronica gazed out the window as she considered her mother's request. Although she could see Harvard's buildings from her laboratory windows, she hadn't set foot on campus in over a decade. She felt a slight pang of nostalgia. She decided to give her half sister the benefit of the doubt. Plus, it could prove useful. "I'll make a call," she said finally.

"Thank you, Veronica. You can't blame Carrie for my mistakes," said Veronica's mother.

It bothered Veronica that her mother had had a thought so similar to her own. "I don't blame her, I don't blame you," said Veronica. "I don't even know you." She hung up the phone without hesitation.

After she hung up, Veronica told her secretary to hold any

more of her calls. She watched the glow of the sunset outside her window. It fluttered and sparkled over the Charles River. Cars roared up and down Storrow Drive, and the trees were bursting with spring greenery. Veronica grinned. It was the right decision to help her half sister. There was no room in business for emotional kid stuff. The president's daughter would make a great contact, and she would be a great publicity engine for StoneCorp's new phones. In six months, every girl in America would want one of the communications models.

She could funnel the necessary money to do more intense research on the weapons design, and in a year, they might change the world. Now, with any luck, she could find out what Nostov's interest in the project was and buy him out of the entire thing altogether.

10

Hiro and Veronica sat at the window at one of Boston's most exclusive restaurants looking over the twilit harbor and skyline. Even at the end of the day, the city still pulsed with energy. Lights floated on the water and ran through the streets. In the far distance, Fenway Park's lights blazed with a night game. Boston's natives strolled up and down Newberry Street.

Hiro seemed more like his old self than the last time they'd met. She'd insisted they meet in Boston, on her turf—she didn't want another unwelcome surprise like last time. She'd also suggested they meet at the restaurant instead of at StoneCorp, so Hiro wouldn't be anywhere near her laboratory. He was a genius and a scientist himself. If he saw the wrong thing, it wouldn't take him a second to figure out what it was and how it worked. She didn't want him to have any advantage over her.

"I'm sorry about the last time we met. I shouldn't have allowed Sergei to surprise you like that," said Hiro, carefully buttering a dinner roll. Even in his modern business suit, he looked out of place in a restaurant without geisha and yellow pine.

"I haven't thought about it at all."

"I'm glad. He's really nothing to worry about. A necessary evil. Like a stockholder."

Veronica took a sip from her wine glass. "Who is he?" she asked.

"I needed him to get the notebook. I knew it was in the archives at one of the central television stations—the Russian communications industry had somehow got hold of it sometime during the 1980s. They wanted to use it for a project on government advertising and mind control. Unfortunately, Mr. Nostov bought the station. When he found out I was interested, he found the notebook, and, unfortunately, he was much more intelligent than I initially thought. He demanded an interest in the project, or he would put the notebook on the market and sell it to the highest bidder. I couldn't say no," said Hiro.

"So why do you keep him on?"

Hiro set his dinner roll on the edge of his plate. "For the time being, it is much easier to keep Mr. Nostov in the loop than to have to keep looking over our shoulders for assassins. I want the project completed more than anything. Mr. Nostov has no interest in science—just money and power in his own little fiefdom. This is no more than a new shiny sports car to him."

"I don't like him being involved," said Veronica.

Hiro sighed and took his dinner napkin from his lap. Then he gestured for the waiter to take his plate away even though he hadn't touched any of his food. He snapped, "Eventually, Mr. Nostov will tire of his game and move out of the picture. He's a bureaucrat trapped in a gangster's body. No imagination whatsoever."

"I'm not worried about Mr. Nostov. I just don't like him. And I am too good of a scientist to put up with his petty thug act."

"I didn't mean to imply you were worried about him. Now, let's try to be a little more social. I read that your sister was going to be inducted into one of Harvard's most exclusive clubs, along with President Monroe's daughter. You must be proud," said Hiro, the timbre of his voice shifting with the tenor of the conversation.

"She's being inducted next week. It's a club I founded when I was an undergraduate."

"It's good to be close to family. If I were to change one thing about myself, I would have remained closer to my relatives. When you become as successful as we are, it is far too easy to let people slip through your fingers."

Veronica nodded, dreamily toying with her silverware. "I guess. But family can be a weakness. Truthfully, I don't even know Carrie. She's my half sister, and my mother made sure we never got close."

"I guess she was intimidated by you. And rightfully so."

"That's one way to look at it. I think it was just easier for her. My stepfather didn't like the idea of other children with some connection to my mother out in the world. And my father stepped completely out of the picture and never came back. None of them ever seemed that interested in my life."

"And despite all that, look how you've succeeded," said Hiro. His voice took on a paternal tone, as if he were trying to make Veronica feel better.

Veronica snapped to attention, suddenly realizing she was on the verge of pouring her heart out to a business partner and competitor she barely even knew. She flushed with embarrassment and took a long sip of water from her glass. "Yes, I am successful" she agreed.

Hiro wiped something off the sleeve of his jacket. He said, "Well, I guess then we should get down to business. I'm sorry, Veronica, but it's becoming increasingly clear the weapon portion of the project is never going to work. We've done test after test on mice, and even some tests on the higher orders of primates. The death ratio hasn't changed at all. No matter what we do, the weapon has about the same effect as standing in front of a malfunctioning microwave oven. Maybe the scientist's mad ideas were just that. Mad," said Hiro, frowning down at the tablecloth.

"You already want to give up?" asked Veronica in surprise. "Is this because of Nostov? We can get rid of him. You've got to give the project more time."

Hiro poured himself another glass of wine and topped off Veronica's. "What are we supposed to do, bankrupt our companies over a stupid pipe dream? We have given it as much chance as any prudent scientific endeavor should be given."

"Nostov still seems interested."

"He owns stations and transmitting towers. He has no idea how they work. And no interest in finding out," said Hiro dismissively. "A new weapon, he understands—a new technology, not in the least. I could have shown him a desk computer in the 1960s and he would have only thought of it as a way to show television."

"I thought you were interested in power as well."

Hiro nodded. "I am. Although the weapon proved to be impractical, there were some interesting suggestions regarding optics and sound technology. If nothing else, we've created one of the most advanced pieces of technology in the last two decades. I'm satisfied with that. The profits will keep our two companies independent for another hundred years. Didn't you say you were seeing the president's daughter next week? It would be a great marketing opportunity if we could get one of the prototypes into her hands."

"I know. I've already thought of that from the communications angle. I still don't understand why you don't want to work on the weapon portion anymore. I thought that was the entire point. It's not like you need the money," answered Veronica.

"Money opens many doors. Maybe next time, we will have the pieces necessary to put together something that shatters the earth. We just don't have it this time. And I have to think of my company. We have many other projects that need attention. I can't spend all my researchers' time and energy on something I know will ultimately fail."

"So you're giving up? I had a different impression of you." Veronica was uneasy. Something wasn't right. She had a feeling she was being played as a pawn.

"I'm not. I've just been in the business a long time. You don't survive very long if you don't listen to the writing on the wall. And here, the writing on the wall says that the project is never going to evolve into a weapon. Let's not allow that fact to taint everything. I have several more ideas for uses of StoneCorp technology. Don't worry, this won't be the last time our two companies work together."

Veronica sat dumbfounded. She wouldn't worry about that. She would never work with Hiro again. She did not like being played with like this. Projects were not halted this quickly in her book. She had to wonder, though. Did it have something to do with her slip about her family? Did she somehow show some weakness that Hiro didn't like? Hiro ordered a cup of coffee and sipped it quietly as he stared out the window at the city's lights. He seemed lost in thought. His eyes looked out at the city as if he were a god staring down at the world from a very great height, watching how his creation ticked along through its day. It seemed as if he already owned the world.

Veronica's eyes narrowed. It had nothing to do with her. At that moment, she knew Hiro was lying about the weapon. She was sure that it worked, but for some reason, he didn't want her to know about it. She decided she would let him think she was done and work on the project herself. They finished dinner and Hiro escorted her to her car.

"I'll call you soon and we can discuss an alternate route for our projects." He smiled and helped her into the car. When her car drove off, he quickly pulled out his beautifully carved Jade cigarette case and puffed hard on a cigarette. Moments later his phone rang and he jumped. He picked up the receiver and stuttered a hello into it.

"H— hello?" He cleared his throat and waited for the person on the other end to talk.

"Yes, it's done," Hiro said as his car pulled up and he got inside. Once inside the car, he leaned back in his seat and continued smoking his cigarette. "Yes!" he yelled into the phone. "I told you I've placed the phone. It's only a matter of time. I must go now." He threw the phone across the car, puffing heavily on his cigarette as if this were his last one. Or maybe he was hoping it would kill him. He looked out the window and longed for the scenery of his native country. He couldn't wait to get home.

11

"I've come up with a new argument regarding Man's inherent bastardness," said Alex. He lay on the hotel bed, his hands propped behind his head. The sheets were twisted around his bare waist.

"I don't really think 'bastardness' is a word," said Veronica.

"If it's not, it should be. It's a nice, ugly word—Germanic sounding. Up there with *schadenfreude* and *weltzschmertz*." He scratched at something on his elbow.

"You're lucky you're a chemist," said Veronica. She stood at the foot of the bed, wearing nothing but her lingerie and thigh-high stockings while searching through her suitcase for a missing earring. Her body looked like one smooth, perfect curve. Although they always had sex whenever Alex was in Boston, as soon as it was over, Veronica seemed to forget Alex was even in the room. Tonight, they were in a hotel room in Boston's Copley Square. Alex was in town for a medical conference at MIT. Veronica had never let him visit her at her apartment or at StoneCorp's laboratory, a few miles away in Cambridge. In fact, the hotel room was hers.

"What is that supposed to mean?" Alex asked.

"I can't believe I can't find this stupid earring."

"Why? Are you nervous?"

"Why would I be nervous? I just don't want to walk in there with one earring dangling off of me like a pirate. My sister is friends with the president's daughter—the two of them are getting inducted into the Athena Club tonight. I have to play good sister if I want to have enough time with Miss USA."

"What's your sister's name?"

"Carrie. Actually, she's my half sister."

"So you're only half related."

"If we were fully related, I doubt I'd be going at all," snapped Veronica. "Here they are. God. I forgot how terrible they really are. I saw a picture of the president's daughter out and about on campus with a similar pair. I thought she'd like them. A little young for me, but I guess they're okay."

"Do you calculate absolutely everything you do?" asked Alex, clearly implying a lewd joke.

Veronica didn't even look at him as she put the earring on. "Of course. I had your physiology and known likes and dislikes fed into our computers at StoneCorp. Just to let you know, I will never dress up as Little Orphan Annie for you."

"Wow, that computer is bloody impressive!" laughed Alex. He yawned and stretched like a cat. Then he rapped a quick staccato beat on the headboard. "You're lucky you're so gorgeous."

"What's that supposed to mean?"

"It balances your astonishing sensitivity to the feelings of others. I'm not sure if I would be interested in you without it."

"That would be heartbreaking," said Veronica sarcastically, disappearing into the bathroom. She continued to call out through the doorway. "I really need to get dressed and get going. I'd appreciate it if you aren't lying around in my way when I come out."

Alex stared at the ceiling and tried to ignore the sick feeling in his stomach. He didn't want her to see how hurt he actually was. When he heard Veronica turn on the water, he swung his legs to the floor. He was sure she was seeing someone else—in fact, he knew she slept with whomever she wanted to whenever she wanted to, either because of tactical considerations or out of boredom or even spite. She had never been monogamous with him, but since he knew she wasn't monogamous with anyone else, it had never really bothered him. He had always thought of himself as above the others, her favorite. But she was acting even colder than usual. Maybe there was someone else—someone more important than all the others. Someone more important than him.

Suddenly, Alex could hear the faint sound of a phone ringing. He looked around for Veronica's handbag. He glanced at the closed bathroom door, then snapped Veronica's handbag open. Inside were two cell phones, an electronic organizer, a sleeve full of credit cards, a passport, some makeup, and a sealed envelope.

Alex held the envelope up to the light. It appeared to be a personal check of some sort. Then he picked up the ringing phone. It looked like one of the new StoneCorp prototypes Veronica had mentioned at brunch that day. She hadn't said too much about them, only that they weren't ready to be mass-marketed yet. Alex figured he was holding one of only a few in existence. He turned it on, and suddenly, the phone in his hand started ringing and buzzing quite loudly.

Alex practically jumped out of his skin. Who else would

have one of these things? Although it might have been one of her research scientists, Alex knew Veronica didn't like to let her underlings have control over prototype technology, in case they got the idea to take the technology to a rival company. If she had given another one of the phones to someone, it would have only been to someone she trusted. Alex had the sudden unshakable belief that Veronica had given another phone to whomever she was seeing. He didn't bother to put on his clothes. If the phone's picture was as clear as Veronica said it was, and if Veronica had given the boyfriend one of her new phones, the boyfriend would certainly get Alex's message.

Alex stared into the screen, ready to face his competition. He hit the accept button on the bottom of the screen to accept the call when, suddenly, a picture of a knight on a chessboard flashed on the screen, along with a series of bright lights and binging ring tones. Then the phone disconnected to a dial tone. A shooting pain raced through his head and ears like an angry wasp.

What was that? Alex thought about calling the number back. The phone had probably taped him staring naked into the screen. Veronica would use it later to make fun of him for poking around in her things like a teenager.

Whatever it was, he decided he didn't need to see it again. He turned the phone off and set it back in Veronica's purse, gathered his crumpled clothes, and got dressed. Then Alex walked out, slamming the door shut behind him.

12

VERONICA STOOD IN the Athena Club's hallway, sipping a glass of wine. She'd continued to send fifty thousand dollars to the Club every year after she'd graduated—in fact, it was a requirement to remain an Athena Alumna. While most of the money had gone into programs and trips for the Club members, a good deal of the money had also been poured into the Athena Club House. The Club had bought an entire block of Victorian buildings just off Harvard Square, connecting them all through an intricate series of passageways. The walls were covered in mahogany and art—in fact, several pieces were being actively pursued by Harvard, Boston, and many other art museums who seemed appalled that internationally important pieces were being kept in a girls' "sorority house." Fresh flowers stood in vases, and signed first editions lined the bookshelves. There was now a party room with a concert hall-quality stage, an Olympic-sized lap pool, underground squash courts, a rooftop deck, workout rooms, saunas, a climbing wall, a center garden, and room for forty girls with huge single suites. Five housekeepers lived on site, along with three chefs, a gardener, and a personal trainer/masseuse. All of them were women. Alex joked that the Athena Club was like some kind of Amazonian temple, and that it was beginning to make the Sultan of Brunei's palace look like a trailer home. In fact, that's exactly what Veronica wanted.

When she'd first arrived for Initiation Weekend, the girls all stared at her as if she were some kind of mythic figure they had only half-believed in, like a centaur or a unicorn. They practically killed themselves trying to please her, showing Veronica books and articles they were involved with, a film one was producing, and a jazz album one of the seniors was soon releasing on Blue Note. Every time she turned around, a different girl was standing near her. They refilled her glass when only a quarter of whatever she was drinking was gone. They brought her different hors d'oeuvres. They gave her armloads of expensive gifts. If she had asked for it, they probably would have thrown rose petals in front of her feet and carried her around Harvard Square in a litter. Finally, Veronica told them enough was enough—she was only here to see her sister inducted. The girls immediately vanished with hurt expressions, as if they were sinning acolytes forced from the Temple of Veronica.

At the end of the hallway, a door opened. Veronica's half sister, Carrie, came walking toward her. She was taller than Veronica, with the same hair and eyes. But her father's darker features shone through, and her face was wide and soft where Veronica's was all sharp angles. She was wearing a very pretty red dress, like all of the other inductees, but she looked awkward in it, her athletic build a little overpowering for the tapered silk fabric. She was pretty, but not gorgeous—a cheap imitation of what her half sister was. Veronica could understand why her mother felt the need to call in Veronica's help.

Carrie seemed to be playing dress up, as if even she knew she didn't really belong here.

"So, how do you feel now that you're an Athena Sister?" asked Veronica.

"I feel good," answered Carrie. She had been terse with Veronica the entire day, as if she were afraid Veronica was simply helping the rest of the girls play a very elaborate joke and the rug was in imminent danger of being pulled out from under her.

"You know, you could be a little nicer to me," said Veronica, smiling. She hoped she sounded more playful than she felt.

Carrie looked at her feet. "Mom said you helped get me and Jessica in."

"That's not what I meant. We're sisters, after all."

"I guess. Half sisters anyway."

"Of course we are," said Veronica grandly. "You know I never stopped thinking about you."

"I didn't think you were interested in me."

"Not my fault. I tried to stay involved. You know that, don't you?"

"I do."

Veronica watched Carrie pull at her lip with her fingernails. There was a scab there—apparently picking at her lips was one of Carrie's nervous habits. Veronica fought the urge to reach out and slap her hand away. She made a mental note to remind some of the older Sisters to cure Carrie of that habit as soon as possible. "I sent you Christmas gifts," Veronica said.

"I never got them."

"Mom intercepted them."

"I know," said Carrie. She sat in one of the large leather chairs that were scattered along the hallway.

Veronica remained standing. Carrie had the manners of a fifteen-year-old boy, and Veronica fought the urge to correct her. Fighting and nagging would have just made the awkwardness permanent. For now, she just wanted her half sister to like her. She said, "I thought your class looked lovely during the ceremony."

"Everyone was staring at you. It's like they think you're the Queen or something."

"I am the founder of Athena Club. All of this was my idea. It wouldn't have existed without me."

"I know," Carrie sighed. "I'm going to have to live up to you. Everyone is going to look at me ten times closer." She looked at the wall as if she were considering kicking it for emphasis.

"So? You just have to be ten times better. I have no doubt that you'll live up to it. We share half of the same genes after all."

"When Mom said you were coming, I figured it was just because I'm friends with Jessica, and you wanted to kiss up to President Monroe or something," said Carrie.

Veronica smiled warmly, trying her best to look surprised at Carrie's suggestion. Veronica answered, "That's ridiculous. I wanted to see you. Mom said she was getting divorced—"

"They're separated. It's not that big of a deal," responded Carrie sharply.

"Right. Separated. Anyway, when she called, she said she was separated, and she had no problems with me coming to see you. And I came right away. It had nothing to do with any favors Mom wanted me to do."

Carrie played with the tips of her fingers in silence. Finally, she asked, "So, what do you think?"

"What do I think about what?"

"About me. What do you think about me?" asked Carrie.

Veronica mumbled, "Well, I—"

"Hey y'all! We're going to celebrate with some pizza!" Jessica Monroe exclaimed, practically skipping down the hallway toward them. She was the president's daughter through and through. She had the same satisfied grin, and the same expression as if the entire world had been built just for her. She oozed privilege and self-confidence. Although the initiates were required to wear their hair down during the initiation ceremony, Jessica had already pulled her blonde hair back into its signature ponytail and bow. When she spoke, it was with an Alabama accent that sounded as if her mouth were full of sweet syrup. She was a cute little party girl, brown eyes flashing with mirth, and her red dress looked wonderful on her, as if she had just stepped out from the pages of *Vogue*. In fact, she was already slated to appear in the spring issue, and she'd been telling everyone she was going to wear only red as a salute to her new Sisters. She'd been very careful to make sure Veronica knew that. Someday, she'd make a fine politician.

Jessica ran the rest of the way and clasped both of Veronica's hands in her own. "I'm so glad I found you," she said. It was an incredibly warm gesture, something gained from having grown up in a furiously political family. Veronica felt a real sense of intimate friendship immediately—she admired Jessica's skill. She would go far. Unlike Carrie, she was a perfect choice for the Club. Once again, she couldn't quite understand what she and her half sister had in common.

"I thought we were having dinner in an hour or so?" asked Veronica good-naturedly.

"We are," exclaimed Jessica. "This is snacks!" She giggled

merrily. The timbre of Jessica's voice made the idea of a trip to the local pizza parlor sound like something incredibly "bad" and wonderful, as if she were suggesting they all go crash an exclusive movie premiere.

"I don't know, we probably shouldn't," said Carrie, looking at her half sister. She seemed to think that what she was saying was what her half sister would want to hear. The Athena Club had very strict unwritten rules regarding body image and gluttony.

Instead, Veronica smiled widely and put her hands on both of their shoulders. "Of course we should! This is a celebration! Where are we going?"

"My favorite is Pinocchio's—their spinach pizza is great! It's right around the corner," said Jessica. Then she leaned conspiratorially into Veronica's ear. "And the guy that takes orders is really hot."

"Sounds great," said Veronica. Carrie was looking at her shoes, obviously disappointed and surprised that she'd guessed her half sister's wishes wrong. But how could she have guessed that this trip was fitting perfectly into Veronica's plans? Veronica reached into her handbag. "Let me just make one call to the office and make sure they haven't blown up anything," she said airily.

Her next few moves were completely rehearsed. Veronica removed the new phone from her bag with a practiced, graceful, and almost seductive motion, flipping open the screen so it was directly in Jessica's line of vision. On the other end of the line, a handsome model she'd hired for the weekend waited for her call, dressed as a StoneCorp scientist. The model was in a room painted in bright blues and greens to set him off to the greatest advantage, with beakers, flowers, and an aquarium just behind him. They'd done weeks of research with a design firm to determine what would be the perfect picture for young Miss Monroe to first see on StoneCorp's videophones, based on Jessica's interviews, her choices in fashion, and the color scheme of her family's ski house in Vail. The model was chosen because he looked like an amalgamation of Jessica's recent boyfriends and Brad Pitt. "Hello, Ms. Stone. Can I help you?" said the man. His voice was rich and deep. He was wearing a white jacket like a stereotypical research scientist.

"Hello, James. How are things at the lab?" asked Veronica. She glanced over at Jessica. Her mouth had dropped open. Carrie stood and peeked over Jessica's shoulder. Veronica had to admit, the picture was mesmerizing. The glass beakers and swimming fish seemed to stick out from the screen, and she could almost feel the hard glass and the wet, wiggling bodies in her hands. The model was also perfect. Veronica thought she might have to keep him working for a few days more.

"Everything is going fine. We're running the beta test on the new fluxus converter. Energy levels have been at sixty degrees Celsius, but we're thinking we can cross-loop the channel with some copper and oxygenate nitrous." The model's words were basically gibberish, a collection of things a sound consultant suggested, designed to use the tones of the model's voice to their greatest advantage. Even though his words were meaningless, it sounded as if he were talking about sex.

Veronica nodded. Then she answered, "Sounds good. We're going to Pinocchio's in Harvard Square for some pizza."

"I love Pinocchio's," said the man, laughing richly. "That's my favorite restaurant from my MIT days." Veronica knew the man had never set foot in a college classroom. Even so, he was a good actor. She'd definitely be paying him more than they had negotiated.

Jessica pulled on Veronica's elbow and whispered, "Let him come! Let him come! I'll treat!"

Veronica smiled and batted Jessica away playfully, as if they were two lifelong friends talking to a boy they had a crush on. Everything was working out just as Veronica had thought. "That will be all. Thanks, James."

James sighed. "Good night, Ms. Stone," he said. Then the screen went blank.

"That was the most beautiful man I have ever seen!" exclaimed Jessica. "He's a scientist?"

"He looks like a model," said Carrie glumly. She seemed jealous of all the attention her half sister's employee was getting.

Veronica kept herself from shooting a look at her half sister. "He's actually one of our best scientists," she answered.

"And he's cute! What kind of phone is that? The picture and sound were incredible! It looked like he was right there, shrunk down in your hand! The fish looked like they were going to fall out onto the floor. I half-expected water to come dripping out! That's totally the coolest thing I have ever seen."

"It's a new prototype made by my company," answered Veronica. She paused for a moment as if she were considering something. "Do you want one?"

Jessica glanced at Carrie and then back at Veronica. "Are you serious? Really?"

"I'll give you this one," said Veronica, handing it to Jessica. "It's a prototype, so the only saved number in it is my office. Consider the phone yours. And, here's the organizer that comes with it. It has the same amount of memory as a Mac, and wireless Internet access from any place on the planet. You could be on a raft floating in the middle of the ocean, and you'll still be able to get a signal."

Jessica cradled the phone and the organizer in her hands and practically hopped up and down. "You are so generous! This is so cool! Carrie, check this out!"

"And I'll send one to your Dad. That way you can talk to each other whenever you want. I know you don't get to see him much," said Veronica, sneaking her suggestion in as nonchalantly as possible.

"Thank you so much. This is so great. Thanks," said Jessica, poking at the organizer while Carrie flipped the videophone open and closed.

Carrie looked at Veronica expectantly. She said, "This is a really nice gift." It was clear she thought Veronica was about to give her one as well.

"Not too many exist, so I can't really give away too many of them. But as soon as StoneCorp starts mass production, everyone in the Athena Club will have a set. Along with our new stereo and television. But right now, these are the only phones I can give out."

Carrie wilted in disappointment, but then smiled widely before Jessica looked up from her new organizer and noticed. Carrie said, "That's cool. I can't wait. So, aren't we going to get some pizza? We have to be back for dinner pretty soon."

"Oh yeah, right, but this is so cool! Look at this screen saver! It's like real 3D!" exclaimed Jessica. She had clearly lost all interest in going to the pizza place. "I feel like I can stick my hand in it."

"Well, maybe it wasn't such a great idea. Dinner is in like an hour," said Carrie sadly. She sank back into the chair, apparently accepting the fact that no one was talking to her.

Veronica leaned forward and started showing Jessica all of the organizer's special features. Then she turned on the unit's sound system. The entire hallway started to quake with Jessica's favorite song, another product of lengthy research in Jessica's likes and dislikes. Carrie got up and started to wander down the hall as if she couldn't quite decide whether she should stay or go. Finally, she said in a voice that was barely audible over the loud music, "Well, I guess I'll go up and check on my makeup and stuff."

"Oh! If you're going upstairs, I have a gift I've been meaning to give you all day!" Veronica exclaimed, reaching into her handbag again. "You can put it up with your stuff so it doesn't get lost."

Carrie looked at the envelope Veronica handed her, apparently trying to decide if it was proper etiquette to open it in front of her or not. Jessica continued to play with her new toy. Finally, Carrie ripped the envelope open. "It's a blank check made out to me," said Carrie in confusion.

Veronica smiled at her. "Write in what you want. We're sisters, after all. My money is your money."

Carrie slipped the check back into the envelope. She seemed suspicious of it, as if she wasn't sure whether it was meant as a gift or as some kind of bribe.

In fact, Veronica considered it a bounty for delivering Jessica Monroe to her, and a purchase of her half sister's loyalty. While Carrie was of little or no use to her, Jessica Monroe was quite a coup.

At least for the time being, Veronica would keep behaving

as if she had believed Hiro's story about giving up on the weapon. That way, she could do a little more research herself, and figure out what was going on with Hiro and, she guessed, Mr. Nostov.

13

When Alex finally got on the phone, his voice sounded distant, as if he were speaking from the bottom of a very large hole. "Hello? Veronica?" he croaked, before falling into a spasm of coughing.

"You sound terrible," said Veronica, absentmindedly twisting a strand of her hair around her index finger. She'd called Alex's office out of boredom. It was late in the day in Britain, but Alex sounded like he'd just woken up from a long nap. Outside her window, two peregrine falcons swooped and dived over the trees in Central Park.

It was two weeks after Carrie's induction into the Athena Club, and Veronica was in her New York apartment. She kept several apartments around the world, but she was rarely ever in them— most of the time, she found it easier just to stay at whatever hotel her hosts put her up in. In any case their rents were good tax write-offs for the company. She was in her New York apartment the least out of them all. Boston was a short hop on the corporate jet, and she didn't like being away from StoneCorp for longer than necessary, so she rarely stayed at the New York apartment.

Consequently, the apartment was beautifully decorated. Each room had several pieces of very expensive furniture and the walls were lined with luxurious artwork, part of her collections from around the world. Her crystal vases held some of the most striking and magnificent flowers. The women who kept her apartment clean were told to keep fresh and exotic flowers out at all times. She loved coming in and smelling that warm sweet flowery air. Her refrigerator had been stocked with a few of the essentials. When she was a few hours away, she called her cleaning crew and notified them of her arrival and of what she wanted waiting for her when she arrived.

She stepped out onto her veranda and leaned down to look into Central Park. She could see the people walking briskly down the street and in and out of the park. It was a crisp day in New York and she loved the breeze that blew past her on her terrace. It was different air up here than down below. Cleaner, purer, softer, and it lacked that grungy hot dog and pretzel smell she loathed.

Alex began coughing again and woke her out of her dreamy stare over the park.

"Yeah. I know I sound awful," he said, before breaking into another bout of coughing. "I thought I had the flu, but now I'm not so sure."

"You'll be fine," she said as she sat down on one of her lounge chairs outside and flipped through a magazine.

"I know. I'm actually trying to get my staff doctors to do something useful and cure me. I am the CEO of a pharmaceutical company after all. It doesn't seem like I should be capable of getting sick."

"Antibiotics."

"I'm so full of antibiotics right now, I feel like someone

could use me to sterilize an emergency room," answered Alex. He turned the phone away from his mouth and coughed some more. "My secretary is avoiding me. I've become the Typhoid Mary of the entire company, and I'm the one that signs their checks, the thankless bastards."

"You'll feel better," Veronica said, flatly annoyed that this was all they were talking about.

"I know, I just always hate being sick. Even when I was a little boy—I think I was the only child who felt very put out by having to miss school," he said. "You sound bothered. Where are you?"

"New York. I had to meet with one of StoneCorp's affiliates."

"You mean you bought another company?"

"They had a fuel cell I wanted. For the phone."

Alex started to laugh, then stopped himself before he started coughing again. "This is going to be some phone."

"It already is some phone. I'm making something no one has even imagined before. By the time I'm done, it will be much more than just 'some phone.'"

"Cool. I want stock."

Veronica laughed. "Okay. I'll give you one or two shares."

"I've always said it was your generosity that attracted me. So what's bothering you? You wouldn't have called me otherwise."

Veronica tapped on the edge of her veranda with her fingernail, as if she were trying to pin down her thoughts. "I don't know. It was weird seeing Carrie. And the last time I talked to Hiro, I started going into my family. It was unnerving."

"I'd blame the wine."

"I'm blaming me. It took me a long time to get to where I am, and I can't lose any ground. In the tech field, you can be on the front page of *The New York Times* and then an industry joke and dinosaur by the next day. The way I look and everything—I can't let people start to think they can treat me less seriously than a man. I am StoneCorp. If it starts going around that I'm telling all my personal problems to everybody, I'm sunk. Hiro must think I'm a fool. It probably has something to do with why they halted the project."

"They halted the project? I thought you just said you were still working on the project?"

Veronica answered, "I said *they* halted. *I* haven't halted anything. Hiro wants to stop where we are and just put out the most technologically advanced cell phone in the world."

"Isn't that what it is?"

Veronica paused. She was suddenly struck with the desire to keep the real nature of the project from Alex. "Of course. But it could have been even better," she answered. She felt like her deception was obvious.

Luckily, Alex renewed coughing. "I can't believe how terrible I feel."

"You should be home."

"I am home. I'm having all my calls forwarded here. At least the ones I want to answer. Which has been one so far."

Veronica smiled at herself in the glass. "Thanks."

"Look. Don't worry about it. You're twenty times the man Hiro Nakashimi is."

"Thanks," answered Veronica, laughing. "I'll try to take that as a compliment."

"I mean it as one. I should go. I think I'm going to lie down for another nap and try to sleep this thing off. Maybe by then my docs will figure out what the hell is wrong with me. Otherwise, I'm firing the whole pack of them."

"It's probably just some weird virus. Don't worry too much. Just rest and drink lots of fluids."

"If you felt like I do, you wouldn't be so nonchalant about it."

"Probably not."

"In fact, I'd bet you'd demand that the CDC come up and look at you personally."

"Probably." said Veronica. An awkward silence engulfed them and Veronica felt it. She shrugged it off. "Get better," she said before hanging up.

"I will. Not really any other option, is there?" answered Alex.

14

A week after talking to Alex, Hiro invited Veronica back to Kyoto. They sat together in the same restaurant as before, looking over binders of advertising material for the new breakthrough cell phone. All of the advertising was mysterious, with no clear indication what was being advertised. Mainly it was pictures of scenic vistas, deep blue oceans, and cosmic backgrounds of stars and planets. The marketers wanted to call the phone "Veronica." Her name floated through all the materials like a ghost.

"The advertisers thought a mysterious name would generate buzz. And they wanted a woman's name. People are more likely to covet or value an object if it is named after a woman instead of a man. Like ships. Or when the Segway was still called Ginger," said Hiro.

Veronica ran her finger over the raised type of her name. She knew in her heart that Hiro had gotten the weapon components to work, but he seemed completely absorbed by the advertising and slogans. Even so, Hiro kept looking at her as if she seemed different than he expected. She guessed he might have assumed she'd be furious about her name over everything, but she wasn't. Over the last week, there had been even more breakthroughs on the prototype phones at StoneCorp, especially with its new fuel source. To her, this version of the cell phone was already obsolete. She didn't care what they called it. The important work was at her lab in Boston. "The marketers are probably right. I can imagine the buzz. People like a little mystery," she said.

"Are you all right?" asked Hiro.

"Why?" Veronica glanced at him in surprise.

"You look a little distracted."

"It's strange seeing my name as an advertising slogan."

"What about StoneCorp?"

"That's not an advertising slogan. That's my baby." She winced as the words left her mouth.

"As TechWorks is mine. I thought 'Veronica' would really give StoneCorp a presence in the worldwide communications marketplace."

Veronica nodded, running her finger along her sake cup. "It already has a presence. Is all this some type of apology?"

"For what?" asked Hiro.

"For stopping the project."

Hiro sat back and looked up at the ceiling. "As I said, it's impossible. A pipe dream. We could drive ourselves mad trying to pursue it. I think that's what happened to the Russian scientist. He didn't know when to stop."

"I still think you're giving up too easily."

"You sound like you're still considering it as a weapon," said Hiro pointedly.

"I'm—"

Veronica was cut off by a man sliding open the room's

screen. It was the restaurant's host. He bowed deeply. "I apologize for interrupting you. Ms. Stone has an urgent call. The man on the other line would not be put off," he said, bowing again.

"What? My cell phone is here with me—"

The man shook his head. "No. No. It came in on the restaurant's phone. He says it's urgent."

Veronica stood in confusion, bowing slightly to Hiro. "I should go see what this is. I apologize."

She took the call in the restaurant's office. The phone was a heavy black rotary from the 1960s. It felt like something from the Stone Age. "Hello?"

"It's Alex."

Veronica gasped. His voice sounded cracked and thin, as if he had aged one hundred years. "What's wrong? How did you know I was here?"

"I had your crew use GPS to find your cell phone. I need you to come to London."

"Why? What's wrong? Why'd you call on a landline?"

"Your cell phone wasn't receiving any signals, and I needed to talk to you."

"Alex, what's wrong?"

Alex coughed for a solid minute before he could gather enough breath to answer. "Whatever I've got—it's killing me."

15

THE HIDEKI BAR was dark and smoky, empty except for the bartender and a waitress so early in the afternoon. Its long silver lines, fox hunting pictures, green velvet chairs, and dark wood floors seemed straight out of the nineteenth century, albeit a nineteenth century on an island almost two continents away. The bar had been built to serve Europeans during the colonial era, and it still retained that era's sense of divine entitlement and menace. Hiro sat in one of the bar's huge crescent-shaped booths, papers and glasses spread on the table all around him. Two of his bodyguards sat discretely at the bar. Another was in a car outside. Five other cars with two to three men each were parked two blocks away with their engines running. Two more guards were in the bar's kitchen, taking over the dishwashers' jobs for the day, machine pistols stashed between the bottles of soap and towels below the sink.

Sergei walked up the bar's front staircase, followed by four other men. He glanced around the room, and then the men fanned out around him. He strode over to Hiro. His brow was knitted into a dark triangle right between his bushy eyebrows. "Veronica Stone is still alive," he said flatly.

"She is. Please, sit down," said Hiro, moving his papers to the side.

"You were to dispose of her."

"And I didn't. Now sit down—I don't like talking to your belly."

Sergei shook his head. "I'm not sitting down. You said your plan was foolproof."

"It was. And it still didn't work."

"You should have just shot her."

"I'm not a killer," said Hiro.

"Yes you are. You just don't like to get your hands dirty. What about the original inhabitants of your little island paradise? How are they doing? I've heard they weren't too keen on giving up their little fishing village. The graves of their elders— something like that."

Hiro frowned uncomfortably. "They were compensated."

"Right. If you count a very long and very deep swim compensation."

"We're not talking about my business dealings."

"No, we're not. We're talking about the way you run your business."

"The way I run my business is my own affair."

"Not when it affects mine. And we can't have Veronica Stone running around alive if our plan is going to work. She could sink the whole thing if she talks to the wrong person. She's been a very good pawn so far. It's time to remove her from the board."

"The phone went off. Clearly, something didn't work."

"We both know it works. That corporate spy you had

skulking around your company's kitchens burning the tuna found that out the hard way, didn't he?"

"That was not my idea."

"No. Because you weren't man enough to have it. When we tried the weapon on him, he died within thirty seconds. His body fell apart as if he were an old Egyptian mummy."

"He faced the maximum amount of exposure," said Hiro.

"Still, the phone should have done something to Miss Stone. We both know it. Someone else must have gotten the call."

"You can't just kill Veronica Stone. She's a very powerful and well-known woman. People will notice she's gone and they'll come looking for us." Hiro's voice was raised. He was annoyed. This was not how things were supposed to go. If the phone didn't work on Veronica, they would have to figure something else out, but killing her outright could not be an option. Sergei and his thugs would make a mess of the whole deal. Then there would be hell to pay. Hiro worked too long and too hard to let everything he'd worked for die because some Russian idiot was going to kill everything that got in his way.

"No," Sergei laughed, "they'll come looking for you. No one knows of my involvement with Veronica Stone."

Hiro shuddered and took a swig of his drink.

"I don't understand it. It had to be her that answered the phone. Her curiosity should have—"

"Curiosity only kills cats. And Veronica Stone is no cat. I will handle this," said Sergei. He picked up his glass. "To Miss Stone. May the skin rot from her bones, quickly." Then he snapped his head back and swallowed his drink.

16

VERONICA DROVE PAST the estate's enormous stone gate and up Alex's gravel driveway. The house had been in Alex's family for generations, from when Alex's great-great grandfather received a royal commission and moved his family out into the English countryside. Green ivy hung from dark granite flag-stone, with small parapets reaching up to the sky and a wide front lawn where Alex sometimes worked with one of his many horses. It looked like a child's idea of a castle full of knights and damsels. Veronica had always loved driving up to it—there was something cheery and magical about the house, like Gaudi's chapel or King Arthur's Camelot, and she could still remember the first time she saw it with Alex. At the time, she half-expected a dragon to come spinning out of one of its high windows, or a unicorn to trot across its lawn. Today, though, the house looked more like a tomb than anything else—melancholy seemed to hang in the air around it like a cloud. It was more than just the rain that had been falling all day. Usually, the house was a hive of activity, cars, friends, business associates, servants, and ani-mals running every which way, reveling in the excitement of an energetic bachelor's home. Now several horse steeples lay scattered in front of the house like ruins, their white beams covered in wet. One of the steeple's bars lay in the grass, apparently knocked from its place by one of Alex's leaping horses. It looked like it had been lying there for weeks. No cars were parked in front of the house. Nothing moved except the raindrops.

Geoffrey, Alex's old butler, childhood guardian, and playmate, helped Veronica take off her wet coat and then led her to Alex's bedroom before retreating back down the hall. Truthfully, she could have found the way herself. Geoffrey knew this. He had acted with somber formality, as if he were conducting Veronica to a funeral. She was beginning to get very nervous.

Veronica slowly opened the door. Inside the room, everything was dark. A radio played low. Veronica couldn't make out a thing. It was as if she were looking into a black hole. The room smelled like illness. Veronica rapped gently on the doorframe. "Are you in there, Alex?"

"Yes. I'm glad you came," said a voice croaking out of the blackness.

"Were you asleep? Why don't you have any lights on?" said Veronica, stepping into the room and flipping on the light switch.

"No! Wait!" exclaimed Alex.

Veronica gasped. Alex's bedroom looked as it always had—dark wood, books scattered along a wall-length shelf, steel lamps, three windows looking out on his back garden—but now medical equipment, IVs, monitors, and computers were lined up next to his enormous bed like attendants. And in the middle of that bed, one that Veronica knew very well, was something that looked like a melting wax dummy lost among the green silk sheets. At first, her mind could barely register what she was looking at. Then she saw Alex's eyes, now rheumy and yellow, staring out at her in fear from the dummy's sunken cheeks and blotched skin. His teeth were gigantic, as if his lips were peeling away from them like old paint, and his chest rattled with every breath. He looked up at her like an animal trapped in a cage it knew it couldn't escape.

"My God! What happened?" Veronica kneeled down next to the bed and took his hand. It felt dry and cracked, like an old piece of leather. It was no heavier than a bird's wing.

"They don't know. They don't think it's contagious," said Alex quickly, as if he had to rush to get the words out.

"I don't care about that."

"I know. I just thought I should say it." His voice whispered like a fluttering scrap of paper.

"What happened to you?"

"You keep asking that. At least you're not trying to make me feel better with some crap like, 'You'll be shipshape in a week,'" joked Alex. He tried to laugh, but only managed a sharp cough.

"Oh Alex—we need to get you to a hospital."

"I've already been. They couldn't do anything. If I'm dying, I'd rather die in my own home than some antiseptic invalid bus station in London."

"You're not dying."

Alex took his hand from hers. "You know, Tip doesn't even recognize me. What good is a dog if it's frightened of you? Man's best friend until the cookies run out."

Veronica fought against the urge to break into tears. "You don't need to act brave in front of me," she said.

A tear rolled down Alex's cheek and dropped onto his blanket. "I'm glad you're here. I was afraid you wouldn't come."

"Why would you be afraid of that?"

"I just was. That's all." Alex coughed again and closed his eyes. It was as if he were trying to keep his body together by sheer willpower, and if he didn't, everything would fall apart like dust.

Veronica brushed a few stray hairs from his forehead. Most of his hair was gone. Only a few yellowish patches clung to his skull like moss. "We don't have to talk. I'll just be here, okay? You can sleep if you want. I'll hold your hand," said Veronica. She picked up Alex's hand again and clasped it between her own, trying to force some warmth into it.

Alex closed his eyes. What had happened to him? A river of terrifying possibilities poured through Veronica's head—AIDS, cancer, poison, sepsis—she'd never seen anyone in the condition Alex was in. She wondered if whatever it was was contagious, or if she had been exposed to some toxin by coming to Alex's home, then immediately felt guilty for even having the thought. She couldn't believe Alex was still holding on. In fact, she kept passing her finger in front of his lips to make sure he was still breathing.

The joyful British pop song on the radio sounded wrong. It seemed impossible that anyone should still be happy, but just as she made the decision to turn it off, the song ended and the midday newscast came on. As usual, the voice of the BBC sounded sufficiently funereal. "Good midday, this is Matthew Carey of the BBC. From America, it has been reported that the president and his daughter, Jessica, have been struck ill with a mysterious wasting disease that American doctors have so far been unable to diagnose. Dr. James Walsh of the Center for Disease Control in Atlanta, Georgia, has said that physicians are working around the clock to discover what is afflicting

President Monroe and his family. In a televised address, Vice President Peter Davis assured the country that the government is still conducting business as usual and that leaked reports of the president's health have been greatly exaggerated, stating 'President Monroe is stable, and, God-willing, will be up and about by the weekend.' The president had spent the last week traveling in Northern Africa. African leaders were quick to deny any connection between their countries and the president's illness. In related news, Tracy Collins, the spokeswoman for Green World, has created a media firestorm with her comments that 'It would serve America right to lose its leader to an African disease when we have done nothing to ease the suffering of over thirty million Africans' on American television's *Nightline* last week. House Speaker Christopher Hand has called for Ms. Collins to be prosecuted under the anti-terrorism Patriot Act . . ."

Veronica stopped listening. Her heart leapt into her throat. The weapon did work! She knew that was why the president and his daughter were so sick. And Hiro had used it! She slowly turned and looked at Alex, then reached into her handbag. The new phone lay in her hand like a smoking gun. Only three people in the world knew its number—herself, Hiro, and Alex. She'd been using her old phone to conduct business. Had Hiro tried to kill her? She flipped open the phone and tried to turn it on, but it was completely out of power, which should have been impossible considering the new long-life batteries she had developed for it. It was as if all of its energy had been sucked out in one huge burst. Someone had called it. Looking at Alex now, she had a sinking feeling that he had answered it.

Veronica stood quickly and paced the room, talking to herself. Alex was looking at her as if she'd seen a ghost. She smiled and started to tuck him in and noticed his water glass on his nightstand was empty. She picked it up and muttered that she was going to get him more water. He was too weak to argue.

She walked into the hallway and right into the bathroom. Once inside the bathroom, she locked the door, turned on the lights, and stared into the mirror. She talked to herself as if she expected her image to answer back. Hiro had called her phone. He had tried to kill her. Worse yet, he had used her as a guinea pig. The only thing that saved her was Alex's curiosity. He must have heard the phone ring while they were together and answered it. It must have been while they were in Boston. If the phone rang, he would have heard it. That was weeks ago, it was so early in the project. Did they want to poison her? But how could she continue working on the project if that happened? Was she the test? Her head was spinning full of questions. She felt dizzy.

She would have to ask Alex if he had answered her phone. She went back into his room. She handed him a glass of water and patted his head with a towel. She sat for a moment, and then pulled out her phone.

"Is that one of your new phones?" asked Alex in a whisper.

"I'm sorry, Alex. I'll put it away. I was just going to check my messages."

She peeked at Alex to see what he was thinking. He didn't respond. She continued. "Someone told me they've been trying to reach me but I never got their call. I never miss a call. It's bothering me, that's all. I'll put the phone away now."

Alex's rheumy eyes opened halfway. "I answered it. It rang once in Boston. I answered it."

"You answered my phone!" she exclaimed with mock exaggeration. "You nosy bastard!" She playfully swatted his arm.

"It was weird though," Alex continued. Veronica went silent. "When I answered it, the screen came on, and it made these weird noises. Then a chessboard came on the screen, and flashing lights, and then it went out. I'm sorry. I know I shouldn't invade your privacy—"

Veronica interrupted him. "It's okay." She stroked his arm and leaned down to kiss his forehead. She felt horrible. Alex was dying and it was all her fault. She hugged him a little too long and then fled the room.

Veronica stood in the hallway outside Alex's room. Someone had wanted her to get that call, but Alex had gotten it instead.

17

Boston was as rainy and dismal as England. Veronica took a cab from Logan Airport to Athena House, unwilling to call and get StoneCorp's limo service to pick her up. She was afraid someone might be tracking her movements. News of the president's illness was constant. No matter where she looked, it stared back at her in accusation. She felt as if everyone knew she had something to do with it, from the stewardess in first class to the cab driver who kept asking her if she had "accepted the Jesus"—her guilt seemed to hang from her face like a mask.

While waiting for her plane in Heathrow, she had been staring at a late edition newspaper headline, trying to come to grips with what she was unwilling to completely acknowledge. An old Irish woman came up to her and offered her nation's condolences, saying, "Don't be upset dearest, I'm sure the man and his daughter will be fine. It's a natural tragedy, it is." Veronica had kept her head down for the majority of the plane ride. Usually, she would have used the time to try and make some business connections, but she was too afraid to talk to anybody.

She'd left Alex too quickly, leaving a message with his butler that she would be back soon, and that the medical staff was to do everything possible to keep Alex comfortable until she spoke with some doctors in Boston. It had been a clumsy lie, implying she'd be staying in London. Alex's butler had seen right through it but, if she were going to save Alex, she had to get moving, and she didn't have time to make up convincing lies.

Two Secret Service agents were guarding the door to Athena House. Veronica almost turned and walked away, but she steeled herself. There was no way anyone could have made a connection yet. She just had to keep telling herself that. She presented her passport. At first, the two buzz-cut men wouldn't let her in, apparently thinking she was simply another paparazzo trying to sneak in to get pictures of Jessica Monroe's room. Finally, Ms. Turner, the Athena housemother, saw Veronica outside and escorted her in, despite the clear disapproval of the two agents.

"I can't believe guards are outside," said Veronica, allowing Ms. Turner to take her bag and hand it to one of the staff porters. Veronica kept the bag containing her computer and phone, as if it contained a body.

"It's been reprehensible what they've been doing. I caught one trying to sneak through the back door yesterday. One even tried to bribe me for an exclusive peak at Jessica and Carrie's room, and they've been bothering the girls on their ways home from class. Bribe me! What do they think I am, some Caribbean castaway with immigration problems? My great-great grandfather was at the Constitutional Convention! Those media vermin, they're utterly without morals," said Ms. Turner, her prim Puritan visage screwed up in a look of incredulity and repulsion.

"You've done a good job keeping them away. I would have expected a pack of them in front of the doors shoving cameras in my face," Veronica said.

Ms. Turner smiled wickedly. "My son is a policeman. He arrested a few and had their cars towed to an impound yard at the end of the Cape. They didn't come back."

"How else have things been going?"

Ms. Turner sighed. "We had a CDC hazmat team tearing the place apart for two weeks. It was ridiculous. The girls would be going about their normal business, having breakfast, studying, reading, and these ridiculous men in yellow plastic suits and oxygen tanks would be tramping around as if they were surveying the moon. They looked at all of us as if we were about to sprout second heads. Tricia, one of the younger girls, got so fed up with it she covered her face in cornstarch and stuck a fake eye to the middle of her forehead. It was all I could do to keep the G-men from hauling her off," said Ms. Turner, chuckling slightly. Then she put her fingers to her lips and turned away. "Although, considering Jessica and President Monroe are still ill, it was in quite poor taste. Ultimately, most of the parents have pulled their girls from school. Actually, the only one left is your sister."

Veronica thought that was typical of her mother. "How is Carrie?"

"Standing as firm as a tree. Would you like some tea or something else to drink? Carrie is still in class."

"I think I might just go up to her room to wait for her."

Ms. Turner put her hand on the stairs to take Veronica up.

"Oh—no no—you don't have to do that. I know where her room is. I'll just show myself up," exclaimed Veronica. She felt she'd spoken too forcefully, as if she were planning on doing something illegal up there.

"That's fine, honey. If you need something, just use the wall speaker. I'll be right up with whatever you need."

"Thank you, Ms. Turner."

"Sisters have to stick together."

"That's why I created this place."

Ms. Turner cocked her eyebrow. "I meant blood relations."

The door to Carrie and Jessica's room was locked, but Ms. Turner had provided Veronica with a key. One side of the suite was wiped clean of everything—there were no books, sheets, clothes, posters, or even thumbtacks left—that side of the room was a void, and Veronica could smell fresh white paint. Why had they repainted? There was a clear line between where the new and old paint jobs met, right below the window frame, as if someone had sawed the room in half. Carrie's side was untouched. A jumble of papers and books sat on her desk under a few snapshots and a poster of some band called *Joy Division*. The poster was against the rules, but Veronica decided not to say anything about it. A fern hung above the window, in need of watering. Everything else was clean and dusted—the bed made, clothes put in their places, shelves cleared of clutter and knickknacks. Veronica guessed the dorm rooms in Athena House were probably the cleanest dorm rooms in America. When she'd been at Harvard, she'd seen other dorm rooms—usually piles of intermixed dirty and clean laundry, scraps of paper, fast-food bags, cigarette butts, and wine bottles with desiccated flowers sticking out of them. Some of the other dorms on campus had called the Athena House's cleaning crews "elitist" and "unbecoming of Harvard." Veronica thought they were a bunch of leftist do-gooders whose trust funds would find them nice jobs in the nonprofit sector. The Athena House paid well, and the women who cleaned the rooms needed to work somewhere— it might as well be someplace that actually gave them health insurance.

Veronica leaned down to look at the pictures, setting her case and handbag on her sister's bed. They were pictures of Carrie and Jessica mostly. One of Carrie, Jessica, and Mrs. Monroe fishing off the back of a boat. There was another of Carrie standing next to the president with one of his signature "president" baseball caps.

"I don't have a picture of you to put up," said Carrie behind her. "You never gave me one."

Veronica jumped. Carrie stood in the doorway, her hands on her hips. She looked angry. Veronica stood and pushed her hair back with her hand, regaining her usual cool exterior. "I need to send you one," she said.

Carrie tossed her backpack onto her bed and then sat down next to it. She was wearing a dark green West German Army jacket, paint-splattered blue jeans, and a pair of purple Dr. Marten boots. She also had a new nose ring pierced through her left nostril.

"Are you dressed up for a play or something?" asked Veronica in shock.

"Yeah right, I'm in a play."

Now it was Veronica's turn to look angry. "That's not Athena code."

"I'm the sister of the founder. What is anybody else going to do about it? Unless you feel you need to take a special interest or something?" asked Carrie, smiling evilly.

"I don't understand why you're acting this way."

"Yes you do. Now why are you here?" Carrie said. "There's enough going on without you getting into the middle of it."

Veronica was taken aback. She felt like she was conducting a hostile business meeting, not talking with her little sister. "I thought you might need some help—"

"Right. You and everybody else that thinks they can make a profit off of this. Some guy from *Playboy* even called—putting out feelers apparently—I'm considering it. Maybe put a big Athena Club tattoo on my ass."

Veronica crossed her arms. "I have no idea why you're acting this way."

Carrie opened her mouth to respond, then froze. "What's that red light on your forehead?" she asked in confusion.

Veronica instinctively dove to the floor, dragging Carrie down with her. The window shattered in a flurry of shots, shredding the room, the posters from the wall, the girls' mattresses. It was as if the entire room were exploding.

"We have to get out!" yelled Veronica, crawling for the doorway. Carrie was curled into the fetal position, her eyes closed as if she could simply will it all away. Suddenly, the shooting stopped.

Through the door, Veronica heard shouts and boots booming up the stairs. The door flew open, and the two Secret Service men who had been guarding the front door came rolling into the room. One fell across Veronica as the other blocked Carrie under the desk and peeked over the shattered windowsill. Veronica could hear sirens and more shouts on the street below.

"Are either of you hurt?" asked the agent lying on top of Veronica. At first, Veronica was too stunned to say anything. The agent repeated himself louder. "Are either of you hurt?"

"Get off! I'm fine!" Veronica shoved the man away and scooted over to her sister, unmindful of the glass and splinters that littered the floor. "Carrie? Are you okay?"

"I'm fine," said Carrie, her voice squeaking out from behind the big agent's shoulders. "Normal day."

One of the agents flipped open a radio. Outside, searchlights started to pierce the night sky. The agent barked into his radio, "Assailant fled. No casualties. The shots came through the window. Check the buildings across the street for any open windows or roof access points. I think we're looking at a high-powered rifle." The agent put his radio away. "You were very lucky. We're going to take you someplace safe."

"Wait. You're not taking us anywhere," said Veronica.

"The federal government is involved. You're coming with us. Orders."

Carrie squeaked from under the desk again. "I say we go with them."

Veronica glared at the agent, who glared back. Silence fell over the room. It was clear they wouldn't be dissuaded.

Suddenly, a poster that had been hanging by one remaining shred fluttered to the floor.

Carrie's scream was bloodcurdling.

18

THE AGENTS LOADED Veronica and Carrie into an enormous black SUV. There was a tinted screen between the driver and the backseat, and the insides of the windows were tinted so they couldn't see out. Veronica had the sense they were headed north, but it could have really been anywhere. Carrie immediately fell asleep against Veronica's shoulder, apparently worn out by the shock of it all. Veronica tapped her fingernail against the glass, lost in thought.

Three hours later, the SUV pulled off onto a dirt road. After bumping along for another mile or so, the SUV stopped. When the door opened, an older man in an Air Force uniform held out his hand in greeting. Several soldiers flanked him, machine guns at the ready, glancing around as if they were waiting for some kind of imminent attack. The older man smiled and helped Veronica from the car. He had a square head and was buzz-cut, with a toothy grin that looked as if it could bite through a beer can. He said, "Sorry about all the cloak and dagger stuff, Ms. Stone, but we really don't know what we're dealing with yet. We thought it best to take all possible precautions. I'm Colonel Gray."

"No problem," said Veronica flatly. They were standing in front of an old farmhouse in the mountains. Veronica guessed New Hampshire. Gray granite peaks stood out over the tree line, where some of the trees were already getting their autumnal tinge. Soldiers were taking her suitcase and bags from the back of the car, as well as a bag someone had apparently packed for Carrie. She got the feeling they were planning on keeping the two of them there for some time.

"I think you'll find the accommodations good. And we have a wonderful cook," said Colonel Gray, leading them toward the farm's wide front porch.

"How long?" asked Veronica.

"Excuse me? How long what?"

"How long are you keeping us here?"

Colonel Gray smiled again. "We just need to find out what's going on first. Someone or someones took a shot at you and your sister—and we can't ignore the fact that you were in the president's daughter's dorm room, and that the two of them are currently facing some type of unknown illness. As my dad used to say, 'There's three too many coincidences flying around for this to be a coincidence.'"

"I have the right to take my sister and go home."

"Don't I have any say in this?" asked Carrie.

Veronica shot her sister a look. "I have my rights."

Colonel Gray turned and stood straight in front of them. "Technically, you don't. This is a potential matter of national security. Now, you're a prominent woman. Don't make me do something like put you under a locked guard or in some kind of special custody. It will just be a day or two until we get things

figured out, then you can go right back to your regularly sched-
uled life."

"This is a violation of our civil rights."

"Now, Ms. Stone. You know as well as I do that we live in a
different world now, and it's a new world that's engaged in a
new war. For the time being, at least, your civil rights have
been suspended. Now let's just all try to sit back and enjoy the
lovely setting," said Colonel Gray. He started to usher them to
the porch steps again.

Veronica stood her ground. One of the following soldiers
almost knocked into her. "I want a phone call."

Colonel Gray turned around on the porch steps. "I just told
you, calling a lawyer or whatever you have in mind is not going
to do you any good."

"I know that. I just want my bag so I can call the office."

"They know you're with us."

"I have instructions I want to give them for my absence. If
I'm going to be sitting up on a mountainside for three months,
I don't want my entire company going down the toilet.
Considering the amount of military contracts we have, I don't
think the 'interests of national security' would like that very
much either."

Colonel Gray studied her for a moment. "Okay. We'll get
you a phone." He gestured over to one of the soldiers.

"I've got a phone in my bag. In fact, that man over there is
carrying it. Just let me make a phone call, and we're all yours."

Colonel Gray paused.

Veronica put her hands on her hips and threw back her hair,
accentuating her body. "What am I going to do, call in an
airlift?"

Colonel Gray waved for the soldier to hand him the bag. He

unzipped it carefully, then took out Veronica's phone. He considered it a moment, then handed it to her. "Keep it quick."

"Don't worry, this isn't a secret machine gun or something," Veronica said sarcastically. "Do you mind if I stand over here for some privacy?"

"No. Of course. I'll show your sister to your rooms," said Colonel Gray. He nodded slightly and led Carrie up the staircase. Two of the soldiers remained on the porch watching Veronica.

She turned her back to the soldiers and looked out over the mountains. She couldn't see a highway or even overhead air traffic. Wherever they were, they were very, very remote.

Veronica knew Colonel Gray and his men would be listening in, probably by intercepting her phone transmission by satellite. Luckily, she'd planned for this type of situation. She dialed her answering machine at StoneCorp, and then quickly plugged in a short flurry of numbers. A man's voice answered. "Hello, Ms. Stone. What's going on?"

Veronica smiled. Even though the voice was computer-generated, it sounded perfect. "I'm going to be away for a few days."

"Where are you?"

"North Carolina, I think," Veronica lied. She wanted the government men to underestimate her and believe they'd confused her as to her whereabouts. She knew that even though she was one of the most powerful women in America, she was still a woman, and she'd use their chauvinism against them.

"You're supposed to be getting rainy weather," said the voice. This was likely true for North Carolina. The voice program was plugged into the Internet and trained to respond with likely answers to Veronica's statements. Right now, the program's artificial intelligence was searching through North Carolina databases for appropriate chitchat. "You'll have to bring me some barbecue."

"I'll try. Listen, while I'm gone, I need you to continue work on the Looking Glass Project." As soon as Veronica said "Looking Glass Project" a computer facsimile of her voice came on the line. Soon, the two computer voices were chattering to each other in barely comprehensible tech speak. Veronica pressed another button, and the voices faded into the background. For all intents and purposes, this was the conversation the military would be listening in to. They would have no way of tracing the second phone line that had just opened up. Veronica should know, since she designed the military's cell call capturing system. She immediately dialed Hiro.

"Hello? Miss Stone, where are you? I heard the news on the television. Let me send you a car," said Hiro, his voice breathless with concern.

"The phone works doesn't it? The weapon?"

"Calm down. Are you calling me on a cell phone?"

"Don't worry—no one can hear or trace this. Answer me— does the weapon work?"

Hiro hesitated. "We're still running tests. Things look good, but—"

"Then what's wrong with the president and his daughter?"

"African fever, I thought," said Hiro, sounding puzzled. "Why?"

"Because someone I know has it too."

"Who?"

She didn't answer. "I think someone's trying to kill me, Hiro, to cover up the phone," she said

"Who would do that?"

She fought the urge to say "You." Hiro wanting her dead

didn't make sense. He had everything he wanted. Why would he suddenly want her dead? If Hiro intended to kill her, she was sure he had much more precise ways of doing it than shooting up a dorm window in Harvard Square. Veronica said, "The Russian. It's got to be."

"But why?"

"You tell me, Hiro. You know something here. And you heard him. I made him mad. I'm a threat. That dog story of his. He clearly meant to put me in my place."

"But we're all working together. It doesn't make sense. I think you should tell me where you are. I can get a helicopter there and fly you out to my island in a few hours. You'll be safe here."

Veronica doubted it. "I'm the guest of the United States Air Force for a few days. I'll get back to you."

"Wait. What do they—"

Veronica switched off the second line and brought back up the computer voices, who were now discussing some 401K problems that would have to be addressed in payroll. As soon as the man's voice spoke again, Veronica cut in "—let's get back to the Looking Glass Project." On the other end of the line, the computer program playing her voice shut off.

"It's under control. You have nothing to worry about."

"I know I can count on you."

"Have fun in North Carolina. Go Tar Heels!"

"Good-bye," said Veronica, hanging up the phone. She smiled to herself. She wondered where the program's artificial intelligence came up with "Tar Heels."

19

HIRO WAS NERVOUS. He didn't like what was happening here. He knew from the beginning that Sergei was hotheaded but he didn't think he would jump to jeopardize their lives by turning into the Terminator. He went for a drive to a remote area of town and pulled up Sergei on his cellular phone.

Sergei's men answered and made Hiro wait for a while before they came back on. "Sergei is busy," they said with their heavy Russian accents. "He'll be in contact with you within the hour." Hiro hung up the phone and reached out to the sky in frustration. "This is ludicrous!" he yelled out to no one. The next hour went by very slowly. Finally Hiro's phone rang and he jumped to answer it.

"Sergei?" he yelled.

"Calm down, my little Hiro," he laughed into the phone, and Hiro could hear the inhale and exhale of the pipe Sergei was smoking. How could he be so calm? He really was not human.

"I will not calm down. Are you nuts? You fire machine guns into the college room of the president's daughter? Are you crazy? You know they have them now, in custody!" Hiro was annoying Sergei, and if Sergei didn't need him quite so badly, he would get rid of him, too.

"It was the only clear shot we had of Veronica, and we were hoping to get both her and her sister. Not to worry though, we know where they are and we're going to get them." Sergei hung up the phone and Hiro almost had a heart attack. He realized then just how weak he was. No matter how successful he became, he now was and forever would be at the beck and call of this madman. His life would never be the same until he could get rid of Sergei. Good, he thought. Let him go after her, and maybe the government will come after him, instead.

20

AFTER THE SUN went down, the air around the farm grew cold. Carrie and Veronica had changed into jeans and sweaters, and several of the soldiers had started a small fire in one of the farmhouse's fireplaces. Colonel Gray, Carrie, and Veronica sat at the farmhouse's main dining table poking at their meals of Cornish hen and mashed potatoes. Colonel Gray had been largely silent throughout, only greeting them when they came to the table and offering them more wine or bread.

The entire farmhouse was built of solid wooden beams, similar to a log cabin, although Veronica guessed the logs were reinforced with steel bars. Carrie and Veronica were placed in a room upstairs, with a window looking out over some horse pastures down in the valley below. The window was nailed into the frame, and the glass was unbreakable plexi. The room had two overstuffed beds with iron frame headboards. A few needle-points and pictures hung on the walls, and a small bouquet of flowers sat in a washing bowl on top of the dresser. Except for the military presence, the window, and the sizable lock on the outside of the bedroom door, Veronica and Carrie could have been staying at any quaint New England bed and breakfast.

"So where are we, exactly?" asked Veronica.

"Classified," said Colonel Gray.

"How can it be classified if we're sitting in it?"

"Well, I won't tell you the location, but we're in one of the old safe houses from the Cold War. You're in a real part of history."

"What's a safe house?" asked Carrie.

"It's where the government was supposed to flee to if nuclear war ever happened. Basically all the congressmen and senators and their families. They got to run to summer camps like these scattered throughout the country. The rest of us got to stay outside and fend for ourselves," said Veronica.

"That's one way of looking at it," said Colonel Gray. "Or you could see it as the best way to preserve the American way of life. Even Noah wasn't expected to get everybody onto the ark."

Carrie looked up from her plate, her eyes still flush with panic. She hadn't been able to calm down since the incident in her dorm room. She was tense, as if she were simply waiting for more bullets to come flying at her from the window. "So, are you guys going to interrogate us or something?"

Veronica almost choked on a bite of potato. She covered her slip by taking a large sip from her wine glass. Would they interrogate them? Is that why they were here?

Colonel Gray seemed puzzled. "Why would we do that? We're just trying to protect you from whatever it is that is going on. We don't think you know much more than we do, do you?"

"What do you know?" asked Veronica.

"That's classified."

"Come on, my sister and I are the ones who were shot at. Don't you think we have a right to know? I mean, you have my sister and me locked up here. You took away our phones and my computer. Who are we going to tell? The squirrels?"

Colonel Gray sighed and drummed his thick fingers against the base of his neck. "Okay. I suppose you have a right to at least know what might be coming after you. We've heard a lot of strange chatter recently. We think a terrorist's cell phone has somehow poisoned the president—perhaps weakening us up for a larger attack."

"Why'd they shoot at us?" asked Carrie.

"Maybe they think you saw the poisoning. Maybe you did. Maybe they just want to cause more fear. Maybe they want to throw us off the track—keep us busy chasing phantoms. Maybe they just needed to destroy something in the room. Frankly, our intelligence doesn't have a clue what's going on."

"I don't know—I thought this might be about the phone or something," said Carrie quietly.

Veronica's eyes flashed. "Why would this have anything to do with the phone?"

"I don't know. Maybe someone's trying to steal it or something. You said yourself that it was the most technologically advanced communications device in the entire world. And you gave the prototypes to Jessica and her dad—"

"What are you implying?" asked Veronica, trying to keep her voice level. She curled her toes hard in her shoes to try and keep focused on not giving her nervousness away. Although she couldn't reach her sister, she almost felt like a little girl wanting to kick her under the table.

"I don't know. Just that the weird stuff started happening after Athena Weekend. And that's when you gave them the phones," said Carrie, moving her fork back and forth through her potatoes. "Maybe terrorists want to get the prototypes. Like Al Qaeda or something. So they can talk to each other or something."

Colonel Gray scratched his chin and cocked his head to the side, as if he were considering taking a shot at a deer. "I didn't know you had given the president and his daughter valuable technology."

"Prototypes," said Veronica quickly. "More toys than anything else. By her logic, you could just as easily say Athena Weekend was the catalyst."

"We're looking into that. Seeing if there were any people left with a grudge against the Monroes."

"I imagine a lot of people have grudges against the Monroes," said Veronica, trying to deflect the subject a little.

"According to the last poll, sixty-eight percent of the country does, but I don't think people pissed off about gay marriage and baby killers are going to invest in a poison that none of our scientists can even see. Most of those kooks just do it the old-fashioned way, with a nice high-powered rifle," said Colonel Gray, sighing.

"The phones looked a lot cooler than toys," muttered Carrie, scraping her food around her plate.

"Why did you give the prototypes to the Monroes? Is the phone in your handbag similar to the ones you gave them?" asked Colonel Gray, his interest clearly piqued. "I think it might be worth my time to take a look at one. As it stands now, we really don't have any other leads."

"No. Completely different. Like I said, the new phone is a prototype—better sound and picture quality. I thought I could generate a little advertising buzz if Jessica and her father were seen using it. It's really nothing to look at."

"If you weren't a trusted component of the defense industry, I might think you were trying to hide something," said Colonel Gray, smiling cryptically. Colonel Gray turned in his chair and snapped his fingers. "Lieutenant. Could you retrieve Ms. Stone's phone for us to take a look at?" One of the soldiers nodded, and marched off toward wherever Colonel Gray had hidden the phone after he confiscated it from Veronica. Colonel Gray motioned for someone to take away their plates. "Would you like some coffee?" he asked.

"Sure," mumbled Veronica. Her mind was going a mile a minute—she didn't think they'd even know what they were looking at, but if they started taking things apart, they would quickly figure out that there were a lot of parts and chips in the phone that didn't belong there. And then they might figure out Veronica's connection to the president. She told herself to calm down. Right now, it was just a coincidence. She still had time.

"You know, we really were all looking at the president's African trip—I mean, until you mentioned the phones, that was really the only thing that was out of the ordinary," said Colonel Gray.

"If someone was doing this to get the phones, I have no idea why," said Veronica.

"Maybe they're not really phones—maybe they're something else," said Colonel Gray.

"Like what? Proof of alien contact? A bomb wired to blow up the entire world?"

"No—but, as you have pointed out, they could be part of a weapon. Are they part of a weapon, Veronica?" Colonel Gray leaned forward on the table. He was physically intimidating, all shoulders and muscles and old, healed scars.

"Don't be silly."

"I'm not."

"I didn't say they were a weapon or anything—I just said they were really cool phones," said Carrie, glancing worriedly between her sister and Colonel Gray.

"You know, throughout American history, the people we've had the most trouble with are our own," said Colonel Gray, spinning his wine around in his glass. "It's rarely these 'outside forces' we're always so scared of. It's our own people who end up handing our asses to us."

"What do you mean?" asked Carrie.

"Every American president who has been shot or assassinated has been shot or assassinated by one of his own citizens. Oklahoma City—some of our guys again. Waco. The Watts Riots. The Los Angeles Riots. The Civil War. The fights over integration. Julius and Ethel Rosenberg. Richard Nixon. Even George Washington had to deal with Benedict Arnold. Attacks and betrayal always come from the inside of the country. It's a cancer we have."

"What about 9/11?" asked Carrie.

"I don't think the final chapter has been written about that one yet."

Veronica smiled. "For a United States colonel, you're pretty pessimistic about America."

Colonel Gray looked at her in surprise. "No I'm not—I believe wholeheartedly in America, and I believe that's why God sends us these tests, and why these tests come from our own sons, daughters, and neighbors. The American Dream could never have been challenged by a boatload of communist spies landing in New Jersey and trying to take over. It couldn't even have been challenged by the Nazis or the Japanese if they had managed to land on our shores. All our challenges must come from our own. We are God's country. The City on the Hill. The world looks to us for guidance, protection, and hope. And as such, we are the ultimate testing ground for Man's bravery, morality, and goodness. We are God's testing place. As such, as with God and Lucifer, we are often tested by our best and brightest." With his last words, Colonel Gray looked pointedly at Veronica. She tried to keep her face placid, lest she give any guilt away.

"That's a tad national-centric, don't you think?" asked Veronica playfully, leaning forward on her knuckles. Maybe if she kept him talking, he'd forget about the phones, and forget about her as any kind of potential threat.

"A little 'United States of Jesus'-centric if you ask me," said Carrie.

"Well, as you said, I am a United States colonel, and I do accept the Lord Jesus Christ as my personal savior," said Colonel Gray. "Honestly, I find it disheartening that two beautiful, smart young women who have been blessed with absolutely everything God has to offer don't think the way I do. Or at least consider the fact that maybe being blessed with so much gives them a moral duty to do as much good in the world as they can."

"That sounds pretty altruistic," said Carrie.

Colonel Gray nodded and raised his eyebrows. "That surprises you? Do you think everyone that works for the military just wants to kill people, or is an idiot pawn of the oil companies?"

Carrie shrugged into her plate. "Kinda."

"Bad 1960s PR. Kennedy. Watergate. The government has never managed to get over it. Oh, now let's take a look at this fabulous phone," said Colonel Gray.

The soldier returned with Veronica's phone and handed it to Colonel Gray. He hefted it up and down in his palm. "It feels pretty heavy. I thought tech was supposed to make everything lighter and smaller."

"Not always," said Veronica. She didn't like some Jesus crusader GI Joe making cracks about her inventions, even if it was in her best interest if he thought it was a piece of junk.

"So, what's so special about this phone?" Colonel Gray flipped open the screen and stared into it. "It looks like one of those little TVs old farts take to football games."

"No—you don't understand—," said Carrie, reaching greedily for it.

Suddenly, there was a commotion on the front porch, followed by a lot of shouting. Colonel Gray leapt up from his seat, setting the phone down on the table in front of him. "You stay here," he said, reaching for his sidearm and striding toward the front door.

Veronica grabbed the phone off the table and shoved it into her jacket.

"Hey! You shouldn't do that!" exclaimed Carrie.

"And you should keep your trap shut about the phone!" snapped Veronica.

Carrie's mouth flopped open. She was clearly bewildered and crestfallen. "What do you mean? I was just saying the phones were so cool maybe someone would be willing to kill for them? Why would that make you mad? I was being proud of you."

"Wait—," said Veronica, pressing her finger to Carrie's lips. Colonel Gray was speaking to someone outside on the porch. Veronica nodded for Carrie to follow her around the other side of the central fireplace.

Outside on the porch, at least a dozen soldiers surrounded three young men and a girl. The four were dressed for camping, with heavy packs on their backs. They looked disheveled and frightened. The girl was lying on the porch. She was blonde and thin, and very pretty. She was bleeding heavily through her right sock. Something white stuck out from the middle of it. Veronica guessed it was bone. "Look man, she's really hurt!" exclaimed one of the college boys in heavily New York-accented exasperation. "Could you guys get off your military-industrial high horse for like two seconds and help us out?"

Colonel Gray stood still. "I will give you another minute to get off this property."

"Are you nuts?" yelled one of the other boys. The girl moaned at his feet. "Can't you just drive us to the nearest road or something?"

"You're trespassing," said Colonel Gray.

"Because we're fucking lost!" yelled the first boy. "They remove your brain when you join the Army, you fascist assholes?"

Colonel Gray squared his shoulders and raised his service revolver. "If I have to tell you one more time, I will be forced to use extreme measures."

"Are you absolutely crazy? What is this, Nazi Germany? What do you have in there, the aliens? I'm not going any-where. Come on, shoot me, I dare you. My dad's a state con-gressman. You'll be redeployed to the Artic Circle!"

Colonel Gray rolled his eyes as the soldiers surrounding them shuffled their feet uncertainly.

"Fine. We'll go," moaned the girl. "This is a stupid fight. Help me up, Johnny." One of the boys leaned down and picked her up by her armpits. "Thanks for the help, big soldier men," said the girl, her voice dripping with sarcasm and evident disappointment. Veronica thought she detected an accent but she couldn't tell.

Although Colonel Gray remained unfazed, the other soldiers looked very uncomfortable. The college kids were about their own ages, and the girl was very pretty. "Colonel—," mumbled one of them.

Carrie grabbed Veronica's arm. "You can't let them do this!" she whispered to her. "That girl is hurt, we have to help them."

"NO!" hissed Veronica. She didn't like the situation and was more than happy to let the Colonel throw them out. Something just didn't sit right. "Leave it alone, it's not up to us. Let's go sit back down at the table." For some reason Veronica wanted to get as far away from this commotion as possible.

"Drop it, Private. They cannot be here," Colonel Gray said. "Now, good day to you four." He motioned them to move away with a sweep of his pistol.

The girl took a step and screamed. Just then, Carrie burst past Veronica and out the front door of the cabin. "This is so wrong! What happened to all that 'moral duty' crap you were spitting back there? Can't you goons see she's hurt?" screamed Carrie.

Veronica took one step outside after her sister. For a split second, she locked eyes with the hurt college girl. The girl smiled obscenely and yelled, "Ostante!" In a split second, the three other hikers had ripped heavy machine guns from their packs. The girl leapt up the staircase, and placed a pistol against Colonel Gray's throat. Then she pulled the trigger. Her fake bit of bone lay behind her on the ground.

The night erupted in gunfire. Veronica grabbed Carrie and fell back through the cabin doorway as one of the soldiers pulled it shut behind her. "Lock it!" he yelled from the other side, before his voice was cut off in a hail of bullets thudding against the door. Veronica reached up and jammed the lock home. "What is going on?" screamed Carrie.

"Calm down! They must have followed us here from Athena House!" Bullets thunked against the windows and door, but nothing broke through. "Come on!" Veronica and Carrie crawled back to the dining room.

Outside, the shooting stopped. Then a flurry of bullets thwocked into the front window. It held, although the plastic and wire of the window were now stretched opaque. "Oh Veronica!" called a woman's voice. Her accent was Russian. "We've come to rescue you! Sergei sent us for help!" There was another single rifle shot—the woman giggled like a harpy.

Carrie glanced at Veronica. Veronica waved her quiet.

"More men are coming up the road right now. All your soldier boys are dead. You can't stay in there forever," said the voice. "If you don't come out, we'll have to start a fire. It's getting cold out here! Maybe we can all make some s'mores when Sergei gets here. Sing 'Take Me Out to the Ballgame.'"

"What's wrong with her?" exclaimed Carrie in fear.

"She enjoys her work."

Veronica looked around the room. Outside, the Russian woman kept talking, clearly trying to drive her out from nerves. She wondered if others were really coming, and if they were, how much time they had to get out of there. Whoever these people were, they'd just obliterated a platoon of secret American soldiers. Veronica and her sister didn't have a chance.

Three more rifle shots ponged into the reinforced front door. "Hey, what are you doing in there? Praying? Calling someone on your famous phone? You should see your president—they won't let out any more photos. There's a rumor his bottom lip fell off."

"We have to find a way out from here," whispered Veronica.

"No one else has said anything. Maybe that woman is the only one left. Maybe we can just run out the back door," answered Carrie hopefully.

"I don't think we can risk it. There's no reason to think those other bastards are dead. Otherwise, she wouldn't be trying to draw us out with all her insane chitchat. She's just trying to break our concentration. Stay with me, Carrie. We won't break if we stick together."

"She blew the Colonel's face off right in front of me. He didn't deserve to die like that," said Carrie, beginning to sob.

Veronica slid her arm over her sister's shoulders. "It's okay. She's not going to do a thing to either of us. I won't let her. Now snap out of it. There's no time for crying." Veronica crawled on her belly over to a glass-front bookcase near the dining table. She eased it open and switched on the bottom-most light so she could see. Its pale glow illuminated her pale face and hands. She hoped Carrie wouldn't notice the tremors that ran through her body.

Carrie crawled over after her. Outside, the Russian woman was singing some obscene song about a pirate and a porpoise. "What are you doing?" asked Carrie.

"Colonel Gray said this was a place for Congress to come and hide during the Cold War. I doubt they were going to jam them all in this log cabin. There must be a tunnel or a secret room or something linking the cabins together, or to the mountain or something," answered Veronica, yanking books from the shelf and tossing them across the floor.

"What are you looking for?"

"This is a government building. Built by government bureaucracy. There's got to be a visitors' manual. Something to list escape plans, hidden food stashes, weapons, neighboring missile silos, I don't know, that sort of thing. Don't you think a bunch of scared bureaucrats would plan for something like that? What if they got here and all the Army was dead? They'd have to figure out things for themselves. Start looking in the other cases!"

Carrie slid on her belly across the wooden floor and started to rifle through another of the cases. Several more shots plocked into the reinforced glass, but Carrie hunched her shoulder and kept looking.

Within minutes, all of the books in the room were piled up against the front door, mainly multivolume histories, collections of crossword puzzles, and mystery novels. They'd found nothing. "Great! Now what do we do?" asked Carrie. Several more bullets punched the window. This time, they beat out the rhythm to "Shave and a Haircut."

Veronica had to admit, the Russian had panache. "It might be in another room," she sighed.

"Or it might not be here at all! Maybe you get it when you become a congressman or something. Maybe they just figured people would figure it out." Outside, they heard several cars honk somewhere farther off. Carrie's eyes rolled like a frightened deer. "They're coming!"

Veronica laid her face down on the floor to think. There had to be a hidden exit door. Logically, it would be stupid to have no escape routes. The cabin was above ground. It wouldn't withstand a blast or fallout, but the tons of granite a couple of hundred of yards away certainly could. There had to be something buried under the mountain, and some way of getting there. An exit door could be anywhere in the building. If it were hidden, there was no way they could find it before the Russians broke in. They really had no choice. "Okay. We have to try to open every door in this place. Yank on anything that could be a knob or a switch—every painting, every light sticking out of the wall, every clock and light switch. The Cold War was a period of extreme paranoia and fear—they probably would have hidden any entrance to the main base in case this cabin was breached. You go to the second floor. I'll hit all the ones downstairs. Be careful not to open a door that leads to the outside."

Carrie just stared at her, her face puffy with tears. "I can't."

Veronica grabbed her shoulders and looked straight into her eyes, trying to will some of her own courage into her sister. "You can and you will. You're a strong girl, Carrie. It's obvious to everyone," said Veronica.

Carrie brushed the tears from her eyes. She took a deep breath as if she were about to jump into the ocean. Then she hopped to her feet and ran upstairs. Veronica got up along with her and started running through the downstairs hallways, yanking on knobs and latches. Outside, headlights started to light up the ruined windows. It sounded as if several vehicles had pulled up into the cabin's front yard. Voices started talking to each other in Russian. It sounded like they had brought explosives, although Veronica's panic was making it hard to translate. "Carrie! Go faster!" shouted Veronica.

Veronica ran through three small auxiliary offices, three toilets, and then into the kitchen, yanking pots and pans from the racks in a complete panic. They banged and crashed all around her, most of them relics from the 1950s. Dinnerware shattered all around her. She no longer cared how much noise she was making. She yanked open the pantry. Inside, the back shelves had been pulled open like a door, showing a dank staircase leading into the darkness. Cans and bottles lay smashed and rolling on the floor. A bag of flour had spilled, and a small set of footprints tracked through it and down the stairs. A row of lanterns hung on a hook by the door. One of the lanterns was gone. It looked like the cook had made a run for it.

Veronica ran back to the bottom of the second floor staircase. "Carrie! Get down here! I found—"

Just then, there was a horrendous boom and Veronica was flying back down the hallway to the kitchen. She smashed against the wall, and dropped to the floor. Plaster and wire fell from the ceiling, and the air was filled with chalky dust. Overhead sirens and sprinklers snapped on, dousing everything in freezing water. Veronica sputtered and got to her feet. The way in front of her was blocked by fallen beams and part of the brick fireplace. The rubble was impassable.

"Hello? Knock, knock?" called the Russian woman's voice. "I think your door is broken!"

It was impossible to get back to the dining room or the stairwell. The only way Veronica could go was back to the kitchen. She looked up at the ceiling as if she could see through it. It was impossible to know what had happened to her sister. Veronica stood with the sprinkler water running down her back, cleaning the blood and the rubble out of her wounds. She couldn't leave her sister. If she was still alive, they'd kill her if they caught Veronica as well. If Veronica escaped, her sister would likely be used as a hostage, and that might be the only way to get them both out of this. If she surrendered, or tried to get to the second floor, they were both dead. They had already shot at them once, and they had been willing to use explosives to get inside the cabin. It was clear this was an assassination, not a kidnapping. Veronica stood in the water, still trying to make her decision.

"Miss Stone? We would like to talk to you. Just for a second," came the Russian woman's voice from the other side of the rubble. A fist-size chunk of it came crashing to the floor. Veronica started, half-expecting the Russian woman to come crashing through.

"Hey! Let go of me!" screamed Carrie on the other side of the rubble.

"Looks like we have your sister. She looks like she's bleeding pretty badly. Come out now, or I'll shoot her dead. Or maybe we'll sew up her wounds with some electrical cord!"

Veronica watched blood wash down her arm until her fingertips turned blue from the cold water. They wouldn't kill her sister. Until they had Veronica, Carrie was valuable. Once Veronica was dead, Carrie was a liability. She was just a girl who had stumbled too close to something much bigger than herself. The best thing to do would be to run.

Veronica squeezed her fists tight and whispered down to her shoes, "I'm sorry."

Then she quietly hurried back down the hallway and disappeared into the pantry, pulling the door shut behind her. There was a heavy iron door to block anyone from coming in. She slid it into place, trying to convince herself the guilt and cowardice she was feeling was unnecessary and wrong-headed. She would meet the Russian and her cohorts again, and it would be on her own terms. It was the only way she'd get Carrie back.

She had to believe she was doing the right thing.

Could she ever forgive herself if she was wrong?

21

AFTER FLEEING THROUGH the pantry door, Veronica lit one of the old gas lamps and followed a long, dark hallway that had been carved straight from the granite mountainside. She walked for what she guessed was a mile or more until she came to a metal grate. Cold, clear air whistled by her. A staircase led deeper into the mountain, to where she guessed the official bunker was, but she didn't want to get herself trapped in there. The Russians would probably guess the same thing she did. She had to get far away as fast as she possibly could. Below her was a highway and a scenic rest area, already lined with truckers going to sleep for the night. She could hitch a ride down there.

She opened the gate and half-slid, half-walked down the steep hillside. From the other side, it looked like an innocuous storm drain. She passed through the parking lot and into the restrooms like a ghost, feeling as if everyone were looking at her and knew exactly what she had done back at the cabin. She told herself leaving Carrie was the right, logical thing. She had made her life with logic. She couldn't stop now. Logic and intelligence was her power. It might be the only thing to get them through this.

The sign on the bathroom said she was in northern New Hampshire. At this time of night, the bathroom's foyer was deserted except for the humming of the soda and candy machines and the buzzing of the overhead lights. She went into the women's room to try and clean herself up.

She stood by one of the cracked and mottled mirrors staring at herself, but without really seeing anything. She was lost in shock and reverie. She had never considered that things could turn like this. Her involvement had been brought on by plain hubris, and Hiro had played her ego like a violin. Hiro had not only needed her imaging technology, he had also needed a patsy—assuming that he was the one behind this. It might have been the Russian on his own. For all she knew, Hiro could be dead, and maybe this was all a rush to grab a potentially earth-changing idea. What was she going to do? She closed her eyes and listened to one of the faucets drip into one of the nearby sinks. Why was it so quiet?

Veronica's eyes snapped open and she felt a chill run down her spin that had nothing to do with the cold water she was still soaked in. Why didn't she hear sirens or helicopters or any emergency response? She wasn't that far from the cabin, and there weren't that many roads to choose from in this part of New Hampshire. An entire platoon had just gone up in flames and she didn't hear one siren. A government building's alarms were screaming on the other side of the mountain, and there was nothing. Police vehicles should be ripping up the highway outside, clearing out the rest area, cordoning everything off and girding the nation for some kind of terrorist threat. With the president and his daughter sick, the military had to be on high alert, waiting for any-thing. But all she could hear outside the bathroom's window was the low rumbling of the idling trucks and the crickets. It was as if what had just happened had been a dream only she couldn't wake up from. The rest of the world remained its normal self, while she was Alice fallen down the rabbit hole. She reached into her pocket for her cell phone, having for-gotten it wasn't there. She was hurt and in the middle of nowhere with nothing. She felt more lost and alone than she ever had in her life.

Someone flushed the toilet in the stall behind her. The stall door banged open and a slight old woman came out, deco-rously fixing her hair as if she had just stepped from a cocktail party and not a sketchy public toilet. Her face was pinched with age, but her eyes were bright. She wore a short strand of pearls and a pink wool cardigan. She looked like the kind of woman who was embarrassed by having to admit she had the same physical functions as the rest of humanity.

The woman walked over to the sink next to Veronica and started washing her hands. Her fingers and wrists were covered in jewelry. It clattered against the porcelain.

The woman looked up at Veronica. "Lord, what happened to you, honey? You fall in the river?" asked the woman.

Veronica looked up at herself again in the mirror. She had a black eye. Blood was running from a gash just under her hair-line, and smoke and ash had stained her cheeks a dark gray. Part of her hair was burnt, and her soaked clothes were ripped and torn as if she'd been mauled. "I, well—"

"Were you in an accident or something? Do you need help?"

Veronica turned on the sink and splashed water into her face. Once she got the ash and the majority of the dried blood off, she didn't look as terrible as she felt. "No. A fight, I guess—"

The woman grabbed Veronica's shoulders. Veronica shrieked and spun, practically batting the old woman into one of the mirrors. "Calm down, calm down. It's all over now, honey. Don't you worry," she said. "This happens to more people than you think. You're not alone in this." The woman grabbed her and pulled her in tight for a big hug. Veronica could hear the woman's heart beating.

Veronica held onto the porcelain sink and tried to regain her composure. She tried to believe the woman's words, although she knew the woman had no idea what she had just gone through. For all Veronica knew, her sister was dead. For all she knew, the Feds were looking for her. For all she knew, Alex was dead. Her entire life had shattered in a week. She doubted she was anything but alone in this. "I'm sorry," she whispered.

"No need for sorry's my dear, you're all right now. My name is Nora." Nora's voice became very stern. She said, "It's not your fault. You must never think it's your fault! Do you want me to call a hospital? Or the police maybe? I've been training at the Women's Center for these kinds of situations. You've just got to get out of it. He's never going to change, and none of that is your fault. There's no children involved, are there?"

Veronica spat more blood into the sink. Apparently the woman thought she'd been the victim of domestic violence. Did she think that Veronica was married to some toothless mountain hillbilly who tried to toss her in the creek? As with Colonel Gray, she had to remind herself it was not in her best interest to tell this woman that she was not the kind of person who'd be beaten by her husband and left for dead at a highway rest stop. Still, as she looked up at the mirror, she realized she looked just like the type of person who would be left for dead at a highway rest stop. If the Russians on her tail had their way, she probably would be. Maybe Nora's misunderstanding was just as well. She didn't think she could really explain what had happened anyway, at least not without sounding completely insane. "I need to get to Boston," said Veronica.

Nora's face spread into a great, warm smile. "My husband, Earl, and I are headed that way. It would be no problem dropping you off. Do you have some people there?" asked the woman. Veronica nodded. The woman steered her by the shoulders to the bathroom's doors. "My name's Nora Wayne Jasper. I'm from Waterloo, Iowa. This is my first time on the East Coast. Earl and I just bought an RV and we're spending our kids' inheritances driving around the country," said Nora. She was keeping her voice high and cheerful, as if it might be a way to make Veronica feel better.

Nora gently took Veronica's hand and led her out of the bathroom. Nora's hand was cool and dry, like a feather.

Veronica followed Nora across the parking lot, looking all around her for signs of being followed. The rest stop seemed asleep, and only a few cars passed on the highway.

She thought she smelled smoke over all the diesel exhaust, but she could have been imagining it. World War III had happened on the other side of the mountain, and nothing at all was going on here. It was as if she were in a completely different world.

Nora's RV was gigantic. Its vanity license plate read "GONE," and the back half of the RV was covered with a large map of the country, with stickers to fill in the states where the Jaspers had traveled. Apparently, they'd been everywhere one could go in an RV without putting pontoons and an outboard motor on it. The RV was bigger than most mobile homes she'd seen. It looked like someone could park a plane in it, and she wouldn't have been surprised if there were a pool and a helipad on the roof.

The RV's big door opened like a bus and Nora's husband, Earl, helped both of them aboard. The inside smelled like face powder, coffee, and newspapers. Earl was a small man, with tight wizened skin and bones that made him look like a wiry tree. He was clearly relishing being the captain of his monstrous vessel. He wore a trucker hat that said "Onward!" Several other hats dangled on hooks behind his head, along with a fishing pole and what looked like a pellet rifle. He smiled at Veronica and immediately started tweaking knobs and flipping switches, as if the RV were a rocket ship he had to keep a constant eye on.

"Now, don't you worry any about Earl. He's a kitten, but not much of a talker," said Nora by way of explanation. "Here, sit down, and we'll get going, and then I'll find you some clothes, blankets, and some food. You hungry? We made some lovely chicken fried steak for dinner—there's a lot left in the fridge. And Earl has some beer stashed away, if you need something to drink. Earl, this girl needs a ride to Boston."

"Aye aye!" said Earl, winking at Veronica. "Just give me a good ship and a star to sail her by!"

Veronica smiled indulgently. The Jaspers were cute, almost what she had imagined her grandparents to be if she had ever met them. Although she imagined no Stone except herself would be caught dead in the Jasper's RV. It was neat and clean, but knickknacks and postcards covered every surface. Veronica guessed they'd raided every junk shop, dollar store, Cracker

Barrel gift shop, and welcome center in the country. Over Earl's shoulder, through the RV's wall-sized windshield, she saw a black military SUV with flashing emergency lights come roaring into the rest area. As the SUV passed under a streetlamp, she saw the blonde-haired Russian was at the wheel.

"That's them!" exclaimed Veronica, ducking down in her seat. Nora and Earl tensed up on either side of her, readying themselves for a confrontation. "Now don't you worry, we won't let him hurt you again," whispered Nora. For a moment, Veronica felt these two strangers turn into something like family. She wanted to tell them everything.

The SUV pulled into a parking space in front of the restrooms. The Russian stepped out, scanning the rest area around her. Two strips of something dark were smeared from the corners of her eyes like makeup—Veronica guessed it was blood. Who was this woman? With the dust and the blood, she looked like an Amazonian warrior or some demon from hell. Incredibly, no one else in the rest area seemed to see her. The Russian glanced up at the metal grate in the hillside. No one else was in the SUV with her. She studied the grate for several moments, and then spoke into a wire dangling from an earpiece she was wearing. Veronica guessed she had made the same assumption Veronica had made about the cabin having an escape route, and had left the men behind to sift through the ruins. Whoever she was, she was very smart. She looked around, and then down at her watch. She had to assume Veronica couldn't have gotten very far yet. The rest area's bathroom seemed like a likely hiding place.

"Well, I'll be—he's a girl," stammered Earl, peering over the RV's steering wheel. The Russian woman marched into the bathroom, holding something in a gym bag in front of her.

"Earl—hush! Don't act like you're some hick from out in the sticks! Remember, Trudie's girl was that way in college," snapped Nora, slapping her husband gently on the back of his wrist. She turned to Veronica. "What you do is your own business. You're just the way God made you. You can't help that. I think the government and whatnot just needs to stay out of people's bedrooms. They don't even read the Bible right."

Earl snorted, "I'm sure she doesn't want to hear you start—"

"Earl, let's get this girl out of here before she gets hurt again. I don't want to watch some strange woman beat you up, as much as you might like it."

"I wouldn't hit a woman. Maybe we can talk to her, get this sorted out here."

"She'd hit you. And there'd be nothing you could do about it."

"I was in the Army," complained Earl.

"You worked in the kitchen. Now stop acting big and tough and let's get this girl back to her home. You don't need to prove your testosterone levels to us."

Veronica said, "Thank you—really. You're both saving my life."

Earl muttered something under his breath at his wife. Then he pulled the RV out of the rest area and started heading down the highway toward Boston. Veronica nodded thanks to Nora and curled back into the fur-covered seat. She immediately fell into the deepest sleep she'd ever known.

22

VERONICA HAD THE Jaspers drop her off at the Dunkin'
Donuts across the street from StoneCorp, saying it was still
too early to go knocking on her sister's apartment door, which
she assured them was very close by. It was almost five in the
morning, and the city streets had changed over from people
just wandering home to people dragging themselves to work.
She had talked Nora out of forcing some new dry clothes on
her, but Nora had insisted on giving her twenty dollars for
spending money in case she wanted breakfast or something
before she went over to her sister's. Veronica finally accepted
the money, and also had them write down their address on a
slip of paper. If she managed to keep herself alive and out of
jail, the Jaspers would be receiving a big surprise in the mail.

Veronica ordered a bagel and a cup of coffee. Then she sat
down at one of the tables by the window. Across the street,
StoneCorp looked normal. None of the employees would be
arriving this early—she ran an open campus with flex time for
all her researchers; it was part of their benefits package. As
long as new projects were being developed, she didn't care

when they worked. They were a pack of night owls who were happier working until two in the morning rather than trying to drag themselves up for the nine-to-five rush the rest of the world was stuck with. The first ones might roll in at ten, at the earliest. Veronica had never been a big believer in the necessity of the company project meeting. She didn't hire her employees for their coffee-drinking and kissing-up skills.

From Dunkin' Donuts' window, she didn't see any suspicious cars, and she could clearly see Manny's, the night security man's, mustache through the window in his little booth at the entrance to the parking lot. She decided it was unlikely someone was waiting for her here, and she was completely sure she hadn't been followed. After the rest and the coffee, she felt like herself again. She had to take action. Otherwise, none of them, Alex, her sister, the president, his daughter, or herself would make it out of this alive.

On the way out of the Dunkin' Donuts, she grabbed another cup of coffee and a box of donut holes with the word "Munchkins" printed on the package. She strode across the street and tapped on Manny's window. He jumped, looking quickly up from the newspaper he was reading. "Miss Stone! What are you doing here so early? Where's your car? What happened to your eye?" he asked. His eyes glanced around the booth, as if he were checking to make sure there wasn't something lying around that could get him fired.

"No big deal. A friend of mine just had a little fender bender, and I was too dumb to wear a seatbelt."

"It happens," said Manny, as if he knew. "Do you need me to call the cops or something? Where's your friend's car? I could get a tow truck." Manny leaned his head out of his booth, trying to see if the car was sitting in the street.

"No—that's fine. It's still running, and she wasn't hurt at all. Just me and my pride," said Veronica, hoping her voice sounded breezy. "I just had her drop me off across the street. Here—for you. I feel like you guys on security never get thanked enough." She handed him the box of Munchkins and the coffee.

Manny looked flabbergasted and clearly pleased with the attention. Like most of her male employees, he sometimes fantasized about a night with the boss. "Thanks Miss Stone. Really, you didn't need to," he said.

"That's okay. I'm sure most of the time all you get is people griping about why their key card doesn't work or something like that. I was up early, in 'double D,' and I wanted to say thanks. So, anything been going on?"

Manny looked up from his donut selection. "No. Not really. A couple of deliveries. Should there be?" He glanced nervously over at his sign-in sheet.

"No—nothing special. I was just curious if anyone different had come by," said Veronica, as carefree as possible.

"Like who? The cops?"

"No—no—why would you think the cops? Have the cops been around?"

Manny was an ex-con, and he answered cautiously. "Well—a cruiser has stopped at that Dunkin' Donuts every forty-five minutes all night. I figured it was because your sister's dorm room got shot up. I kinda thought that was why you were banged up too."

"You knew about that?"

"It was all over the news. I figured you were off at the hospital with your sister or something. Is she okay?"

Veronica looked down at her shoes. "She's fine, but I wasn't there for the shooting. What did the news say?"

"Just that someone took some shots at your sister's dorm room. They didn't say if your sister or anybody else was there. It's the same old crap—they don't know, so they're interviewing every political talking head from here to Virginia. I assume they're saving the real news for the early morning shows—you know, so one of their big boys can have the scoop. So, your sister's okay?" asked Manny, his eyes narrowing just a little.

"She's fine. I sent her to my mother's," answered Veronica. She knew full well that as soon as she was gone, Manny would get on the phone and see if he could get any money for his exclusive information—something he could take to the dog track at Wonderland later. "I'm going to go collect some of my stuff and clean up. I'm supposed to be back at my mother's by breakfast. I'd appreciate it if you didn't tell anyone I was here until I leave."

"Will do, Miss Stone. So, you think it's terrorists, like they say?"

"I don't know, but I have been seeing a lot of unusual and out-of-place-looking men around the Athena House. And the police told me the rifles used were Saudi Arabian," said Veronica. Manny looked thoughtful, as if he were trying to compute how much his inside dirt was worth. Veronica's lie about the men would further confuse things. Nowadays, it was what people wanted to believe. Boston would go into panic mode, and everyone would be looking out for another Al Qaeda. It might buy her some necessary time, and throw the Russians and the government off her track until she could figure out her next move.

Even without her wallet or access cards, Veronica could still get into the building using the fingerprint, voice, and retinal scan reader. All other entrants needed the access card as well, but she had left herself out of that part of the security system. The access card was really just to make employees feel less nervous about StoneCorp. Although they were all perfectly aware that major parts of their private information were in the company's databases, Veronica always felt the access card allowed them to think they still held some small bit of control over their personal information. Of course, they didn't—but the access card was a good crutch to use to ignore the obvious.

Veronica switched on the lights in her lab. Surprisingly, it looked just as she had left it. Before she took another step, she reached into a hidden drawer in the doorway behind her. She took out an aerosol can and sprayed the air in front of her. On the floor at ankle-level was a red laser beam. It wasn't one of hers. She guessed it was a government plant, probably set to trigger a silent alarm. It was low tech, but clever. Veronica had every door entry and security camera encrypted with unbreakable codes that necessitated a deep familiarity with Zoroastrian mythology (a book she'd picked up on a whim, and paid for in cash, making the codes that much less likely to be discovered by someone trying to guess using knowledge of Veronica's personal life and interests—incredibly, most code systems were easily breakable if you knew the name of the person's kids, dog, or hobby). Consequently, the government would have been unable to break into her own computer systems to use them against her. A small laser would just have to do.

She stepped over the laser and sprayed the rest of the room. There was nothing else. Then she switched the overheads to black light. Still no visible wires or trace chemicals. She imagined one of her assistants had let the Feds in, but she wasn't angry. StoneCorp was a legitimate business, its leader was in some type of danger, and the country was under attack. If her assistants had done anything else, StoneCorp would have looked complicit and guilty. She imagined the Feds could have gotten a warrant if they had to, although she doubted they would have bothered. The president was ill and America was the brave new world of homeland security. Veronica smiled— she had trained her staff well.

As much as she wanted to get on her computer and check on the news and see how Alex was, she knew she should just grab the Russian's notebook, a computer, a phone, and her emergency money. She walked over to the wall next to her desk and stared straight at a StoneCorp recruiting poster. It showed Einstein looking wistfully into the clouds. She spoke straight at it, in a loud, clear voice: "Albert, looks like trouble." The wall and poster swung open, revealing one of Veronica's many secret hiding places. Inside was a black duffle bag, twenty thousand dollars in cash, a .38 caliber pistol, five rounds of ammunition, a laptop with direct access to StoneCorp's mainframe, two prototype phones, a selection of fake passports and untraceable credit cards, and the Russian's notebook. She slid all the items into the duffle bag and closed the hiding place, and then stuffed the duffle bag under another cabinet.

She found two large jars in a cabinet next to her desk. They were full of clear liquid, an iodine derivative that was explosive when poured on something and allowed to dry. The Manhattan Project scientists had used it for practical jokes on each other, like pouring it into keyholes, or empty desk drawers. Making her own had actually been one of Veronica's first real science projects when she was in high school. She opened both jars, dumping one on her desk and one on the floor in front of it.

The derivative dried quickly. Within a few seconds, anyone who scraped or slapped it would be in for a big surprise.

Veronica grabbed the duffle and then went over to the closet where she kept some extra clothes she wore when she went running. She slipped out of her wet things and piled them in a drawer full of various small parts, in case someone poked his head in the lab—she didn't want to leave too many obvious clues for people to find. Before she closed the drawer, she rigged a very small stink-and-smoke bomb to the handle. Her interest in toys had left her with many potential booby traps.

She dried herself some more with a towel, and tried to shake some of the ash and debris from her hair. Then she bent down to slip into her panties. Out of the corner of her eye, she saw something moving reflected in one of the beakers on the table in front of her. She spun. Standing behind her was a masked man holding a syringe gun at her throat. "Don't make this harder than it needs to be," said a gruff man's voice. Then his head tilted down, clearly taking in her naked breasts.

Once again, she praised men's predictability. She braced herself against the cabinet and kicked hard, sending the man falling backwards through the lab. Glass shattered and papers scattered everywhere. The man stumbled to his feet and came at her with a roar. She ducked to the side and ran along the center cabinet, pulling doors open behind her. Toys fell out of every nook and cranny, rolling and beeping, and cluttering the floor with marbles and wheels. The man stumbled after her, slashing at her with the syringe as if it were a broadsword.

Veronica yelled "Night!" and a giant black screen fell over the window, blocking out the morning sunlight. All the lights in the laboratory winked out. Then she yelled "Music! Loud! Louder! Louder!" The hidden stereo system started pumping out Beethoven's Fifth Symphony. She could hear the man crash into something else in the dark. "Industrial! Dance!" The music switched with a click. Suddenly, the room burst with ear-shattering guitar bursts and drum beats. "Loud! Loud! Loud!" she kept screaming until the entire room was awash in painful white noise, drums, and feedback. She slid around the counter. She wasn't sure where the man was in relation to her. She thought about risking a flash of the lights, but it would be too dangerous. She also imagined the government's laser had been tripped. How long would it take them to get here?

She felt incredibly vulnerable in just her panties. Even though this was her room, it was completely black, and it was completely impossible to hear anything, she still felt like the man had an advantage over her. For a moment, she simply wished she were wearing a pair of shoes.

She crawled toward where her desk should be, thinking that she might be able to get around him and get to the bag with the gun in it. He hadn't been carrying a knife or a gun, so she guessed someone wanted her for something. Was the man's voice Russian? She couldn't tell. How long had he been in here? How did he get in?

She edged forward. She reached out with her fingertips and brushed against something that could have been the duffle bag. She started to close her fingers.

Suddenly, a hand wrapped around her ankle. She was wrenched backwards across the slick tile floor. Veronica screamed and tried to dig her short fingernails into the floor. The man pulled her to her knees and then banged her head against one of the cabinets. She scrambled to her feet. He spun her around. She reached behind her and grabbed a full vial of something. She smashed it over the man's head and scrambled away, sweeping her arm along the cabinet to knock all the jars and equipment into him. She kept moving, cutting her feet on broken glass and plastic and scraping her chest along the hard edge of a cabinet. The man grabbed her again and she snapped her head back hard. She felt the man's nose crunch behind her. She spun and kicked the man in the chest. He fell away from her.

A huge bang and a flash of fire and light cascaded through the building. The man had crashed into the desk and set off the motion explosive. The entire room smelled like smoke and ash. The man took two steps forward, and then the back of his jacket sparked into orange flame. In the firelight, Veronica reached around her and threw another vial of liquid on him. The fire roared up like a candle. The sprinkler system snapped on and doused the room with fire suppression foam. The room lit up with emergency lights. Veronica grabbed a sharp metal hammer and brought it down between the man's eyes. The man gasped and fell to the floor.

Veronica grabbed her clothes and the duffle bag. A pool of dark blood was starting to cover over the floor. She dashed into the hallway and ducked around a corner, shaking foam out of her clothes as she pulled them on.

She heard voices and shouting. The fire alarms were screaming. She guessed Manny and whatever other guards were on duty were trying to clear the building and get things under control before the fire department came. There were some trade secret rooms that locked automatically when there was a fire. The guards were also under order to check and see the secret rooms' SOS beacons in case someone had been trapped inside. Everyone had to be clear before the fire department came. Otherwise, unwanted eyes might get a look at

StoneCorp's secrets. She would have several minutes before the fire department arrived.

Veronica barked out the password and ran out the backdoor of StoneCorp toward the back fence. The fence shared a boundary with the Charles River running trail, which, at this time of the morning, already had a few joggers glancing up at StoneCorp through the chain-link fence trying to see what was going on. She slung the duffle bag over her shoulder and ran full-speed at the fence. She jumped and caught it halfway up, then scrambled over and dropped to the other side before she ran out of momentum. The gathered joggers stared at her.

"There's a fire—you'd better evacuate. God knows what kind of stuff they were making in there," said Veronica, before sprinting off down the path.

She'd made it three hundred yards before one of the joggers behind her even thought to yell "Stop!" or "Police!" She cut quickly up the bank in case some public vigilante tried to follow her, cutting through the scrub and onto Storrow Drive. She ran through the intersection and then down through Fieldler Park and over the ramp into Boston Common. Joggers and pedestrians passed her on either side without giving her a second look. For all intents and purposes, she looked like one of them, albeit with a huge bag slung across her back.

As she slipped into Boston Common T Station, she snagged a FedEx envelope out of one of the street vending boxes. She bought a token and then jumped on a train heading to South Station. She found a seat. No one even looked at her. They all stared straight ahead, or into newspapers or books.

There was still blood on Veronica's hand, which she rubbed off using a piece of newspaper. She stuffed the bloody newspaper in the duffle bag along with everything else, and hurriedly wrote out a secret address in Brooklyn and a private StoneCorp corporate account number on the FedEx envelope as the train pulled into South Station. She slid the Russian's notebook into the envelope and then bought a ticket on the local commuter train to Cape Ann, figuring that might throw whoever was chasing her off. She was sure they'd check the trains to New York or Chicago. She walked through the main waiting rooms to the trains and dropped the envelope into a FedEx mailbox. She just had to get away. At the moment, she didn't care where. She needed some time to figure out what to do next. She had to save her sister, find a way to cure Alex, and clear her name. She didn't have much time for any one of them. She was livid that things had gone so wrong and that she was caught up in this mess. She kicked herself for not using her better judgment.

This was the last time she would ever work for someone else again. From now on, if she ever got out of this, she would make her own fortunes on her own terms, in her own way, just as she had always planned to. It was obvious Hiro had gotten her so deep into this mess. She would make him pay for that.

23

"But I don't know anything!" screamed Carrie at the cell door for the hundredth time. She didn't know where she was, or how long she'd been there. She was in a small concrete room with some blankets and pillows and a hole in the ground for her to use as a toilet. She thought there'd been a plane ride, but they'd drugged her soon after they captured her at the cabin. She wondered if they'd captured Veronica, too, or if she was even alive. The last thing she remembered was running in a panic through the second story of the cabin. Then she'd seen a maid ahead of her, waving for her to follow. She'd heard Veronica yell something, then the floor fell away from her feet. She was dragged out of the rubble by the girl who had been pretending to be hurt. Carrie's arm was broken, and the woman had dug in her fingers between the split to keep her under control until someone stuck her with a needle and she passed out.

Carrie paced across the room. As scared as she was, her adrenaline was pumping so hard she could run a marathon. She held her hand against the poorly tied splint on her arm.

She wondered if there'd be permanent damage. She'd just met her sister, and she already regretted it. Carrie had been alone all her life—her parents were uninvolved, busy with their own very public lives, and her sister was a mystery.

The cell door creaked open. The blonde Russian woman strode through the door, smiling and holding a pitcher of water, two cups, and a plate of cookies. She looked as if she were just on a friendly neighborhood visit. "Good afternoon," said the woman, her Russian burr grinding away just under her English. "My name's Svetlana."

Carrie immediately started rambling. "Look, I don't know anything. I have no idea what is going on. I have nothing to do with my sister. I don't know any national secrets. I just want to go home." Her words were coming out faster than she could say them.

Svetlana sat cross-legged on the floor and poured water for the both of them. Then she set the cookies in front of Carrie. "Please. I'm sure you're hungry," said Svetlana.

Carrie took a butter cookie and nibbled at it like a mouse. "You killed Colonel Gray. Why did you do that?"

Svetlana nodded. "I had to," she said matter-of-factly.

"It was murder."

"It was war. He would have done the same to me in a heart-beat, I assure you."

"I guess," she said, pausing to consider her thoughts. "I've seen people die on television and the movies, but up close and personal was really scary."

"I know, honey," said the Russian, her voice oozing with sincerity. "You know, you don't know anything about the late Colonel Gray. How do you know I'm not the good guy?" asked Svetlana, sipping her cup.

Carrie took another cookie. "What have you done with my sister? Is she dead?" asked Carrie

Svetlana looked at her in surprise. "Why would you think we have her?"

"Well—don't you? I mean, where is she?"

"She ran, dear. We told her we'd kill you, and she ran. I imagine she's having a hot bath in a hotel somewhere," said Svetlana with a mocking smirk. "Another cookie?"

Carrie glared. "She wouldn't have done that."

"Really?" asked Svetlana. "Of course. She's always been there for you."

Carrie didn't say anything.

"Where do you think she's run off to? Any ideas?"

"I'm not going to help you."

"Truth is, you wouldn't know, would you?" asked the Russian.

"No. I guess I wouldn't," said Carrie, looking at her fingertips.

"I'm wondering if she left the country entirely. You know, she has connections—maybe Aruba—the South of France— New Zealand—New Zealand is beautiful, have you ever been there?"

"No."

"Maybe one day you'll get to go," said Svetlana. "Maybe Veronica will take you. If she ever bothers to come back and get you. More to drink?"

"Well, you think she's coming back to get me," answered Carrie.

"What do you mean?"

"You wouldn't be keeping me here if you didn't."

Svetlana smiled. "Smart girl. Well, I really must be going," said Svetlana, standing and brushing off her pants. "Here, keep the cookies. The food around here is abysmal."

Carrie took the plate of cookies and looked up. "So what happens next?"

"I really don't know. Maybe we'll cut off an ear and send it over to StoneCorp. Not that that would probably make too much of a difference. We threatened to kill you once already. It's really up to Sergei."

"Who's Sergei?" asked Carrie, as Svetlana banged on the cell door to be let back out.

"You'll find out. Unless your sister comes back for you. I'm sure she will, aren't you?" asked Svetlana, smiling over her shoulder. "Any minute now. Just rushing in with the Army and the Air Force. Just like she's always done for you." The door slammed shut behind her.

24

Veronica got off the bus at New York's Port Authority at three in the morning. She had on a blond wig she'd bought near the train station, and a baseball cap on tight and low over her face. She was hoping no one would recognize her. She'd used cash the entire way. No one seemed to have picked up her trail yet. Hopefully, they still thought she was heading north, possibly to Canada. There was a small StoneCorp subsidiary office in Montreal. She imagined the Russians were already lying in wait for her there. It would buy her some much-needed time.

She caught a taxi over the bridge into Brooklyn. She kept a small basement condominium in a converted brownstone in Park Slope, a place she'd never told anyone about. Veronica made sure maids kept the place clean and a gardening service kept the flowers in her tiny garden alive. She also paid a local boy to pick up her mail and newspapers and forward them on to a PO box in Boston. She also had him take care of the inside plants. She paid the boy so much, and he was so terrified of losing the job, that he would never tell anyone she didn't usually live there. Of course, to him, she was Susan Miller, Associate Editor at some publishing company.

"Susan Miller" and the condominium had started when StoneCorp landed its first seven-figure contract. At the time, Veronica was only twenty, and despite all her preparation and desire, she'd been a little freaked out by how easily it had all come to her. If it could come this easily, she thought, couldn't it disappear just as quickly?

During one weekend when she was in New York on business, she strolled past a condominium for sale only a few doors down from Prospect Park. On a whim, she bought it outright, using the name Susan Miller. With her technical skills, it was easy to make a believable driver's license, passport, business records, credit cards, etc., all in Susan Miller's name. In one afternoon on her computer, she gave birth to an entirely new person, who happened to be a beautiful woman with long, raven hair.

She was still a little unsure why she had done it. It had almost seemed that fate had landed her there. Susan Miller's condominium was something she could never lose. No matter what, she'd have a roof over her head, a place to go, and, most importantly, a place to disappear. Even if StoneCorp were ground into the dust, she had someplace to go. Susan Miller was like a comfortable robe she could slip into whenever she needed to get away for a while. Not even Alex knew about it.

She unlocked her door and stepped inside. It smelled clean, yet stale. She guessed she hadn't been there in at least two years. The plants looked healthy, and she'd have to remember to put a note on the door so the neighborhood boy didn't come barging in on her. She wasn't sure what time of the day he usually came.

Veronica went into her bedroom and stripped off her clothes, tossing them into the empty hamper. She turned on the shower as hot as it would go and stood under it for a long time, trying to clean off the dirt and the grime, trying to relax, trying to melt away her sense of guilt and failure. She closed her eyes and silently went through a Buddhist meditation exercise she had learned from one of her old lovers. By the time the water went cold, she had regained some of her stability.

She knew she should eat something and rest. But she didn't know how much time she had, and she didn't know how long she could stay hidden. Then she went into the front room and took her heavy copy of *Ulysses* from the built-in bookcase. A lever snapped up on the bookshelf, and then the bookcase slowly came away from the wall.

Behind the bookcase was the condominium's former second bedroom. She'd spent a weekend gathering books and tools to make her own secret laboratory. During the infancy of Susan Miller, she woke early one bright Saturday morning and decided she needed a laboratory here, too. Her secret identity seemed to set loose a flurry of childish impulses. She went to the used bookstores around New York and stocked up on all the old books she'd loved—*The Canterbury Tales, Moby-Dick, Brave New World, Tom Sawyer, A Tale of Two Cities.* They were intended to fill up the new case, but they were also something of a recognition of her past. In a way, her book collection mirrored her toy collection back at StoneCorp. But while the toy collection was simply something practical for work, the books in Susan Miller's apartment were a way for her to completely escape everything.

So, she built a secret laboratory behind the fake bookcase. And although it was built on childish impulse, there was nothing childish about the equipment inside. It was not quite as sophisticated as the one at StoneCorp, but it was functional, and for the time being, it was the only place she felt safe working on a cure for Alex and the Monroes. If she needed anything else, she had a city behind her of eight million people who likely had the necessary equipment and would be willing to sell it to her for an exorbitant amount of money, no questions asked, no records kept. She wasn't going to fool herself that she could keep her location hidden forever, but for now, she just needed time.

The lab was dusty. She'd decorated the walls with old movie posters and a cartoon painting of Wonder Woman she had commissioned by a very expensive comic book painter, something she could sell for almost fifty thousand dollars if she ever wanted to. She smiled up at Wonder Woman. She was ready.

First, she'd go pick up the Russian's notebook at the post office. Then she'd figure out a way to fix everything.

25

CARRIE CROUCHED IN the dark corner behind the door in her bra and panties, squeezing the metal bedpost she'd bent from the bed. It had taken her all night of bending it back and forth, back and forth, until it finally snapped off in her hand. It was thin steel, about the size of a ruler, but it would do. She relished the feel of the bicep of her good arm flexing as she squeezed the bar, getting herself pumped up for what she had to do. She tried to keep her mind away from her broken arm and any weakness that that might allow into her head. She went over in her mind every self-defense class she'd ever taken. She thought about all the push-ups and wind sprints and weightlifting for sports. Even with one good arm, she was strong enough to do what she had to.

Her thighs were tingling. Dinner was late, and she'd been crouching in the dark for forty-five minutes. Her clothes and shoes were piled up under the bed's blankets to make it look like she was sleeping. It wasn't a perfect likeness, but it would be enough to give her the element of surprise. If there was one thing she had learned from her sister, surprise and a quick, strong strike won most wars before the other side even knew a battle had begun.

Finally, she heard the thump and clang of the door lock. The door opened, and a young soldier came strolling in with a tray of food. He was Russian, about her age, with stunningly bad teeth that looked as if the dentist had replaced them all with gray lead cubes. His name was Ivan. He'd spent the last few days commenting on her skin, her hair—asking her if she would like a bath, some soap or perfume, or maybe some better clothes to wear. He always asked about her arm, and promised it would be better soon. He flirted with her, but as it became clearer and clearer that Carrie wasn't simply going to fall into bed with him, his eyes started to cloud with anger and he started to treat her with contempt. She was afraid if she didn't get out of here this time, or if he stopped her, he was certain to rape her.

"Miss Priss? Time to wake up and have your cat food," said the soldier. "Come on, get your lazy American ass out of bed." The soldier kicked the bed. With its missing leg, it went clattering against the wall, spilling out her clothes. "What! Alarm!" he yelled. He dropped the tray and turned, but it was too late. Carrie smashed him right between the eyes, shattering his nose in an explosion of blood and cartilage. He collapsed to the floor like a rag doll. Quickly, she yanked off his pants and shirt. Then she gagged him with his belt and one of his socks, wrapped him in the sheets, and rolled him under the bed, tying the ends of the sheet as if he were in an envelope and wedging it down with the broken bed frame. Her broken arm burned like fire every time she had to use it, but she pushed it from her mind. On top of the mattress, she arranged his clothes to look like she was sleeping, and cleaned up the mess from the tray, stuffing it on top along with the clothes. Then she draped the blanket over the edge of the bed so no one would see the guard if they glanced inside the cell. Hopefully, no one would miss him, and no one would come to see her for some time—at least enough time for her to find some way to escape or some place to hide until she was rescued. She tugged back on her old clothes. They were still damp and covered with dried blood and globs of dirt and masonry dust.

She lay on the floor and poked her head out the doorway, guessing no one would notice someone peeking out at floor level. There was a desk and some file cabinets about ten yards down the hallway. Another guard was sitting at it with his back to her, watching television and eating a bag of potato chips. He had his feet up. His rifle was four feet away, leaning against the wall.

Carrie stood up and squeezed her iron bar for luck. She crept along the hallway. On the television screen, some fifteen-year-old was singing a Whitney Houston song to rapturous applause. The guard shifted in his seat. She froze. He took a chocolate from the top of his desk and popped it into his mouth.

She crept closer. Just as she was right behind him, she bumped into one of the file cabinets with her thigh. She froze again. She glanced at the rifle, wondering if she was strong and fast enough to get it and use it against him before he used it against her.

The guard spoke without turning to look at her. He spoke English, and his accent was American. He said, "That was fast. I thought today was going to be the big wedding day, lover boy. I thought you were going to show her the 'Russian Bear.'" The guard made little quotation marks in the air and laughed. "I guess the 'Russian Bear' is quick shot. As long as there's some left for me. Hey, silent guy, what—" The guard started to turn in his seat.

Carrie smashed the bar into his cheek, bouncing him onto his desk. The television smashed to the floor.

The guard glared at her, his face covered in blood. He was still standing. "You're going to pay for that, bitch. I don't care who wants you kept alive." He lunged at her. She ducked to the side and kicked the desk chair at him, but slipped and fell flat against the floor. He grabbed her ponytail and yanked her to her feet. Then he ran her into the brick wall. Carrie felt as if the world had exploded. Then the guard punched her splinted arm. She screamed and fought to stay conscious. The guard tossed her onto the desk like she was a slab of meat. Papers and a lamp crashed to the floor.

"I guess we're going to have to do this here," snarled the guard, starting to unbuckle his pants.

Carrie couldn't focus her eyes. She was disoriented and dizzy and her head felt split down the center. Her broken arm felt dead. The guard's fingers tore at the top of her jeans. She could barely move. He pulled her up to yank her pants down and she slid farther across the desk until she was hanging upside down with her good arm on the floor. She had to get herself together. She kept thinking, *He will kill you!* over and over again, trying to get her mind around the pain in her body. She swept her hand back and forth across the floor, trying to find anything she could use as a weapon. His grimy hands dug into her thighs. Just then, her fingertips touched the smashed desk lamp. With the last bit of willpower she had, she jabbed it with all her might into his neck. The broken bulb and socket cut straight through his skin. There was a "Pop," and the man groaned and rolled to the floor. His eyes bugged open in shock. His neck smoked slightly. The lamp had still been plugged in. He was electrocuted before he even knew what hit him.

Carrie lay on the desk until she thought she could get to her feet without throwing up. She pulled her clothes back together, and stood, taking a few wobbly steps as the guard lay dead and bleeding on the floor. His burning neck smelled like bacon. She retched, and quickly grabbed a wastebasket, throwing up three days of prison porridge until she couldn't throw up anymore. This wasn't like the movies. In the movies, you couldn't smell death, no one really died, and no one's life was truly in danger. But suddenly, she felt a surge of power. She was stronger than some stupid movie hero. This was tough, but she'd survived. She'd beaten two men—killing one who was trying to rape her. For a moment, she wished Veronica could see her. She wondered if Veronica would have handled it so well. Veronica had never had to fight for anything—to be noticed, to be successful, to win awards, to wow the world— nothing. Carrie had had to scrap for everything she ever achieved under the shadow of her famous sister. And being a scrapper had made her strong.

She grabbed the potato chips, chocolates, and two bottles of water from the desk, stuffing it into one of the men's backpacks. The rifle was too bulky to sneak around with only one good arm, but she found a knife strapped to the dead man's boot, and a pistol in one of the drawers. She'd never shot a gun in her life, but she'd dated a boy obsessed with some first-person-shooter videogame—she hoped it was basically the same. She was so pumped with adrenaline and pain and fear, she almost couldn't think straight. She had to find a place to hide. If she tried to make a break for the front door now, she'd probably just run straight into a hail of gunfire. As it was, she had no idea where they were keeping her. She stuffed the dead guard's body under the desk and spun his chair in front of it to cover it a little. She figured they'd be on to her soon enough, and if the lamp had popped a circuit breaker, someone might already be on their way. But any little time she could buy was worth it.

She took several deep breaths, and looked around for anything else that might be useful in covering her escape. She found some thin twine in another of the desk drawers.

She smashed the hallway's light bulbs and jammed the rifle under the desk with the dead guard. Then she tied one end of the twine through the rifle's trigger, snapped off the safety, and tied the other end to a bent nail sticking from her cell door. If she was lucky, someone would trip over it or open the door, the gun would fire, and, in the shadowy darkness, that someone would think they were under attack from someone under the desk. It was a trick Carrie learned from her father, who had rigged up a shotgun to take care of some raccoons bothering the trashcans at their summerhouse. The raccoons had been obliterated. None ever returned.

After everything was set, Carrie trotted down the hallway, with the pistol held out in front of her like a light. She'd find someplace where no one could ever find her until she wanted to be found.

26

COLONEL DEWITT STOOD looking down at the bodies of his friend Colonel Gray and his men. They'd gone to the Academy together, and now the only way he could identify his friend was from the nametag on his uniform. The rest of his face was gone.

A soldier trotted up to Colonel DeWitt and saluted. "Colonel, the entire safe-house structure is destroyed. It looks like someone hit it with a missile."

"What kind of missile?"

"Too early to determine."

"How come we didn't see this?"

"All alarms and communications cords had been severed, even the ones that lead down through the congressional safe room. And something knocked out our satellites for over two hours."

"Were any other cabins damaged?"

"No. Just this one."

Colonel DeWitt nodded. Then he crouched down and patted his dead friend on the chest. "So—someone, some terrorist, came onto American soil and completely destroyed an elite Army force and a safe house unknown to the entire rest of the country—and we know nothing about what happened?"

"It appears that way, sir," said the soldier, flinching as if he expected the Colonel to hit him.

"We are the most technologically advanced fighting force in the world and I have lost my best friend and the godfather to one of my children," said Colonel DeWitt as he stood. "Lock down the rest area on the other side of the mountain and use the security cameras and trucking manifests to get a list of everybody who has been there over the past several days—and cross-check those names with any known terrorists. Get CIA and FBI on the horn and ask them if there's something they've been neglecting to tell us in this presidential illness situation. Once you get the list of who was here, notify the local police forces to go interrogate them and find out if anyone saw anything. I want helicopters in the air, and put some dogs in the trees. Somebody better give me an answer quickly, or there's going to be heads rolling. We are not going to get caught with our pants down again!"

The soldier ran off and started shouting orders to the other men. Just as he left the colonel, another soldier scampered up the slight rise from the forest tree line, carrying a large box of radio equipment and sensors. He saluted the Colonel. He was panting with excitement. "I think I've got something."

"What?" barked Colonel DeWitt.

"Well, I used the overhead satellite—"

The Colonel cut him off with a swat of his hand. "If you go techno dialogue on me, I'll break your hand. Just tell me what you found out."

The soldier gulped, then regained his composure. "A call

was made from here—on a cell phone. Colonel Gray had it intercepted and taped. This is the weird thing—it was made by Veronica Stone, the tech guru, telling her office she was in North Carolina."

"What was Veronica Stone doing here?"

"She said something about a 'Project Looking Glass.'"

Colonel DeWitt asked, "Did we find her body in the ruins?"

"Not yet, sir."

"I've met Veronica Stone. Stunning woman. Her company is quickly becoming one of the country's largest defense contractors. Find out who sent Colonel Gray out to get her and find out what projects StoneCorp is working on for the White House—especially what Project Looking Glass is. Get some people to her known addresses, family members, etc. If you can find her, I want her at my office in the Pentagon by tomorrow. If she is missing, track her down. Good work, son."

"And sir, there was one more weird thing about the cell phone transmission."

"What?"

"As she was talking, there was a secondary bounce as if someone was trying to break into the line."

"What's weird about that? Can't you find out who it is?" asked the Colonel.

"I traced it—and it seems to be coming from the dead center of a jungle in South America."

"What city?"

"That's just it—the closest city is 350 kilometers away, and there's no official towns. It's basically a big wasteland."

"Okay. Find out exactly where that point is in the jungle. We may need to go down there for a little visit."

"Yes sir!" exclaimed the soldier, stepping away.

"Soldier—also find out who else might be interested in whatever it is StoneCorp is working on, and which of those parties might settle their trade disagreements with a missile. Especially anyone in South America."

"Yes sir!" shouted the soldier, before trotting back to the cluster of jeeps along the road.

Colonel DeWitt reached down and removed a bloody medal from Colonel Gray's chest. Then he slipped it gently into his shirt pocket. "We'll get the bastards who did this—I promise you that," he said.

27

"So our little captive proved to be more resourceful than we thought," said Sergei, prodding the lifeless corpse of the guard at his feet.

The hallway in front of Carrie's former cell was splattered from floor to ceiling with blood. Her trick with the rifle had worked perfectly, and in the darkness and confusion of who was shooting at them from under the desk, one of the guards pulled a hand grenade. Four corpses lay on the ground. A fifth was under the desk, shredded unrecognizable by machine-gun fire. The only guard to survive was found under the girl's former cot, half-deaf from the explosion, bleeding heavily from a blow to the head. Two guards stood on either side grasping him by the shoulders so he wouldn't collapse to the floor. His head lulled to the side as if his neck were rubber. "Shouldn't we get him to the infirmary," asked one of the men holding up the stricken guard.

Sergei cut him off with a glance. "First, I would like to know how an untrained, American college girl did this to my men."

"I think he must have helped her," purred Svetlana, stroking her blonde hair with her hand. She sat on what was left of the guard desk, her chin resting coyly on the muzzle of her machine gun. "I left her with a couple cookies. She was as good as broken."

The wounded guard gurgled something. Then he shook his head no.

"What? What did you say?" snapped Sergei, wrenching the man's chin up. "Look into my eyes when you want to speak to me!"

The wounded guard screamed in pain.

"Let's just shoot him and go find where the little bitch has run off to. She's probably making a run for the front door, or trying to find a phone to call daddy," said Svetlana, hopping from the desk.

The wounded guard started to shake his head again. "We didn't help her—I swear. She—"

Sergei got right in the guard's face and yanked his chin up again. The guard screamed. "Do you really want me to know that you were defeated by a little girl?" asked Sergei.

The guard tried to shake his head. He seemed panicked and unsure of any way to get out of this.

"You know what I think happened?" asked Svetlana, bending down to peer into the guard's eyes. "I bet our little friend here tried to have himself a little fun, didn't you?"

The guard shook his head.

"I bet you thought you could get away with raping her. She's a beautiful girl, about your age, completely under your control. Did you fall in love with her? Did she fall in love with you? I bet you let your guard down along with your pants and she kicked your insect-little ass," sneered Svetlana. "Isn't that what happened?"

The guard shook his head slower. "Please—," he spit out. "I wasn't going to hurt her."

"You weren't going to hurt her? You weren't going to hurt her? You think she would have enjoyed your little insect penis inside her? Is that what you thought?" asked Svetlana. She slapped the guard so hard his head popped back against his shoulders. "That's what all you military men think, isn't it? You think she wanted it!"

The guard kept shaking his head no and started to cry, "Please—"

"Maybe you'd like this!" shouted Svetlana, drawing a small pistol from her belt. She put it against the guard's forehead and fired.

Sergei glared at her. "Must you do things like that?"

"The new world will have no place for rapists," answered Svetlana, wiping some blood from her forehead. "Besides, he told us what we needed to know. She escaped because of male stupidity, not because anyone was helping her."

The guards holding up the man's body looked too stunned to move. Sergei waved them away. "Take him—along with the others. And get a clean-up detail here. Also, find Roskilnov and tell him we have a prisoner loose on the grounds."

When the guards had disappeared down the hall, Sergei turned to Svetlana. She was leaning against one of the walls, running her hand through her hair, preening herself like a cat. Sergei said, "You shouldn't do that in front of our men."

Svetlana's eyes flashed. "That's exactly the kind of thing I need to be doing in front of our men. If they're going to help us with our plan, it's EXACTLY the kind of thing I need to be doing."

Sergei drummed his fingers against his chin. "I don't have time to argue with you. We must find Veronica's sister now before she does any more harm. We can't afford to lose her— it's the only way we'll get Veronica back."

"What do we need Veronica for? We have the technology—Hiro is working for us. Let her run if she wants to."

"She might alert the Americans before the weapon is completely ready."

"So? She'd never do it. She built it, gave it to the president and his daughter herself—there's no way she'd go to the authorities. Even if she did, the stupid Americans would probably just call her a terrorist and ship her off to some military base never to be heard from again. By then, it would be too late. We would have Mother Earth by her tits, and no one would be able to resist our demands."

"I still think we need her," said Sergei.

Svetlana's eyes narrowed. She patted her machine gun like her favorite dog. "You think we need her? For what? You think she's pretty?"

Sergei snorted. "Don't be ridiculous. I just want her around in case we need her technical expertise."

Svetlana could tell Sergei wasn't being entirely truthful. "Fine. I will capture her, alive, for you—under one condition."

"What condition, Svetlana?" asked Sergei warily.

"I just want to make sure it's just her mind you're interested in." Svetlana giggled and planted a kiss on Sergei's neck. Then she said, "You'll find out when I bring her to you."

28

Veronica stared at her laboratory computer screen. There had to be an antidote, a way to reverse the process. She'd been too scared to phone out, so she had no idea how Alex or the president or his daughter were doing. She kept her eye on the obituaries, and kept her tiny AM radio tuned to the news. Alex was an important enough man that if he died, she was certain the BBC would broadcast news of it. She desperately wanted to call Alex, but if she did, she might lose all chance to work on a cure to save him. A lot of people were looking for her.

She'd tried to get the phone to repeat the call that Alex had seen, but after the call, it had apparently been sent a kill signal that erased any chance of seeing it again. She turned the pages in the Russian's notebook and sipped at her tea. She skipped over the pages showing the resolution necessary to use images as a weapon. They made her feel too guilty, and were too close to her own early drawings and ideas for the phone. After the resolution requirements and sketches for delivery systems, there were pages and pages of drawings and doodles, with equations and diagrams representing certain wattages and colors. Music notes floated above the equations with dotted lines connecting one to the other, and a drawing of a digital clock counting off microseconds. It all seemed tied together—she just couldn't quite make out how.

Veronica had been working for twelve hours straight, and her sister had been gone for forty-eight hours. She didn't let herself think what could be happening to her. She had to focus.

She leaned back in her chair and flipped the pages of the notebook through her fingers. For a moment, it seemed like the pictures were moving. She sat up and did it again, this time holding the pages tighter, flipping it like a children's book showing a horse jumping over a stile or a man flying in a plane. The pictures definitely had some type of order, although she couldn't have described exactly what they were doing. Were they a man flying a spacecraft? Were they monsters battling each other? Were they some kind of stream of binary code built out of hieroglyphics? Was it a coded message?

Were they the scientist's idea of a joke? They were definitely doing something. And even just by flipping them under the bright light of her desk lamp, she could feel something quivering at the base of her brain, as if she'd just gotten off some sort of fun-house ride.

She flipped the book over and then scrolled through the pages again. This time, in the corner of the pages, almost too small to notice, she saw a picture of a face slowly sloughing off to leave a grinning skull. It reminded her sickeningly of Alex. She flipped the pages again, this time reversing the order. The skull magically grew its skin back into a smiling portrait of Lenin.

She looked at the numbers and the equations, all the lines connecting these pages with the strange drawing in the corner. She flipped back and forth. The skin fell off. The skin grew back. The skin fell off. The skin grew back. Then it hit her like a bolt of lightning.

These pages were the exact rings, tones, sounds, and colors needed to turn the phone into a cellular disrupter—and if you did the exact reverse, that would be the cure!

Somewhere, there was a broadcast tower set up with the exact sequence to kill someone, reachable by some secret phone number.

She had to build one of her own.

Before they found her.

29

BRAVO COMPANY PIERCED through the jungle like a giant, many-headed snake, punching through the scrub and brush to where their orders told them they had to rendezvous. Their packs were strapped hard against their backs, and they held their rifles close against their bodies, making no sound but for the hushed footsteps of their boots on the jungle floor. All of them were young men, cherry-picked from many different units into an elite squad of ghosts and killers. Their muscles, and the rising and falling of their chests moved in perfect harmony under their uniforms and camouflage makeup. This was what they had signed up for. They were unstoppable supermen.

The squad leader suddenly held up his hand. Everyone froze. He pointed with three fingers off to the left, then with three to the right, before crouching down into position. Three soldiers peeled off in each direction, while the rest lay down on the jungle floor. It was as if all twenty men had disappeared.

The moving soldiers circled in front of the others until they came upon a group of old vehicles smashed in the ditch. They were an assortment of old jeeps that had apparently simultaneously driven off the nearby narrow dirt road and crashed into the trees. Skeletal remains were scattered all around the wreckage, as were old rusty weapons and tattered pieces of clothing.

One of the soldiers held his hand to his ear. "Sir, we've come across five to seven vehicles destroyed along the side of the road," he whispered. He reached into one of the jeeps and studied a necklace one of the skeletons was still wearing. It looked like it was made of human vertebrae. "Bones—looks like most of the flesh has been picked off by whatever scavengers and insects live around here. Some rusty weapons. There's no sign of an explosion or any gunfire—no holes in the vehicles, and no damage except for crashing into trees. Some of the tires are still inflated, so I don't think the tires were punctured. I'm guessing drug dealers—maybe they were ambushed. Or a deal gone bad. There's a lot of coca that runs through this jungle."

"Forget about the jeeps. Your GPS transponder shows you should be right on top of the target," said a voice on the other end.

"We'll shadow the road. Out."

The soldier stood and waved his waiting comrades forward. They passed through the wrecked jeeps and ran along the edge of the dirt road, keeping themselves hidden in the tree line. Suddenly, a clearing opened up in front of them. In the middle of it was a small gray building with a large satellite dish on top. The jungle was already starting to encroach into the clearing from the sides. It looked as if no one had been there in a long time. The soldiers fanned out along the perimeter.

The leader waved two fingers forward and two soldiers ran across the clearing until they were on either side of the only door. One readied his weapon as the other grasped the knob.

Suddenly, the air filled with an ear-splitting wail that knocked the soldiers to the ground. Birds and insects burst from the canopy all around them.

The squad leader rolled onto his back and dug desperately in his jacket pocket until his fingers touched a packet of chewing gum. He dumped the entire pack in his mouth, his shaking hands unable to unwrap it, and chewed as hard as he could. He extracted globs of the gooey stuff and jammed them in his ears. It didn't completely silence the noise, but it dulled it enough so he could get to his feet. His men lay all around the clearing, screaming in agony. On top of the building was a small loud-speaker. He drew his pistol and fired. The loudspeaker shattered into bits of metal and plastic. The clearing returned to silence.

He took the gum from his ears as his men tried to collect themselves. He yelled out over the tall grass, keeping his head down in case there were any other surprises. "So, we know this place is booby-trapped! No more touching things until we've completely secured the area!"

"Sir! The door's open," said one of the soldiers closest to the building. The leader craned his head over the grass. His men were pressed against the wall on either side of the open doorway. The door banged slightly in the stagnant air, as if some ghostly breeze had just passed it. One of the nearby soldiers pointed at it with the muzzle of his rifle, but he kept the rest of his body securely behind cover. The other soldier was rubbing his ears with a bandana, as if the ringing sound was still lodged inside.

"Okay. Everyone get his act together! I want two sound and light shows inside that door, then four in to follow. Ten seconds!"

The still-stunned soldiers dragged themselves to their feet and readied their weapons, pulling small air filters over their mouths. The two by the door removed two small devices from their packs and got ready to toss them inside. Their leader held up one finger, and the men threw the devices in and spun away from the doors.

There was a loud bang, then flashes of lights like firecrackers before black smoke came billowing out. The two soldiers by the door remained in position as four men leapt from the grass and sprinted inside. There were several shouts. Then complete silence.

After a moment, one of the four soldiers stepped back outside. "No one in here. And our initial sweep revealed no other booby traps. But—well—"

"What, soldier?"

"It's pretty strange in here," said the soldier, apparently at a loss for an explanation. "I'm not really sure what we're looking at."

The squad leader nodded his head in resignation. "Okay. Let's try to figure out what the hell is going on before we call in the support staff. Colonel DeWitt wants to know what's going on up here before the spook agencies shut everything down. You six up there start checking the inside for surprises— I want the rest of you checking the roof and walls for any wires or detonators. I don't want this whole thing crashing in on us while we're inside."

The men fanned away from him. The squad leader stood and made a visual check of the clearing one more time. None of his men were looking in his direction. He quickly removed a small spy camera from his jacket pocket and entered the still-smoking doorway.

30

VERONICA SAT IN the laboratory among piles of empty cardboard boxes, mailer envelopes, and Bubble Wrap with her long brown hair tucked up under a baseball cap, walking a small screwdriver across her fingers as she thought. The air was hot and greasy with solder, and the entire apartment smelled like electricity and ozone. In truth, it was one of her favorite smells. It meant that she had an idea and was working on something—that some new device would soon be brought to life.

She rubbed her temples. She wasn't sure how long she'd been working. When things were really clicking, and her thoughts were coming fast and furious, she could lose days as her laser-like intensity focused in on a problem. Alex called it a "V-trance"—Veronica didn't think he was far from the mark.

She'd ordered several television sets and had them all set to the different news channels—but news about the president and his daughter had gone strangely silent. It was as if everyone were too afraid to say anything, lest the Monroes' condition hint at a larger and more deadly attack on America. Even the usually bellowing cable news talking heads kept it out of their performances, finding it easier and more comfortable to attack their usual targets of the liberal media and gay marriage. It was as if the sick president had gone from being the top concern of the country to being swept under the rug. The only information was from daily press conferences with the administration's press secretary, who was always full of smiles and jokes, assuring the country that the best minds were working on the situation and that the president was getting the best care in the world. Every so often, they'd release a picture of the president and Jessica Monroe taking a walk through the hospital's grounds, or the president tossing a football with a Secret Service agent, or Jessica, in bed, but laughing at some story of her mother's, looking as radiant and young as ever. With her trained eye, Veronica could tell they were digital fakes, and the first whispers were already crawling across the Internet—before long, some kid would post up the real pictures and how they had been pasted together. Veronica guessed the Administration was growing desperate if it was trying such tricks, obviously simply buying time for itself. Like her, it needed to rally its forces.

On the news channels, she had seen no mention of herself or StoneCorp. Either no one had made any connection yet, or everything was on lockdown, and they weren't telling the public anything. Veronica wondered how far the classified orders ran. She smiled to herself, imagining tight-lipped officers trotting around the Pentagon, no one saying anything, everyone completely confused and paranoid over who should be told what. She imagined they felt very lost, and were as close to a governmental collapse as they'd ever come.

Veronica was leaning down to solder a new circuit when she saw a familiar face on one of the televisions. She grabbed the

stack of remotes and silenced the other screens. Her old friend
from college, Mary O'Donnell, was on one of the talking head
shows, engaged in a shouting match with its bilious and fas-
cistic host.

"You have no idea how much goes on under the surface
of our American government. History is made in the clandestine dark, not with ridiculous bills about flag-burning
and abortions—all of you are being snowed—your eyes are
being averted to other things, to keep you from asking the
really dangerous questions," spat Mary, sitting back elegantly on the couch. She looked prettier than she had in
college, but harder, as if any bits of childish innocence had
been finally worn away. Her face and eyes were as hard and
angular as diamonds. Next to the overweight host, she
seemed capable of actually doing something, not just
talking about it.

"But aren't those some strong words, considering how your
company has made its money?" asked the host.

The screen switched back to Mary's face. Under her was a
banner reading "Marilyn Moriarty, President of Moriarty
Intelligence Incorporated." Mary rolled her eyes. "Out of
anyone, who else would know what's going on but me? That's
my business."

"But aren't you afraid of repercussions?"

"Like what?"

"Well, if what you say is true, you're a dangerous person to
dozens of organizations and governments. Why don't they
stop you?"

Mary laughed as if the host were being extremely foolish.
"One—I sell to everybody equally, on the same terms. That
makes me something of an 'Internet' between all these

organizations. If they cut me out, they lose their contacts and eyes over each other. Most groups can't afford their own intel, so I am a necessity for most governments, like air. They take me out, it would be like cutting off their noses to spite their own faces."

"It can't be that simple."

"Occam's razor. Everything is that simple. If it weren't, we would have all killed each other years ago. Society is not big on complication. There are two other reasons as well. One: I die, all the information I've gathered gets dumped to the publicly accessible Internet—lots of reputations and plans would then be destroyed. Two: now that I've shown that such a service can be done, another person would just pop up in my place. At least this way, I'm the devil they know. Every single bit of information, every little secret, every little misstep, every little indiscretion and three a.m. loss of self—everything is out there—and I can get it with a snap of my fingers."

"You sound extremely sure of yourself," laughed the host.

"I am. Here, I just want to prove something to you. Give me a question."

"What? I don't understand you."

Mary rolled her eyes again. It was a habit she apparently hadn't been able to shake since college. It made her look like a petulant girl. Still, it was intriguing in its own way. Veronica guessed men found it alluring.

"Ask me a question about yourself," Mary said. "Something I couldn't possibly know from one of your standard bios. Something that's not in the public domain—or at least that you don't think is in the public domain."

The host laughed and scratched his chin. He looked as if he

were uncomfortable with where this interview was going. "Well—I—"

"Anything," said Mary. She looked at the man as if he were an ant she was torturing with a sunbeam and a microscope.

"Okay. The address of my high school sweetheart."

Mary smiled. "Clever not to give me her name. Okay. My people should be running the information through our computers right now. Can we have a few minutes?" asked Mary coyly.

"Of course. It's time for a commercial break. We're here with Marilyn Moriarty, President of Moriarty Intelligence Incorporated. Just how much of your personal information is out there, and what can you do about it? And are we being duped by information overload to miss the important things going on in this country behind the facade? We'll be back in a moment."

As the program went to an investment commercial, Veronica plugged Mary's name into her specially-designed Internet search engine. Within seconds, she had every posting and public record on Mary O'Donnell, Marilyn Moriarty, or Moriarty Intelligence Incorporated. Mary had changed her name, but hadn't married. She pulled up Mary's archived Harvard thesis on "Commercial Branding from Society's Collective Subconscious"—and there it was—Mary's argument that you could subconsciously tie in to people's thoughts and feelings on things if you picked a name that could trigger those emotional memory responses. However, the human brain, being what it was, couldn't be fooled by something with far too many obvious connotations, such as Elvis Presley, or Sherlock Holmes. The trick was to dodge the initial firewall of familiarity and dip directly into the subconscious. Veronica continued paging through the old thesis and its charts, graphs, and evidentiary points. She should have given Mary more credit as an intellectual when they were at school. Mary was the beautiful owner of a clandestine information service— Marilyn Moriarty. It was really a kind of genius. While Veronica had made herself rich with hardware, Mary had used software and the Internet. Veronica had heard of Moriarty Intelligence, and she remembered signing off on some of her employees using some of its services. But until she saw Mary's face, she hadn't connected the two. Suddenly, she realized Mary must have taken the business plan they had drawn out in college— tech-oriented, mysterious owner, absolute power within an industry—and used it for her own fortune. In a sense, Mary had been riding Veronica's coattails and Mary didn't even know it. The idea pleased her.

The commercial was over. Mary was taking notes and talking on a cell phone, which she quickly put away. The host smiled. "Okay, for those of you just joining the program, I've put a challenge to Ms. Marilyn Moriarty, the President of Moriarty Intelligence Incorporated, to find the current address of my high school sweetheart. That's all the information I have given her, and she assured me that by the end of the break she would have an answer. Let's see if Moriarty Intelligence is all it claims to be, or simply another technological promise yet to be fulfilled. Ms. Moriarty." The host sat back in his chair, smugly sure of himself.

Mary smiled back with the same assurance. "How much info do you want?"

"All of it! Let's see if your computers can really dig up my life in two minutes," said the host, practically winking at his television audience.

"Okay," said Mary, sitting back smugly herself. Suddenly, the host seemed a little shaken. Mary said, "Your question was a little bit of a trick, but I won't hold that against you. You went to senior prom with Kelly Brotzman, who later married and changed her name to Fine. She lives in Austin, Texas."

The host started to smile and sit up.

Mary held out her hand. "But—that was not your high school sweetheart. In fact, that was the only date you ever went out with her on. Her high school yearbook picture is dedicated to a "Darren Fine," now also of Austin, Texas— they've been married since they were twenty-two. We guessed they were fighting at the time of the senior prom and you got asked to fill in. Which begs the question, why would you be available?"

The host started to cut her off. "Well, that's extremely impressive! I don't think anymore needs to be shown. It looks like you can really get into just about anything. So, how do you—"

"Wait—there's more. It turns out your yearbook dedication was to a K.C.—now there were only three 'K.C.'s in your high school—one black girl, and two boys. Considering your high school's location in South Carolina in the 1950s, and your conservative views, we took the girl out of contention immediately. Out of the two boys, one was a special-ed student you seemed to have little contact with, and one was the pitcher on the high school baseball team where you played third base. He dedicated his picture to 'I don't know'—which we guessed was a reference to the classic Abbot and Costello routine. Now, living in the genteel society in South Carolina at that time, we guessed people just wrote the two of you off as very close friends—the team had three winning seasons, after all."

The host looked as if he were about to have a heart attack. Mary grinned like a shark.

"There's two police records and a school file—seems the two of you were caught doing something. They were expunged as 'ethical lapses' and involved arrests at a popular make-out point near your hometown. All in all, the town seemed to accept you as you were. I'd say they acted fairly commendably."

The host's face was beet red. He looked all around the studio for help, as if he expected one of his staff members to come out and stop all this. He gave the "kill" signal to his staff members and immediately jumped out of his seat. The cameras were shut off and the television program went to commercial as the show was terminated from the air. Before the man's name was mentioned or the ridiculous woman completely ruined his life, the host wanted her out of his studio. He stood up, exacerbated, and shook his head at her. Mary just sat there, smiling. She had proved herself, and on national television. There was no telling what her company was capable of now.

The host leaned over to her and very quietly hissed, "I don't know what you're trying to prove here, Miss Moriarty, but if you don't want to be sued for every last dime you have, I suggest when we come back on the air you make sure to fix this situation."

She smiled and nodded. He didn't have any grounds for suing her, but she wasn't about to waste her time fighting this man.

The lights came on and the camera crew gave them the "on air" signal. The host apologized for the commercial break and gave a final introduction of his guest. This time, he didn't really let her talk. Finally, he thanked her for her time and said, "This has been a conversation with Moriarty Intelligence."

Veronica grinned at the television. She admired Mary's flair. Maybe she could enlist her help in finding where Sergei may have taken her sister.

31

THE NEXT MORNING, Veronica met Mary at her office, which was high in a skyscraper in the Meatpacking District. The office itself made her feel as if she were stepping into a computer. After the grit and trash on the street below, the elevator opened on the top floor to reveal a single receptionist sitting behind a silver desk. The woman smiled at her. She was darkly pretty, with a phone earpiece and microphone wrapped around her right ear like a piece of exotic jewelry. Behind her head was the company's name. Other than that, the foyer was empty.

"Ms. Miller, I presume?" asked the receptionist, smiling even wider. "You're here to see Ms. Moriarty." The woman looked down at her computer screen. Her eyes grew wide.

"That's enough, Valerie. Just forget what you saw. Ms. Stone and I are old friends," said Mary, striding quickly into the room.

"But—the president—the entire world is looking for—" Valerie stammered.

"And it is our secret," stated Mary, rolling her eyes. She

cocked her head to the side and stared at Valerie. "I don't need to say anything else about this, do I?"

"No, Ms. Moriarty," answered Valerie quickly. She changed the screen on her computer and shuffled some papers on her desk.

"Thank you. Now, Veronica, good to see you," said Mary, giving her old friend an awkward hug. "Come on, follow me to my office—we can have some privacy there."

Veronica followed Mary through the door and down a long silver hallway. Through glass windows on either side, she could see banks of people sitting at desks, staring into computer screens and typing. Mary said, "The heart of Marilyn Moriarty. I've got two hundred people here and another five hundred in India, searching and compiling. We're like a giant human search engine."

"Interesting—what about Valerie back there? How did she—"

"Your face was scanned in the elevator. It's something we do to impress new clients and keep out the riffraff. She's ex-Navy Intelligence. She knows how to take an order. And don't let her size and looks fool you. She could have killed you with her stapler if I asked her to," said Mary, smiling back over her shoulder. Veronica had the disconcerting impression that Mary was imagining what such an assault might look like.

"Wouldn't it be more effective to just station a couple of goons in the room as security?"

Mary smirked. "So, what kind of trouble have you gotten yourself into?" She sat down on the couch and motioned for Veronica to do the same. Instead, Veronica walked over to the window and looked down at the people walking on the streets. This was not the Veronica that Mary was expecting, and that put her off a little.

"Mary, I need your help," said Veronica. Mary sat up on her couch and gave a quizzical look at her old friend. Veronica never needed help from anyone, and she was shocked as well as honored that she came to her.

"Veronica," Mary said, and walked up to her friend. "You look terrible. Have you eaten? Are you hungry?"

"Well, I could use a cup of coffee," said Veronica, sitting down. Mary's office was as slick and clean as the rest of the building. There was one metal desk, a metal tray with several liquor bottles on it, three chairs, and a huge window with an incredible view of the water. "I would have pictured your office different from this."

"What do you mean?"

Veronica accepted the hot cup of coffee from Mary's hand. "I always thought you were more of an antique and old furniture type. You were in college."

Mary frowned slightly. "My room had a futon and one photograph of my family. You don't remember, do you?"

Veronica grimaced. "I guess not. It's been a hard couple of weeks. I do remember your Paddington Bear sheets."

Mary smiled. "Yes, those were my favorite sheets. I'm sure you're not here to reminisce." Then she said, "So how can I help you?"

"I saw you on television the other night," answered Veronica, looking into her almost already-empty coffee cup. She suddenly felt incredibly tired and stressed. She hadn't realized how on edge she was until it looked like Mary wouldn't help her. She'd been running on pure adrenaline for days.

"Oh, that," said Mary, evidently pleased. "I really nailed that bastard to the wall, didn't I? I didn't even get into the really juicy stuff."

"It was impressive."

"Another thing I got from you. 'Think laterally.' Anyone can surf the Internet and look up names in phonebooks—our trick is that we get into things other people don't think of. Like yearbooks. We have almost every high school yearbook scanned into our computers. That's how I got that guy."

"Clever."

"The trick is to get stuff before people get old enough to realize they shouldn't write their true, secret feelings in year-books or whatever. Now, with the Internet and blogs and mes-sage boards, it's gotten insanely easy. If some sixteen-year-old declares her love for her best girlfriend, we hold on to the information—the girl might be the first female president for all we know. And by the time she becomes an adult, all that stuff will be long-since buried."

Veronica nodded. "It must take an amazing computer system."

Mary smiled. "We have the best. A specialized StoneCorp. I bet you didn't even realize you were making it for me. I thought you might have, though. I half-expected you to put something special into it."

"I never thought I meant that much to you—for you to think about me," said Veronica.

"We were best friends, remember? I might have been a little cold sometimes, and you were definitely a rival and someone I very much wanted to beat, but you were still my best friend," said Mary.

"Thanks. That means more than you know right now."

Mary nodded. "I know. Now tell me what you need me to do."

"I need you to find my sister."

"That's funny."

"Why is that funny?"

"Because someone has just asked me to find you."

32

LATER THAT DAY Veronica was rushing through the airport looking for a private jet of some of Mary's more personal clients. They were on their way to Prague and giving Veronica a lift. She didn't know how Mary had done it, but in the middle of one of the largest international manhunts in history, Mary had gotten false documents and a plane ticket to Prague on a private jet belonging to some young rock band Veronica had never heard of. The band was friendly and oblivious to who she might be, mainly concerning themselves with the mass amounts of drugs and girls on the plane, and, since she was "cute," whether she would be willing to "party" with them. Veronica begged off and sat in the back, claiming she was scared of flying. When the pierced and tattooed bassist still wouldn't stop offering her champagne and hits of ecstasy, she went into a long and detailed description of the problems caused by her genital herpes. After that, no one got near her.

When the plane landed at Czech customs, Veronica just hung back with the pack of drunken groupies, letting herself dissolve in with them as the band's harried manager struggled to get the unruly mass of people in her care through customs. It was astonishingly easy. After Veronica was through, the manager walked up to her, handed her her bag, and said, "Take a different taxi from the others. Tell Marilyn Moriarty I'll remember this one." Veronica thanked him and disappeared into the airport crowd.

She hurried through the darkened Prague streets, keeping her shoulders hunched and her face covered with a baseball cap. She pulled out her map and quickly turned right at the next street. The bar was in the Old City, near the Charles Bridge. Veronica finally found it at the end of a winding back-alley of ancient cobblestones and medieval walls. At this late hour, the streets were deserted except for drunken students and the gypsy pickpockets stalking them. Everything looked closed. But the bar door she was looking for hung open. There was no signage or indication of what the place was—just a simple wine bottle, with a rose in it, in the window.

Veronica walked past the door and glanced inside. It was too dark to see much more than a few tables, some booths, a bubbling Wurlitzer, and the bottles behind the bar. But it looked empty—except for the barman. Veronica did another walk by. If it was a trap, she'd never discover it by simply walking back and forth in the street until morning. She took a deep breath and stepped inside.

The barman looked up from washing a pint glass. He was broad and beefy, hairless but for a walrus-like mustache twisting above his upper lip. He barked something in Czech.

Veronica took off her hat and said in Russian, "I'm here to meet someone."

The barman's eyes narrowed. He picked up a paring knife

from the bar and held it out threateningly as if he intended to skin her.

"The old wounds run deep. I don't think I'd be using Russian around here," said an unmistakably familiar voice behind her. She turned around. Hiro was sitting alone in one of the large booths, his back to the front door. He was pointing a small pistol at her.

"I knew he would understand me," said Veronica.

"I'm surprised you don't speak Czech."

"I'll put that on my list. Did you get me here just to shoot me?"

"Of course not," said Hiro, putting the pistol down on the bench beside him.

"It would have been a lot easier just to shoot me or blow me up in America. Not that you haven't tried that already."

Hiro shook his head. "Look, sit down. I brought you here to talk."

Veronica slid into the booth on the other side of the table from Hiro. "How come you didn't have some goons frisk me? Aren't you being a little cavalier?"

"You're the one who failed to bring a weapon."

"How do you know that?" asked Veronica.

"You walked through a clandestine metal detector when you passed through the front door. Unless you have a gun made out of paper or wool in your pocket, I'm fairly certain you're unarmed." Hiro gestured at the barman.

Veronica sighed. "I knew you wouldn't invite me all the way to Prague to just kill me. It's not your style."

"Neither is carrying a gun yours."

"So—what do you want?"

The barman set two beers on the table. When he had left the table, Hiro handed Veronica a slip of paper.

"What's this?" asked Veronica without touching it.

"It's a phone number, and the antidote to the cellular disruption the Monroes and your boyfriend are currently suffering from. I'm afraid some of the damage might be permanent, but this will stop the progression from continuing and slowly begin to reverse their condition."

Veronica looked warily at the paper. "How do I know it will work?"

"Would I call you all the way to Prague to play a schoolboy prank?"

"Why?"

Hiro sipped his beer. "It seems our friend Sergei has put some forces into motion which I had not anticipated. And he has effectively blinded the both of us."

"What do you mean? My lab in Boston was broken up, but—"

"Sergei had several moles on my island. The man acting as an assistant chef was the squadron commander. It took them less than two days to dismantle everything from the inside while I was away," said Hiro. He spoke as if he were merely reporting the weather.

"So the island is under Sergei's control?" asked Veronica cautiously. Maybe that's where she would find her sister.

Hiro looked aghast, as if Veronica had just said something incredibly foolish. "Of course not. I had the Japanese Air Force carpet bomb the entire island into oblivion. From what my people have told me, not even the birds survived. A pity really—we had two unique endangered species which I guess are extinct now."

"What about your own people?"

"Carpet bombing is a messy business," said Hiro obliquely.

Veronica stared at him. "You're as inhuman as Sergei."

Hiro grimaced. "I don't remember you having any qualms about making the weapon. You are just like we are."

"I'm nothing like you."

Hiro glanced at the jukebox and popped his forefinger. "Fine. Believe what you need to sleep at night. But I remember the look in your eyes when I first proposed our little project to you on the beach—and I knew you would have the affinity with the mad Russian scientist we needed. You were an integral part of our little doomsday scenario, and a more-than-willing participant. Now, I've done what I came here to do." Hiro stood up from the booth.

"Hey—we're not done yet. You didn't give me an answer. Why are you giving me the antidote?"

"Maybe I would just like a possible ally out there who hates Sergei as much as I do," he said, moving toward the bar. The barman was holding a large assault rifle. Hiro turned back, his voice almost wistful. "But, even so, you really should get going. I had to make a quick phone call to the local authorities. I couldn't have you hanging around or following me. It seems that the entire world is looking for you in connection to the president and the murders of several American soldiers. If I were you, I'd start running. This street is a dead end, you know? It would be very easy for them to box you in."

Veronica started from her seat in shock. She could already hear sirens in the distance. She took two steps to the door and then turned. "This isn't over between us," she said.

Hiro smiled. "Of course it isn't. I see a long and fruitful relationship ahead of us. Provided you don't get caught and put in jail forever. Or executed. They seem to love doing that in America. Now, good night and good luck." Hiro opened a door behind the bar and disappeared. The barman gestured at her with his rifle. "Get out, Russian whore!" he spat in English.

Veronica stuffed the strip of paper in her jeans and pulled her baseball cap over her hair. "I'm American, jackass," she answered in Russian. Then she sprinted out the door.

The bar was the last building on the street before it ran into a stone wall. Veronica glanced up at the top of the street. Already, she could hear voices and sirens at the end of it. The police cars' lights flashed on the roofs of the buildings all around her.

Next to the wall was a stack of crates just high enough to get over the wall. She sprang up them just as the sound of heavy boots came running down the lane toward her. The wall simply split the street off from a narrow alley that ran along the waterfront. She dropped down on the other side. Several hundred yards away, police boats were converging toward her. There was nowhere to go.

The cell phone she was carrying rang in the pocket of her jacket. She almost jumped out of her skin. It was one of the untraceable throwaways she has brought, and someone had programmed the ring tone to some Czech rapper. She cut the volume and cupped the screen with her hand so she could read the incoming number without giving away her location. It was Mary.

Veronica snapped the phone open. "Mary, unless you're sending me a helicopter, this isn't a great time," she whispered into the phone.

"She's there!" exclaimed Mary on the other end of the line.

"What? Who?"

"Your sister. She's in Prague! That's where they're keeping her!"

Veronica gasped as a searchlight from somewhere on the bridge swept over the wall above her head. She stuffed the phone back in her pocket and tried to think.

Suddenly, she heard splashing and screaming out in the dark river in front of her. A flashlight turned on, illuminating a small motorboat bobbing along in the middle of the water. There were more shouts and splashes. People were skinny-dipping—daring each other to jump into the icy water. Veronica recognized one of the voices. It was the rock band from America.

She opened the scrap of paper and memorized it as quickly as she could, keying the numbers to letters so she could spell out a word—a memory trick she had taught herself in junior high. She smashed the throwaway phone under her heel, stripped off her clothes, wrapped them in a loose brick, and tossed them into the water. Finally, she jumped in after them.

The water was so cold it burned. She quickly splashed out to the motorboat. Someone shined a flashlight in her face. "Oh, hello. Fancy meeting you here." It was the band's bassist. All his words slurred together. He said something else that was lost in the giggles and laughter of the other naked people around him.

"I saw you from the shore. I thought I'd say hello," said Veronica as seductively as she could under the circumstances. The police boats were getting closer, and she could hear someone yelling through a bullhorn in the lane she had just escaped from. "Do you have anything to drink?"

The bassist switched off the light and offered her a bottle of champagne. "Of course. Come aboard. You should have seen the show tonight. And these Czech girls are nuts!"

Veronica accepted his outstretched hand and clambered into

the boat. With the police closing in, she didn't really care if this pack of drunken boys ogled her nude body or not. One of the Czech girls came dripping out of the water like a seal and pointed at the boats. She said something in Czech.

"I thought all these Czech girls knew English," said another of the band members, who was desperately trying to keep the boat from running over several people who were still in the water.

Veronica said, "She says the cops are coming. It's illegal to swim in the river, and it's illegal to be nude. And she's fifteen and a virgin."

The bassist's eyes widened. "Crap—we've got about six pounds of skunk weed and some other stuff. Hey, Rhett! We'd better get out of here, man!"

The one behind the wheel yelled for everyone to get back on board. He gunned the engine, but the police were already on top of them. Suddenly, they were surrounded by search-lights and shouting.

"Whoa! Hey! Guys! We were just swimming!" exclaimed Rhett.

The lights slowly crept over all of them. Veronica heard voices. She kept her head down as if she were merely embarrassed to be naked. Men were arguing on the police boats.

"Seriously—we were just leaving. No problem. We're a band. We played a show tonight. No biggie," said Rhett desperately.

Finally, the lights switched off. A voice shouted at them from the police boats. "Is everybody on that boat with you?"

"What do you think? It's not like we just found some other naked people floating along in the river!" yelled Rhett.

"Where are your clothes?"

"In the river. Look, we'll pay for the clean up or whatever."
There was a long pause. "Okay. Get out of here. We'll be
paying a visit to your hotel tomorrow morning to talk about
this little incident. I suggest you be sober." The police boats
backed away and then turned to swarm along the edge of the
river.

The bassist looked at Veronica. "Are you some kind of crim-
inal or something?" he asked in a whisper as the boat pulled
away downriver. His voice sounded a little afraid.

"No. I'm more like a secret agent," answered Veronica,
accepting a towel and a beer from one of the other girls.

"Cool. And the cops are after you?"

"Yep. I uncovered some nasty Soviet stuff."

"Wow. This is so totally 007. I didn't know we really had
stuff like this," he said, his voice filled with drunken awe. "And
you're so totally hot."

Veronica toweled off her hair, then tried to wrap the towel
around her. It was obviously something stolen from whatever
hotel they were staying in. "Thank you," she said. "And thanks
for your help. You've helped save the world from nuclear
annihilation."

"Really? Awesome!" The bassist took a long sip from his
beer. "So, you don't really have herpes, do you?"

Veronica shook her head no. "Later. Right now I have to
think about my report to double-o ten."

"Oh right. Secret spy stuff first. I totally understand."

"Thanks," said Veronica, watching the flashing searchlights
get smaller behind them. When she saw Mary again, she'd
have to thank her. These guys were perfect—dim witted and
willing to believe anything. "When are you guys leaving
Prague?"

"Oh, we're playing another three nights, and then it's off to England and France—do you need another lift?"

"I would love one," said Veronica, kissing him lightly on the nose. The bassist smiled back at her, deliriously happy. "I just have something I have to do first," she said.

33

Veronica had taken a room at a local but, more importantly, quiet hotel in Prague. She'd borrowed some clothes from the band, picked up her gym bag from the train station locker she stowed it in, and checked into the hotel under a Russian name, speaking in Russian the entire time. Luckily, it was late, and the man working the front desk didn't seem to be aware of the manhunt going on right under his nose. He seemed more interested in letting her know by his words and gestures that he didn't like Russians. She'd caught another lucky break, but her luck couldn't hold forever. Eventually, she'd be caught in a situation she couldn't wriggle out from. Life as a scientist had taught her that. At some point, the puzzle became too difficult, and the answer evaporated, unintelligible, into thin air. She just hoped she could save Carrie and Alex before she was caught.

She took a quick shower and changed her clothes. Then she called Mary.

Mary answered the phone groggily. "Hello?"

"Mary, did you send the number and phone to Alex?"

"I did. But MI-5 is watching the house. I tried to sneak it in there with a milk delivery, but it got snatched. So—I don't know. If he's got a phone in there—"

"He doesn't. And why is MI-5 watching his house?"

"His connection to you. Apparently, they know all about you two. And when they went to ask if he'd seen you, they noticed he had the same 'wasting' as the Monroes."

Veronica gasped. "So—did they take Alex to the hospital? Are they trying to help him?"

"No. My contact in MI-5 says they're keeping him there as bait. They figure you might return to gloat over your handiwork or that he might be an accomplice to the assassination attempt on the Monroes."

"What assassination attempt?"

"Yours, honey."

"Why would I assassinate the president?" asked Veronica.

"I don't know—neither do they—you're the one who gave the president the phone. Supposedly, Fox News is going to break the story in about six hours that you are part of an Al Qaeda sleeper cell—deep, deep undercover."

"That's crazy!" Veronica gasped.

"The world is so scared of Al Qaeda, they'll believe anything. It looks like they're making you into some kind of 'Manchurian Candidate.' You were brainwashed in a religious cult in college, etc., etc.," said Mary. She almost sounded bored, as if this kind of thing happened every day.

"What cult? There's no proof—"

"They make it," said Mary. "In fact, they hired a world-famous information specialist to do it."

"You can't—"

"I have to. If I refused, they'd guess something's up. It's

something I do for them all the time—insert just enough truth to make it hard for the target to refute. I can drag my heels a little, but that's it. In about twelve hours, you're going to be a starry-eyed jihadist—a liberal idealist sucked into a worldwide power struggle she is too naive to understand by a boyfriend with a shadowy past. But don't worry; I'm leaving Athena House out of it."

"Great. That takes a lot off my mind," answered Veronica sarcastically. "Although I'm a little ticked about the naive part." She lay back on the incredibly opulent bed, staring out the window at the lights of the city below her. Her room-service order remained untouched on the tray. Everything was crashing down around her. She switched the new throwaway cell to her other ear. Luckily, she'd brought ten, all with different numbers, all untraceable. "How am I going to get to Carrie? It's not like I can just go in and ask them," she said. "Did you check up on Sergei and the woman I described?"

"Yeah, I did. I couldn't find too much solid information. But the dog story he told you is apparently true. There were reports of an official's family and friends disappearing under unusual circumstances. A peasant broadsheet blamed it on werewolves."

"Great. I guess he wasn't kidding with his threat."

"Do you know any Green Berets?" asked Mary.

"I was hoping you did, to be perfectly honest. I thought Marilyn Moriarty would have her own private army."

"Unfortunately, no. I have some contacts with some African militias, but I'm not sure how reliable they would be. They're more of a 'blow up everything and let God sort it out' bunch. Plus, most of them are fifteen-year-old drug addicts, and they'd sell you out in a heartbeat."

"Sounds like a fun bunch," said Veronica. She was desperately holding onto her bravado. If she really thought about what she was doing, and the odds against her, she wasn't sure if she could hold on to the courage to continue. She rolled over on her side and watched the news crawl across her laptop screen—again, an untraceable Internet connection, courtesy of Mary. Mary had planted a couple of news stories about Veronica being sighted in Canada, but so far, it didn't look like any of the news media had bit. It seemed most people believed she was still in Prague. As soon as she was rested, she would find another place to hide.

"It's all I've got, really. I'm in the information business, not search-and-rescue."

Veronica was silent for a long time. "Thanks for helping me, Mary."

"Don't get too excited, I'm also destroying your name and reputation."

"But you're helping me—and risking a lot—just accept the fact that I'm grateful."

"You're welcome—I'm just glad I'm the one getting to help you for a change." She paused for a second and then added, "Maybe I can throw them off a little more. I'll see what I can do."

Veronica glanced at her computer screen; a man in military fatigues was giving a news conference in front of an air base. According to the type at the bottom, his name was Colonel Harland R. DeWitt of the United States Army.

"Who's this DeWitt guy?" asked Veronica, reaching for the sound button on her computer. She heard a knock on her hotel room door. "Room service—can I get your tray?" called a woman's voice from the other side.

"He's the lead man on finding you. I can run more

information, but it would take a little time. He's not the normal guy they use for this kind of stuff, so I'd need to do a little checking."

There was another knock at the door. Veronica tapped the phone against her head in thought. "Colonel DeWitt has an army," she said.

"What are you thinking about?" asked Mary.

"What if you were to tell him where I was going? Where Carrie is?"

"What would that do?"

"Maybe he can break her out for me."

"They'll probably shoot you first."

"That's a chance I'll just have to take. Look, room service is about to break my door down for the tray. Give me two hours, then call in Colonel DeWitt with the tip. If he gets Carrie out—then at least she'll be safe. Use me as bait—say I'm in league with Sergei and we're holding my sister together—I'm going to lay low and see about hopping a plane to England."

"Okay. But I think this is not the best—"

"I've got no other options. Just do it for me, please." She waited for an answer. Finally Mary said okay. They hung up the phone and Veronica sighed her first sigh of relief in a long time. For a brief moment she thought her sister would be okay.

Veronica rolled off the bed and walked to the door, dragging the tray cart behind her. She was exhausted. If she didn't get some sleep soon, she'd probably collapse. "Look, here's your—"

Standing in the open doorway was the blonde-haired Russian. "Hello! Funny meeting you here!" Before Veronica could move, the Russian jammed a Taser into her neck, knocking her to the floor.

34

Carrie woke up to voices echoing through the aluminum air vent where she had been hiding. Her legs and neck were cramped, and her broken arm was swollen blue. She licked her lips and tasted dried blood. She heard the voices again. They echoed around her, both of them speaking in low tones, as if they were simply two people having a conversation on the street. One she recognized as the Russian woman's. The second was Veronica's.

Carrie checked her swollen arm. It wasn't strong enough to hold her weight anymore. She rolled onto her side and pulled herself along the vent. Its rivets and sheeting made it slow going, and every time the metal creaked, it sounded as loud as a gunshot to her. She kept waiting for the bottom of the vent to rip open with bullet holes. She knew they were looking for her, and she knew they'd want blood. As she pulled herself along, the voices grew louder.

"Where's my sister?" asked Veronica.

"I thought she was your half sister," said the Russian woman. She held an orange in her palm. She started to peel it with a large hunting knife. She did it slowly, as if she were skinning a small animal.

"She's my sister." For the hundredth time, Veronica tried to get her fingers into the knot tying her wrists. She was tied to a wooden chair, her ankles bound to the chair legs with duct tape. She'd awoken in this room, tied to this chair, the Russian woman studying her face with a strange expression, as if she were studying a painting. Her neck still burned from the Taser. Since she couldn't touch it, the pain was maddening, but she tried to keep her mind focused on it. Otherwise, she was afraid she might pass out again.

"Right. But you left her, didn't you? I wouldn't do that to my sister."

"I didn't have a choice."

"Right. Of course. You didn't have a choice," said the Russian woman. She tossed the orange peel aside. "The favorite excuse of the guilty."

"Where's Sergei?" asked Veronica.

The Russian woman cocked her head to the side, like a dog listening to a strange noise. "Why do you care?"

"He's in charge, isn't he? You're just his servant girl."

"I am not his servant girl. You haven't asked about your half sister."

"If she wasn't alive, you would have said something."

"True. But there are worse fates than death."

"I don't believe you."

"Fine—aren't you going to beg me to let her go?"

"No. I know you don't have the power to do that. Where's Sergei?"

The Russian woman touched her knife to Veronica's cheek, just below her right eye. Veronica tried not to flinch. "We have some business to attend to first—then I will take you to Sergei. And I can do what I want. Sergei and I are equal partners."

"Really? Then how come he isn't here? I bet you haven't told him I'm here, have you?" asked Veronica. The more she kept this woman talking, the more time she would have. She prayed that Mary had sent out the tip to Colonel DeWitt. Otherwise, she was dead.

The Russian woman removed the knife and leaned back in her chair. "I wanted to talk to you first, woman to woman," she said, eating another slice of her orange.

"Why?"

"To offer you a choice."

"What kind of choice?"

"To work for me."

Veronica's eyes widened. "You're insane."

The Russian woman nodded. "I know. People more qualified than you have told me that."

"What makes you think I would ever agree?"

"You have no place else to go. I'm not sure if you have been watching the news, but you are a wanted woman. The American president is hours away from death, you've been linked to terrorists, and StoneCorp has been burned to the ground."

"What? What do you mean?" exclaimed Veronica.

"A mob attacked the building. They killed the security guards, then firebombed the place. Apparently, it was a spontaneous display of patriotism by your fellow Americans. They had lovely pictures on the television. I don't know what you had in that lab of yours, but the flames were beautiful—so many different colors," said the Russian woman.

Veronica thought for a moment. Could this really be true? She knew this woman would say anything. "Who did it?"

"Well, they might have had a little help, you know. There are quite a lot of Russian immigrants in Boston. Good people— and they're just dying to prove their loyalty to their new country."

"Why?" Veronica imagined all she had ever built destroyed— erased from the earth just as if it had never been there. She didn't believe her. It just couldn't be true.

"We couldn't leave any evidence behind, now could we? Hiro has proved to be very unreliable, and, if we are really to have a new world, we can't leave any loose ends. Oh—and they got that girls' club of yours, too. Luckily, no one but the care-taker was there."

Veronica shuddered. The thought of the Athena House burning down was too much to handle. She had to assume this psychopath was lying, or she would never have the strength to continue. She would have to play the game to live.

The Russian woman finished her orange. "Look, for all intents, the Veronica Stone you once were is dead. Where else can you go? They'll kill you the minute they get the chance, or lock you away in some dirty prison for the rest of your life. You'll never be able to work again—but, if you work for me, you can keep doing what you were put on earth to do—change the world."

"Where's my sister?" spat Veronica.

"So, I'm to take that as a no?"

Veronica stared hard into the Russian's eyes. "Just tell me where my sister is and we'll talk after that, you hideous mon-ster," she said, slowly and coldly, refusing to answer.

The Russian woman nodded. "Yes, maybe I am a monster, but then, so are you. You should hear the things they're saying about you on the news. It's incredible. And that poor little

Monroe girl—not so pretty anymore. Well, if that's the way you want it, we have to take care of one thing before we go talk to Sergei." The Russian woman removed a small bottle from her pocket.

"What's that?" asked Veronica.

"Oh, this? Nothing. Just some sulfuric acid."

"What are you planning to do with that?"

The Russian woman smiled wickedly and stood up from her chair. She walked over to the door, spinning the bottle in her palm like a top. "Oh, I need to take care of something, and then I thought I would touch up your makeup before we go to see Sergei," she said. "I know you'd want to look your best. I'll give you a few minutes to think over my earlier offer." Then the Russian woman stepped out the door and slammed it shut behind her.

35

COLONEL DEWITT STOOD in the bridge of the *U.S.S.* *Davenport* running his forefinger over a map of the Czech Republic. The bridge buzzed with the activity of keeping a ship like the *Davenport* afloat, but all of it was shut out by his thoughts—he might as well have been alone, and the sailors around him kept out of his way, one of them already suffering the brunt of Colonel DeWitt's frustration and anger. He'd only been able to sleep a few hours over the past few days. Veronica Stone could be anywhere—and it was still a mystery how she got out of the United States without being flagged. He guessed she had used a private aircraft, but Miss Stone was proving to be a more formidable opponent than he had originally thought. At first, he had believed she was simply a pawn caught up in world events, but now, with the news reports of her early involvement with Islam, he was beginning to wonder if she was the one who had massacred his friend. Colonel DeWitt studied Veronica's photograph again. He could barely believe that someone as smart, successful, and beautiful as

Veronica could be a cold-blooded killer. He was old enough to know looks were often misleading, but still—he looked at the picture again—someone like Veronica Stone killing his friend was hard to stomach.

One of the ship's ensigns came into the bridge, carrying a cup of coffee. He handed it to the Colonel, who accepted it with a slight nod of his head. "Is there anything else you need, sir?"

"No—thank you, Ensign." He tapped the map hard with his finger, as if he could pin Veronica down with his nail. "Wait—I want to ask your opinion about something."

The ensign stood with his hands behind his back. He looked as if he were preparing himself for a very tough question from the Colonel. "Yes, sir."

"Does this whole Veronica Stone thing smell right to you?"

"I wouldn't know, sir. I'm not really trained—"

"Just your opinion. I'm not grading you."

"No, sir. But everyone says she's a terrorist, and, when President Monroe dies, she'll be an assassin."

Colonel DeWitt tapped the map again. "The first successful one since Oswald. Do you believe in that as well, Ensign?"

"Believe in what, sir?"

"That Oswald was the lone killer of Kennedy."

"Before my time, sir. I couldn't guess."

"Believing so requires a lot of faith in the opinions of other people, doesn't it?"

The ensign's face softened from its hard facade. "Well, you have to, don't you, sir?"

"When I was a young man, I remember standing down on the deck, waving in my buddies' planes when I wasn't flying myself. This was during Vietnam. Every time I walked out on that deck, I checked to make sure the jump net was there in case I had to jump out of the way of a crashing plane. I checked it every single time—even between landings."

"That seems reasonable, sir."

"Reasonable, yes, but I really believed that one day I would jump from the deck and it wouldn't be there, and that the only one capable of making sure the net was there was me, and my own two eyes looking at it. Maybe it was serving in Vietnam, becoming a man in that era—I don't know. Colonel Gray and I used to argue about that a lot—he had the faith to believe in things he couldn't see with his own two eyes—I didn't." Colonel DeWitt took another sip of his coffee before continuing. "That little argument was how most of our fights about religion started. His faith with a capital F, and my lack of any. That will be all, Ensign."

The ensign saluted. Just as he turned to leave, he crashed into another sailor rushing into the room with a sheet of paper in his hands. The sailor saluted Colonel DeWitt and exclaimed, "Sir, we've found Veronica Stone, sir! She's still in Prague!"

36

VERONICA CLOSED HER eyes and yanked on her ropes. She was tied tight. Now how in the hell was she going to get out of this? She thought she was running out of time.

"Hey!" came a whispered voice above her head. "Hey!"

Veronica leaned back to look up at the ceiling. "Carrie? Is that you?"

"Yeah—I'm in the vents—"

"How did you—?"

"Long story—"

"Carrie, I'm so sorry! I'm so sorry I left you!"

"You did what you had to do," said Carrie. "I'm going to get us both out of here."

Veronica heard banging over her head.

"I've got to get you out before she comes back," whispered Carrie.

There was a sound of scraping metal and more banging. "Just hang on—I'll untie you!"

"Carrie, don't—," whispered Veronica, just as the door started to open. "Hide!" She threw all her weight to the right, throwing herself and her chair to the floor with a loud clatter to cover up the sound of Carrie in the vent. She screamed as if in pain.

The Russian woman walked into the room with a curious expression on her face. "Trying to escape, Veronica? I thought I heard you talking."

"So you're hearing things now?" she yelled. She just hoped she'd made enough noise so the Russian woman hadn't heard Carrie. Veronica struggled on the floor and kicked her feet, banging the chair harder against the floor. Her arms burned from the pain of being stretched behind her, all her weight on her elbow. "I hope Sergei kills you! You bitch! You go to hell!"

The Russian woman looked around the room without approaching closer. "That's two strange comments in a row— why would Sergei kill me, and since when does a scientist like you believe in hell?" The woman looked up at the vent above their heads. "I'm beginning to think we have a rodent problem."

"You stupid Russian bitch! I know Sergei will kill you when I escape!" screamed Veronica, trying to draw the Russian's attention away from the vent. She held a finger to her lips and circled around Veronica.

"Where are you going? Don't you want to touch up my makeup?" shouted Veronica, trying to make as much noise as she possibly could. She jerked the chair from the floor, cracking it on the concrete.

The Russian woman smiled, her eyes locked on the grate that opened into the vent. "If I were you, I'd start crawling, little girl," she growled at the grate.

Veronica kicked at the chair to try and stand, but it was no use. She was helpless. "Get away, Carrie! Go!"

The air duct started to bang and bend as Carrie tried to

crawl away, clearly outlining her body as she fled. The Russian woman grinned and unholstered the pistol on her belt. She slid it from her belt as if it were made of silk. "I've been wondering where you had gotten to. Come to help? You're much more resourceful than I would have thought—and a good deal braver, I would say," she said. She stuck her tongue from the side of her mouth in an obvious parody of a child taking aim with a toy gun and pointed the pistol at the duct.

"No! Carrie!" screamed Veronica.

The Russian woman fired through the duct near the wall in front of Carrie, popping a clear dark circle through the aluminum. The duct convulsed as Carrie jerked away from the bullet. Then the Russian woman fired again, this time near the opening in the vent. Carrie screamed. The aluminum bent and clanged. It was clear the Russian woman was playing with Carrie.

"Oops—how silly of me. I really should try to get better at this," mocked the Russian woman. Then she slowly moved the pistol, aiming it at the middle between the two bullet holes. She let it hang there at the end of her arm and grinned down at Veronica. "I'm guessing I'll get her this time," she said. "What do you think? Want to make a bet?"

Suddenly, the entire building shook. Veronica heard shouting and several loud bangs. The building shook again as if some huge creature had just picked it up and shaken it hard. The Russian woman brought her pistol down and glanced around the room in surprise. At the same instant, the duct pulled loose from the ceiling in a rain of plaster and stone. With a squeal of metal, it ripped in half and Carrie shot out of the opening, slamming into the Russian woman and knocking her to the floor. The pistol slid across the room. Carrie scrambled to her feet and dove for the pistol just as the Russian woman grabbed her ankle. Carrie fell flat against the floor with a scream as she landed hard on her bad arm. The room shook again. Carrie lay on the floor, grasping for the pistol, while the Russian woman lay next to Veronica, dragging Carrie toward her. The Russian woman grinned maniacally. A thin trickle of blood ran down her cheek from a cut on her forehead. Between Veronica and the Russian woman lay the bottle of acid.

Veronica yanked hard against the chair legs, and with the last bit of her strength, she wrenched the chair from the floor and fell hard on the bottle. It shattered—spraying glass and acid against her shoulder and straight into the Russian's face.

The Russian screamed and lunged for Veronica, giving Carrie the chance to kick free. The Russian grabbed Veronica by the throat, pressing her thumbs hard into her neck. The acid had already made angry pink splashes running down one side of the Russian's face. She grinned even broader. Pale blue smoke rose from her skin. Veronica could smell something like rotting apples and bacon.

The Russian jerked Veronica toward the puddle of acid on the floor. The room shook again. The Russian woman's mouth was right against Veronica's ear. "I will make you die slowly," she growled. "But first we need to even things between us."

Suddenly, there was another bang, sharper and more compact than the others. Something warm splattered across Veronica's face.

Veronica blinked her eyes, trying to see through what she knew was blood. Carrie was standing above Veronica and the Russian woman. The Russian woman's pistol hung limply in her hands. The smell of gunpowder filled the room.

Veronica shook her head to clear it. She looked up at Carrie standing there holding the pistol still at the dead woman's head. She had a look of satisfaction on her face. "Carrie—untie me!" she yelled.

Carrie looked at the gun, and then at her sister. She was breathing heavily. Her face was a mix of incredulity and power, as if she couldn't believe what she had just done, but was relishing the power and realization that she was capable of doing it. She suddenly looked very old. Veronica spit the Russian's thick blood from her mouth. Carrie's girlhood innocence was going up in smoke, and Veronica had been the one to light the fire.

On the other side of the door, they could hear the pops of gunfire. Carrie shook her head in an unconscious imitation of her sister and shoved the pistol into the waist of her pants. She yanked on the ropes until Veronica's hands were loose. Then they both tore the duct tape from Veronica's ankles. Veronica wiped blood from her eyes. The Russian lay on the floor, her face staring placidly up at the ceiling. There was a red hole the size of a quarter between her eyes. Except for that mark, she could have been sleeping.

Veronica stood up. "Give me the pistol!" she yelled, sticking out her palm.

Carrie put her hand protectively on the grip. "I'm okay with this," she said, smiling at it like a pet.

Veronica stared at her. Carrie looked as if she had lived through a war. All of the goofy girlishness that used to dance around behind her eyes was gone. Veronica had only gotten to see it for a short time. She said, "Carrie, I'm sorry—"

"Don't apologize. Let's just get out of here," snapped Carrie, self-consciously wiping her hair from her eyes as if Veronica were embarrassing her.

"Not without the gun." Veronica held out her hand.

"I'm not afraid to use this."

"I know you're not. I just don't want you to have to anymore. This is all my doing—let me be the one that has to suffer."

Carrie looked at the floor, then handed the gun to Veronica. It felt as heavy as stone. "None of this is your fault," said Carrie.

"All of this is my fault," said Veronica, dropping the gun in her pocket. "But that doesn't mean I'm not going to try to make things right."

"How? Isn't it a little too late?"

"No," said Veronica forcefully.

Veronica led the way to the door and put her hand against Carrie's chest to stop her. The hallway was empty. In the distance, they could hear shots and yelling.

"What's going on?" asked Carrie.

"I think Mary called in the cavalry," replied Veronica, glancing up and down the hallway.

"Who's Mary?"

"An old friend from college—we need to get out of here without anyone seeing us. Do you know any way out?" asked Veronica. There was another building-shaking boom. Plaster dust rained from the ceiling.

"I just hid in the vents. I didn't find anything."

"Okay. We just need to be logical about this," said Veronica. "The gunshots sound this way, so we go toward the gunshots— let's go!"

"Shouldn't we be running away from them?" gasped Carrie, pulling on Veronica's arm with her good hand.

"A way out has to be that way. That's how the cavalry is coming in—that's the way we have to go to get out," answered Veronica. She took hold of Carrie's hand and squeezed it. Then the two of them ran down the hall toward the sound of the battle.

37

THE INTENSIVE CARE unit at Walter Reed Hospital was in a continual state of lockdown. The White House had effectively moved the business of running the government to the hospital, and aides, officials, and soldiers hurried around Walter Reed's dark hallways, forcing the doctors to move patients and offices to other floors. Everyone worked in a whisper that covered the building like a cloud. The president's long, unexplained illness was unprecedented in American history, and no one knew how to manage the crisis. In their indecision, they chose to defer to the president. He lay in bed surrounded by machines and tubes, his steely blue eyes glaring furiously from the wreckage of his body, like Ahab steering his ship farther into the sea. The president had insisted that as long as he was still breathing and thinking clearly, he was still the elected leader of the free world. His daughter lay in a bed in a large, sunny room down the hall that the First Lady refused to leave. The president demanded hourly reports. He forbade the doctors from telling him about his own condition.

"How are we doing today, Henry?" asked President Monroe. His closest ally and friend, Senator Henry Gibbons, stood at the side of the bed, frowning down at him.

"Not so good. The Crimson Tide got clobbered yesterday," he joked in his soft Tennessee accent.

"Too bad. I bet Air Force One on that one. Tell Larry that Notre Dame owns it now," said the president. He tried to smile. His skin was yellow and stretched taut against his skull. Dried blood was clotted in the corners of his lips. His eyes were pink.

"Will do," answered the senator. He pulled a chair up behind his friend and sat.

"How's my little girl?" asked the president.

"Doing fine."

"You're a damn terrible liar."

"True. But I keep managing to get elected. They've found Veronica Stone."

The president tried to sit up against his pillow, but the effort was beyond his strength. He flopped back against the bed. "Where is she?" he asked.

"Prague. We don't know why yet. Colonel DeWitt got a tip from one of our outside intelligence contractors. Apparently, he and his men have walked into quite a fire fight."

"So, who's behind all this? Al Qaeda? North Korea?" The president spasmed into a violent coughing fit. He spit green bile into a small towel by his bedside. "Domestic loonies?"

"We still don't know. It looks like the Russians."

The president's expression turned incredulous. "The Russians? Why? I thought we got all our competitive crap out during the Cold War."

"The spooks are saying it's an independent operator. We've

got a couple wet operatives inside the government, but they know nothing about this guy. A few rumors of some youthful strong-arm stuff. He's a businessman who has managed to get hold of a big part of the privatization of the Russian Telecom Agency—from the outside he looks no different than any other of those petty thugs that grabbed up everything after the Soviets left town. Up until this moment, he has been completely overlooked by our intelligence. We're not even sure of his name yet."

"That seems about right," said the president sarcastically. "If I wasn't the president, I'd think America and the world were all part of some larger conspiracy myself. How come we know nothing about this guy?"

"The spooks are screaming budget cuts as usual."

"Was he behind Colonel Gray's murder?"

"They think so. They're not sure."

"I'd have guessed that. What's Veronica Stone's connection? And why is she killing me?"

"Trying to kill you, Jack," said the Senator reassuringly. "And we're not so sure it was her."

The president spit into his handkerchief again. This time, his phlegm was black. "Wasn't StoneCorp a big donor to the campaign?"

"StoneCorp was a big donor to both campaigns."

"I guess you just never know what tree the kooks are going to fall from next, do you?" asked the president, sighing with resignation. "I want you to promise me something, Henry, in case I die."

"Of course. Anything."

"I want you to get these bastards. I want this Russian and Veronica Stone and whoever else hung from meat hooks. Not for what they've done to me—for what they've done to Jessica. You understand?"

The senator nodded. "Colonel DeWitt has been instructed to take out these terrorists with extreme prejudice. Gray was his best friend from the Academy. This is a personal mission for him."

"Good. Good," murmured the president. He spit into his handkerchief and closed his eyes.

The senator stood from his chair. "I'll tell the nurse you're not to be disturbed," he said, laying his meaty hand on the side of his friend's pillow. He hoped his face didn't betray how horrified he was at the president's appearance. He wished that his friend could hold on to whatever hope he had for as long as he could. It might be the only thing that could save him—although he knew it was far too late for that.

The president's eyes snapped open. "I have a Cabinet meeting in five minutes. I'm not giving up."

"I know you're not."

"I'm still in charge."

"I know." The senator started for the door.

"And Henry—"

The senator stopped and turned. "Yes?"

"I could give a rat's ass about plausible deniability and insulating myself from whatever dirty measures Colonel DeWitt may feel compelled to take. I want everyone to know that *I* want their heads on a platter. I want the word to go out that I'm not giving up the ghost until they have," he croaked, nodded once, then closed his eyes. "I might be a simple sinner going to hell, but I want them there first to hold the door for me."

38

DUST FELL FROM the ceiling. There was another loud boom and the hallway's floor shook like a carnival fun house. Veronica and Carrie managed two more steps before there was another searing roar that sent them diving for cover. At the end of the hall, a closed door disintegrated from its hinges. Hot metal and wood skimmed their backs and stuck into the wall like smoldering toothpicks. Through the open doorway, they could hear guns going off and men shouting. They'd found them. Veronica pushed Carrie back down before she could stand up.

"Listen to me: We can't be caught by either side. If we are, Alex and the Monroes don't have a chance," said Veronica.

"I know," answered Carrie. She was covered with soot. A cut over her forehead made a muddy rivulet down her cheek.

"So you need to do what I say, okay?" asked Veronica, drawing the pistol from her pants. "No matter how wrong it may seem."

"Okay."

"Ready?" asked Veronica.

"Ready."

Veronica pulled Carrie to her feet and the two of them ran through the still-smoldering doorway. They found themselves in a large garage, standing on a platform about forty feet above the main floor. A hanging steel walkway joined the platform to a grid-like set of walkways. Below them were dozens of shipping containers, along with forklifts, trucks, and several black luxury sedans. Some were on fire. On the other side of the garage, she could see Sergei and a group of his men behind a steel wall on top of the walkway, dropping hand grenades and firing into a bottleneck created by two lines of steel cargo containers that stretched from the middle of the room to what appeared to be the only exit. One of the container doors was open. The container looked to be filled with steel girders, a fabricated portcullis like the ones used to protect medieval castles. The soldiers trying to push their way in were ingeniously trapped by Sergei and his men. Sergei and his men were grinning, dropping bullets and explosives onto their enemies as easily as if they were pouring boiling oil onto them. Outside, there was another loud boom and the side of the garage shook. The soldiers were trying to break another way in. The ones trapped between the walls of the containers fired as fast as they could, using the bodies of their fallen comrades as shields. Bullets clattered against the metal wall. Rocket-propelled grenades arced wildly past Sergei and his band of killers. No soldier coming through the doorway was given more than a second before they were taken down. Veronica guessed one of their frantic shots had destroyed the door Carrie and her had just come through.

"This is crazy—why do they keep coming?" yelled Carrie over the gunfire.

"They're trying to save the president."

"We've got to help them."

Veronica shook her head. "Absolutely not. We're going to lay low until we get a chance to sneak out of here. Look, we'll hide behind those crates in the corner."

"We can't just let them all die. They're coming to help us."

"No they're not—and what are me and you and this pistol going to do about it?"

"I don't know—but we can't just let them all die!" Carrie exclaimed, running down the stairs to the floor below. A stray bullet broke a hanging light bulb, missing her skull by inches.

Her sister would get them both killed—but Veronica had already left her once. She wasn't prepared to do it again. "Wait!" yelled Veronica, leaping down the staircase. She grabbed Carrie by her good arm and pulled her behind some boxes. "We can't just run at them. We'll do something. Just let me think." Veronica looked all around them. A black sedan only a few yards away exploded in a torrent of orange flame and smoke. Her nostrils filled with the smell of burning tires and gasoline. On one side of the boxes they were hiding behind was a small pickup truck. On the other was a stack of propane canisters. Another stray shot could incinerate the both of them. It gave Veronica an idea.

"Stay here!" she ordered, sprinting from the cover of the boxes to the pickup. More shots rattled the roof beams over-head. The room shook. She glanced in the pickup's cab. The keys were in the ignition. She tried the door. It was locked.

She ran back to Carrie. "Grab those propane canisters and toss them into the bed of the pickup!"

"What are you planning to do?" asked Carrie.

"Something incredibly stupid!" yelled Veronica, slinging two of the canisters into the bed of the truck. They were heavy, but she was full of adrenaline and fear. The flesh from her fingertips ripped against the canisters' hard metal handles. "Help me!"

As Carrie heaved another propane canister into the truck, Veronica used one to smash the window. She opened the door and jammed the canister behind the gas pedal. A bullet hit the windshield. It shattered, raining down on top of her.

"Veronica!" screamed Carrie, pulling her sister out of the cab to make sure she was okay. Veronica shook her off and tore the sleeve from her silk blouse. She yanked off her belt and opened the truck's gas tank, jamming the buckle in to keep the tank open. Then she stuffed the sleeve into the tank so it was hanging out like a fuse. The room shook again. A chunk fell from the ceiling and crushed the burning sedan flat, snuffing the fire out into a plume of dark smoke.

"Get back behind the boxes!" yelled Veronica, taking advantage of the screen of smoke. She took the pistol from her waist. She snapped out the clip and yanked out a bullet. Several more bullets scattered across the floor. "Keep back!" she yelled to her sister. She ripped off her other sleeve, lay it across the bullet, and smashed it hard with the butt of the pistol. The bullet split and sparked. The delicate silk smoked, then burst into flame.

Veronica lit the sleeve in the gas tank, then turned the truck's ignition. The truck shot forward like a rocket, straight at the walkway where Sergei and his men were standing.

Veronica dove behind the boxes. She looked up. Sergei saw the truck roaring toward him. He aimed his AK-47 at the truck cab, peppering it full of holes. In the smoke and confusion, he apparently couldn't see that there was no one behind the wheel. Then it was too late.

The truck smashed into a metal column under Sergei. Then the gas tank exploded.

Fire roared straight into the air, followed by several other explosions as the propane canisters heated and burst apart. Veronica heard screams as the walkway ripped from the ceiling and fell into the inferno. Sergei and his men were gone. Wreckage leaned in twisting pretzel-shapes against the former bottleneck. The soldiers were already pushing against it, trying to get farther into the building. The garage filled with thick burning ash. Veronica could hear American voices shouting.

Veronica put the clip back in the pistol. "I need you to do something for me," she said to Carrie. "But I'm only leaving you because you're safer without me."

"What? Are you nuts? What are you thinking? We're almost out of here!"

"I can't get caught. They're not looking for you. I want you to create a diversion so I can get out that door! I wouldn't ask you to do this if I could think of any other way," said Veronica, pushing the pistol into her sister's hands.

Carrie stared at her, her eyes filled with distrust and disbelief. "You're leaving me again?" she asked. Then she added, "I understand, you have to, I understand."

"I do have to," said Veronica. She stepped forward and kissed her on the forehead. "You saved my life. I owe you for that. You'll be safer without me. Please, just listen."

"Okay. After all, you're my sister."

"I wish I had been—now, listen to me. When the soldiers break through, take a shot at them from the doorway. One shot only. Then toss the pistol and run. They'll think some of Sergei and his men are alive. They'll follow you. When they catch up, just let them get you out of here and to a hospital."

"What about you?" asked Carrie.

"Tell them I was in the truck. It will buy me more time."

"You can't do this alone—I can help you."

Veronica glanced over at the wreckage, which was quickly being pushed aside by the soldiers. "I have to do this myself. Now go!"

Carrie started to say something, but Veronica stopped her, laying her hand gently across her mouth. Men shouted. Someone fired several shots into the fire where Sergei and his men lay. Veronica smiled. Then she sprinted toward the soldiers, disappearing into a cloud of greasy smoke.

The last thing she saw was her sister standing there holding the pistol out in front of her like a woman on the frontline ready to shoot. She was so proud.

39

Colonel DeWitt stood over the body of a blonde woman. She'd been shot once in the head. A chair lay next to her, bits of duct tape still sticking to it. The aluminum air duct was ripped from the ceiling. A haze of plaster and dust floated around his head in a cloud. The room smelled like fire and blood.

"Any idea who she is?" asked Colonel DeWitt, leaning over the body. Her pockets were empty. Her clothes gave no clue to her identity.

"We don't know, sir. This building belongs to a telecommunications corporation operating out of Russia. We haven't been able to figure out much more than that," said the lieutenant standing next to him.

The lieutenant was just out of the Academy, but smart and ambitious. He reminded Colonel DeWitt of himself when he was younger. Colonel DeWitt had a sudden picture of his friend Colonel Gray pop into his head, a time when the both of them were in school and had driven all the way to California just to see the ocean. He wondered if the woman laying at his feet had killed his friend. If she had, she was lucky someone else had gotten to her first. "Any sign of Veronica Stone?" he asked.

"None."

"Any more resistance?"

"There was another shot fired as soon as the men broke through into the main garage. They pursued, but they haven't turned up anyone alive yet."

The door burst open. Four soldiers walked in, surrounding a disheveled young girl. Her arm was black and blue and she was covered with soot. Her clothes were torn. She looked young, as if she were only a girl who had stumbled into some adult's nightmare. She was young enough to be Colonel DeWitt's daughter. Even so, there was something in her eyes. She'd seen more than she should have at her age. That much was obvious. As she entered the room, she stared at the body as if she were afraid it was going to leap back to life and try to strangle her. It was clear the girl knew who she was.

One of the soldiers saluted. "Sir, we found her hiding in a closet. She had a pistol in her possession. She says she was held hostage."

Colonel DeWitt nodded in greeting. "Hello, Carrie."

The girl looked surprised. "How do you know who I am?"

"Good guess. Are you okay?"

"I think my arm's broken."

"Find the medical officer," ordered Colonel DeWitt. Two of the soldiers disappeared back down the hallway. DeWitt turned back to Carrie. "Where is your sister?"

Carrie looked down at the floor and swallowed. "She was in the truck when it crashed into the men firing down at the soldiers. She didn't make it out."

Colonel DeWitt stared hard at her. Finally, he said, "You've been through a lot."

Carrie glanced back up at him. She seemed even more surprised than she had before. Her mouth hung open as if she wasn't quite sure what to say, as if this discussion wasn't going quite the way she expected. "I'm okay."

"I know. But you've been through a lot," Colonel DeWitt repeated, still weighing her reaction. He'd seen trauma victims in Carrie's state before. He had only a few minutes until the girl's adrenaline ran out and she realized she was finally safe. Then she would fall to pieces. "I'm sorry we couldn't save your sister."

"It's okay."

Colonel DeWitt gestured at the body on the floor. "This woman hurt you."

Carrie nodded. Her eyes started to water. She wiped her nose with the back of her hand, leaving a black smudge of grease and plaster on her cheek.

"Were you the one in the chair?" he asked.

Carrie looked around uncertainly.

"Could you leave us alone for just a moment?" ordered Colonel DeWitt. The lieutenant nodded and he and the other two soldiers stepped from the room. They closed the door behind them. Carrie stared as the door banged shut. Watching her body movements, Colonel DeWitt stepped away to make her feel more comfortable. "You make a terrible liar."

"What?" asked Carrie. "What do you mean? I had nothing to do with any of this!"

"I know you didn't. But I also know we're not going to find your sister's body in that burning wreckage in the garage."

"But—"

"Don't worry—you don't have to cover for her. I know she's not here. I also have a pretty good idea where she might try to go."

"She didn't mean for any of this to happen. It's not her fault—it just started happening—she just got in over her head and they tricked her—she—she had nothing to do with the soldiers dying—this woman was the one who shot Colonel Gray—!" Carrie pointed at the body on the floor, then closed her eyes in horror.

The girl was starting to get hysterical. Colonel DeWitt stepped forward and gently put his hands on her shoulders. "I believe you. I'm giving her a ten-hour head start. What she does with it is her business."

Carrie stammered, "You believe me? You're going to let her go?"

"No. But I'm going to give her a chance to make things right with herself. After that, well, we'll see."

"But, she—"

Colonel DeWitt looked sharply at Carrie. "She's a big girl, and she knew what she was doing. You can't protect her any-more. Without her, none of this would have happened. And it's my job to make sure she faces some justice for what she's done. Lieutenant Rodriguez, where's that medical officer?" he yelled at the closed door.

"I thought you were—"

Colonel DeWitt stepped back. "I'm sorry—but there will be no place for her to hide."

40

CARRIE HAD DONE just what Veronica asked, and in the smoke and confusion, Veronica had managed to slip out. The building turned out to be in the center of the old section of the city. Firefighters, police, and onlookers surrounded the American soldiers, all of them trying to get information out of each other. A notebook lay on the ground near the door. She scooped it up. Just as Veronica reached the outside, a Czech policeman stopped her, grabbing her arm. "Who are you? What are you doing here?"

Veronica flipped open the torn book, and pushed her hair from her face. She gave the policeman her most enchanting smile. Then she held her hand over the notebook as if she were about to write something, shielding her hand with its pages. She prayed he wouldn't notice she wasn't actually holding a pen. In Russian she said, "Can you tell me what has happened here, officer?"

The officer blinked. "Wait—who are you?"

Veronica tried to look as if she were hiding something, poorly. "I'm just a reporter wanting to get some information— is it true the Americans have taken over the city?"

"How did you get into the building?"

"The press knows no boundaries! You can't stop the truth!"

The policeman rolled his eyes, as if he couldn't believe the ridiculous woman in front of him. "Get out of here, you damn Soviet reporter. Go back to your own country," said the policeman, shoving her toward the crowd of people. "Go clean yourself up and stop acting as if you're anything more than a vulture." He ran his finger harshly through the ash on her cheek, seemingly implying that she'd put it on herself to sneak past him.

"You can't silence the press!" yelled Veronica, acting as if she were struggling to get past him and into the building.

"Get going," he said, roughly shoving her past the police and soldiers. An American soldier gave her no more than a passing glance.

The policeman shrugged. "Enjoy yourself—now, if you don't move along, I'll arrest you right here."

Veronica acted as if she were about to say something, then skulked past the crowd. She turned and made an obscene gesture at the policeman. He studiously ignored her, clearly relishing throwing the know-it-all reporter out of the area. No one questioned why she was so disheveled. If one acted fast and decisively, one could get away with almost anything.

Veronica made her way through the city streets, leaving the beautiful Old City and heading out to the Soviet-block outskirts. She wanted to get as much distance between herself and the warehouse as she could. She wasn't sure how long it would take for someone to figure out she had slipped away. Luckily, she guessed the policeman who let her go would be more interested in saving his own skin than in catching an American terrorist. She doubted he'd tell anyone he had seen her.

Once again, she had left Carrie behind. She went into a public restroom, washed her face, and blotted some of the dust off of her clothes. She wasn't sure how she would get to Alex or the Monroes. Part of her wanted to simply disappear—let someone else save the day. But no one else knew what she knew, and no one else had access to the antidote and the system that had the strength and clarity to deliver it.

She found a laundromat. After watching the women working there, taking in and out the clothes of mostly American tourists who could afford to have someone else wash their clothes for them, she found a dryer that looked unwatched. She opened it as if the clothes were hers. One of the women glanced suspiciously. She smiled back and said something cheery in English. The woman shrugged her shoulders, figuring it was just another American doing American things.

The clothes were men's—they looked as if they belonged to a student. Veronica grabbed a pair of jeans, a T-shirt, and a ragged baseball cap. Then she slipped into the bathroom and changed. With the oversized clothes and bleached-out T-shirt, she looked inconspicuous, like a young college student on her year abroad.

She walked down the street, swiping some oranges from a fruit market, and a cup of coffee and a croissant from someone's table at a street café. In a small park, she found some young men playing Frisbee. Luckily, they spoke English, allowing her to keep her cover going. She borrowed one of their cell phones and called Mary.

"God—where are you? What are you calling me on?" asked Mary. "I've been watching some of the intelligence feeds. It seems like there was quite a firefight. CNN is telling people it was some sort of Al Qaeda cell."

"I'm borrowing someone's phone," answered Veronica, walking a little away from the Frisbee players. They watched her and nudged the owner of the phone, as if he were definitely going home with the beautiful girl who had asked him for help. She smiled back at them. "They won't be looking for someone calling in on this number, but I don't have much time. I need one of my phones. Put it in the bear's house." She heard something clicking on the line, and then a strange silence. She guessed someone was trying to trace the call. The government was getting much faster. She couldn't count on them making stupid bureaucratic mistakes.

"Will do. You'll also want the yellow rain hat?"

"Yes, please."

"Oh, I have to go—it's really good hearing from you, Anne. Have fun in Spain," bluffed Mary, trying to confuse whoever was listening. Then she hung up the phone.

Veronica thanked the Frisbee players, and allowed one of them to program in a fake phone number for her on the cell phone. Then she kissed him quickly on the cheek and sauntered out of the park. A police cruiser slowed down on the other side. She didn't think they could have traced her that quickly, but she wasn't taking any chances.

Under the circumstances with Alex, she knew Mary would guess what she meant by "bear's house"—Paddington Station, London. The question about the "yellow rain hat" had been a test to make sure she understood her. Mary had slept on her childhood Paddington Bear sheets, and Veronica had teased her mercilessly for it. Mary knew it was the only thing she remembered about her college room. Veronica wished she had known when she was a girl how smart Mary was, and how much she would come to depend on her. Hopefully, if she made it out of this alive, she would have more than enough time to make things right. Now she would have many people to help build her empire. They could all share in the growth together. They would be unstoppable. If, she reminded herself, she made it out alive.

But for now, she had to get to England.

41

VERONICA HITCHHIKED OUT of Prague, and then took a quick series of local trains to Belgium. She found a train car with several young American women traveling together, and made friends quickly by helping them with some translation problems and with some suggestions on what to do in each city they were planning to visit. Whenever they crossed a border, Veronica simply handed the border guard a messy stack of everyone's passports. While the girls continued to play Hearts or write in their journals, she would secretly swipe back one of the passports the guard had already seen. Luckily, three of the girls had dark hair like her, and with a few bats of her eyes and a well-chosen pleasantry in the guard's native tongue, they were sent on their way with a nod and a wink and a promise to look up the guard in whatever small town they had just passed through.

When she reached Belgium, she chopped off a good deal of her hair in the train station bathroom and traded hats with a young Rastafarian, switching her cap to a knit beret made up of bands of gold, red, black, and green. Then she slashed two holes in the knees of her jeans and shoplifted a Grateful Dead patch from a head shop three streets away from the station. She also shoplifted a small sewing kit, and sewed the patch onto the seat of her jeans. Then, while passing a small brownstone, she swiped some wool socks drying from a line and a pair of paisley-patterned Birkenstock sandals. Finally, she grabbed an old denim jacket off a sleeping man at a bus station. With her new ensemble, she looked like every peacenik American college student who had ever gone to Europe to check out the legal marijuana in Amsterdam. She guessed customs agents looking for a world-famous terrorist would pass her right over. She'd blend right in.

She hitchhiked to the Belgian ferry station. She loitered around until she figured out who the guys working on the ship were, and then went down to where they were having their sack lunches on a small patch of grass. She watched the water with the group of them, making jokes, and purposely messing up her French in such a way as to appear charmingly sexual yet naive. They offered her some beer and a sandwich and tried to find out if she was holding any drugs. Instead, she told them a sob story about losing her passport and her money to some bad boyfriend back in Brussels. They all nodded and shook their heads, appalled at the treatment such a beautiful girl had had in their country. They all assured her the man who had done this to her was an aberration to Belgian manhood. She patted their shoulders and thanked each of them vociferously. Then she told them she had to get back to England, where she had an apartment and some money, but there was no way she was ever going to be able to get there now. Finally, for the small price of a peck on one of their bearded cheeks, they let her help them with the ferry ropes and stow aboard the next ferry over to England.

The Belgians had radioed ahead. Their British counterparts were there at the dock to meet her and let her out of the locker the Belgians had hid her inside of. They walked her down the side of the boat past customs without any of the border patrol even raising a head. After some good-natured ribbing about pretty women and their preference for men who were bad for them, and the phone number and address to her apartment, they let her go on her way up the road over the Cliffs of Dover. Veronica waved behind her. They all waved back, their leathery skin hard and brassy under the gray English sky. They'd clearly reveled in the power they had in their small jobs—basically having a say on who gets in or out of their country. But, if they'd known who it was they'd been helping, they might have had many second thoughts. Veronica Stone, the terrorist, was all over the news.

She snuck onto a local train into London and ducked her way past the policemen and cameras on her way out of Victoria Station. She decided to walk the few miles to Bayswater and Paddington Station. It had been incredibly easy to get into London—almost too easy. She couldn't let herself get too paranoid. Of course, in her case, everyone was really out to get her. She giggled aloud, and abruptly cut across Hyde Park to avoid two chatting policemen who had glanced over at the sound of her abrupt laughter.

The park was beautiful and green. She stayed away from the Kensington Palace side, wary of the video cameras that were hidden in the trees. As she walked, she watched the passersby—children Rollerblading and running in the grass, couples together, men walking their dogs. No one even looked up at her. In a big city like London, it was easiest to be invisible by staying out in the open. People were always expecting criminals and terrorists to skulk around in the darkness, dressed in robes and black masks, not to be traipsing happily through the sunlight dressed like a beautiful young hippie.

The sun was warm and the grass smelled sweet and cool. She knew her euphoria was mainly the product of lack of sleep and the continuous stress she'd been under, but she held onto it, knowing it was her best shield against being recognized. She was afraid that if she let it go, she might simply collapse to the ground in a puddle of nerves and fatigue. She waved at a baby in a carriage and cooed at a passing dog. She needed all the energy and strength she could muster. She still had quite a way to go.

She crossed through Speaker's Corner, and then scurried across the street surrounded by a busy pack of Japanese tourists. She stopped at a newsstand and scanned the front pages, carefully covering her face with a pop music magazine. All of the headlines screamed lurid details of the American president's illness. There were several pictures of him in good health, along with his beautiful young daughter, smiling and laughing at political rallies and at their family farm. There were no pictures of them sick, but there were plenty of descriptions from "Washington insiders" and various news personalities. Members of Congress were calling for a military strike, while the implicated countries they were threatening issued vehement denials regarding their involvement. The Left blamed American foreign policy, while the Right saw the attack on the president as a vindication of everything they'd been warning about for years.

From Islamic Jihadist terrorist groups to American White Power, everyone claimed responsibility. Famous movie stars offered condolences, while religious leaders claimed this was proof of God's anger at the immorality of the modern world. Some television pundits even tried to blame the American Democratic Party, while different groups tried to tie President Monroe's sickness to racism, AIDS, environmental degradation, and even lax immigration policies. Everyone was scared, and everyone was pointing fingers and throwing blame, but no one really knew what was going on. There was no news of Carrie, Alex, or even Hiro. No one had yet reported the firefight in Prague.

Veronica started a little when she noticed the news vendor's eyes on her. He smiled, flirting shamelessly with her. She grinned and took a chocolate bar from the stand, holding it up and shrugging her shoulders. The old man smiled back and waved her on, giving her the candy for free. She blew him a kiss, put the music magazine back, and continued down the sidewalk, just as a policeman rounded the corner and stopped at the stand for a package of cigarettes.

She congratulated herself on her policy of not using her photograph for StoneCorp. None of the papers had more than fuzzy shots of her speaking at tech conferences. The pictures were blurry and taken from far away. They were nothing the average person walking down the street could use to identify her. Most of the papers had had to make do with a written description, but even though they all pointed out her great beauty, it was quickly overrun by descriptions of her achievements and power. Veronica guessed people would focus on the technology and business aspects of her story, and assume a "beautiful, powerful technologist" was several steps in beauty below a "beautiful model"—when "beautiful model" might have been a more apt description for the actual Veronica Stone.

When she got to Paddington Station, she entered through the back-alley entrance. She stopped at a flower stall. There were three video surveillance cameras between where she was standing and the lockers, and she guessed there was at least one in the locker room itself left over from the IRA bombing days. She guessed that even with everyone looking for her, that nine times out of ten she could rush right by the cameras without anyone noticing until she was long gone. Video cameras in public places were notorious for only being good at catching the aftermath of a bombing or attack. No one was watching the literally millions of hours of tape to stop any crime from actually happening. It was too expensive and would take more man-hours than any police department on the planet could hope to offer. In fact, StoneCorp had been working on a face-recognition system that would have solved the problem. Luckily, the US military hadn't been willing to part with any of the powerful new technology, so it was locked up in some underground office at Strategic Air Command, probably until it was obsolete. Still—she'd been incredibly lucky so far—she guessed it couldn't hold on forever.

She picked a path directly underneath the cameras, keeping low and out of sight of their viewers. If anyone was looking, all they would see was the absolute top of her head. Even if the US had allowed England to use the StoneCorp recognition software, no software on the planet could match people by the tops of their heads.

Another camera hung from the ceiling over the entire locker room. There was also an attendant seated behind a bombproof plexiglass screen, his face buried in a racing form. He glanced up at her as she walked in, and then went back to his paper. This was the one moment where Veronica was most vulnerable. She had to get the locker key from the attendant. She just hoped her luck would hold out.

"Excuse me, sir? I need to get into my locker?" asked Veronica, with all the squeaky-voiced uncertainty she could muster.

The man didn't look up. "Name?"

"Moriarty."

The man sighed and swiveled in his chair to a huge ledger book on the counter behind him. He moved like a glacier, licking his finger between each turn of the pages, every muscle in his body letting Veronica know that he was being very put out by her request. Finally, he found the name. He left his finger on it and stretched across the tiny office to a wall covered in keys. In one deft motion, he pulled the key from the wall and spun in his chair, dropping the ledger book into the metal pass-through basket. "Sign, please."

Veronica let her hair dangle in her face as she signed. She guessed any camouflage was better than nothing. She signed "Molly Case" as broadly as she could, trying to conceal her normal handwriting in a series of ornate loops and broad strokes. She closed the pass-through. The man on the other side looked at it once and threw it back on the desk behind him. He dropped the key into the pass-through with a dull clunk. "Fifteen down, three up on the left. It's already been paid for," he said, sounding as if prepaid boxes were certainly something to be curious about.

Veronica laughed a little too loudly. "Oh, my Dad! I left my stuff here when I went over to France for the weekend. Lost everything else on the train. He really wants me to come home."

The man studied her for the first time, looking her up and down through the plexiglass. "I bet he does," he leered.

Veronica fought the urge to pop the glass with her hand. She couldn't give herself away, but even so, she wasn't used to being treated this way by poor dirty old men. She wanted to flash her eyes at him—"Do you know who I am? I have enough money to buy you and your entire family. You will never see the things I have seen, and you can't even imagine the things that I've done!" But she kept up her appearance. She backed away, giggling shyly as if she didn't know what to do in the face of such an obviously powerful personage.

She found the locker and slid the key into the lock. Inside was an expensive leather backpack. She unzipped it and glanced inside. There were two of Veronica's phones, a pouch full of money, and a tiny Paddington Bear stuffed animal. She smiled and patted the bear's head.

"Oi! Come over here, missy!" yelled the locker room attendant.

Veronica slung the backpack over her shoulder and sauntered back to the man. She could try to run, but she didn't know what he wanted yet.

The man on the other side of the glass squinched up his eyes and stared at her as if she were a particularly intriguing chip he'd just plucked from his fish and chips lunch. "What's your name again?"

"Why?"

"I'm the one asking the questions," he said, tapping his dirty index finger on the security patch that was sewn on to his jacket.

"Molly Case."

"Where are you from?"

"Canada."

"Where?"

"Vancouver."

"I got a niece in Vancouver. She can't get enough of those Grizzlies," said the man, leaning forward in anticipation of her next answer.

"It's a long drive to Memphis." Luckily, Veronica knew the basketball team had moved. She realized it was a cheap trick from the man trying to get her to mess up. She wasn't going to mess up. She guessed if he was going to try to trick her again, it would be with a sports reference. From the racing form and his general demeanor, she guessed he was the kind of misogynist who could never imagine a pretty woman had any knowledge of sports at all.

The man looked disappointed. "Indeed. Shame they had to go."

"Well, basketball never really seemed to belong in Canada. Too much ice."

"So, you're a hockey fan?"

"I'm more into curling."

"Right." The man studied her suspiciously one more time. "I don't know you from somewhere, do I?"

"I don't think so. Maybe just walking along on the street. Do you ever go to the drum circles for peace in Hyde Park?"

The man snorted. "Right." An old woman rounded the corner and made her slow way toward his window. The man put his head back down in his paper and waved his hand at Veronica, apparently unwilling to let the next customer see him actually doing any work. "Okay. Off with you!"

Veronica walked away as slowly as she could will herself to do. She'd dodged a bullet. She guessed he would call the police just to make sure, but he'd definitely recognized her. He still wasn't matching her face with the terrorist reports. It would come to him soon enough.

She would have to hide out for a while.

42

VERONICA WALKED HALFWAY across the city to get away from Paddington. Then she lay low for several hours in a small corner pub, her face buried in a philosophy textbook she'd snatched from another table, her wrist looped protectively through the straps of the backpack. It was dark and empty. There was one man sitting at the bar nursing his cider and another sitting at a corner table reading a paper. The bartender seemed to be engrossed in cleaning the pilsner glasses when she walked in. She sat at a table in the back. She lay her face down on the table and dozed a little, trying to catch up on some rest while she had the chance, anonymous among other exhausted young people studying for their exams. She lost track of time and had a waking dream of being chased down a hallway, Sergei alive and on her heels, waving a machine gun and screaming in some language she couldn't understand.

When she woke up, she was even more exhausted than before, but she knew her body needed at least that little bit of rest if she was going to be able to make it all the way. She bought a cup of tea and a scone. The minute she paid, her stomach exploded in rumbles. She couldn't remember the last time she had eaten. As she walked back to her table, she caught the eyes of the young men at the table next to her tracking her from the till all the way back to her seat. At first, she was worried they had recognized her, but then she remembered her chopped hair and the way she was dressed. She struck up a conversation with them. They were a couple of flirty university boys, lost in a textbook on basic computing. She asked some foolish questions about computing that she knew they would know the answers to until they were all sitting at the same table, thick as thieves. At one point, two policemen stuck their heads in at the entrance, but they didn't even look twice at her. The boys were already leaning in closely, each of them trying to win her over. To a stranger, she probably looked like the girlfriend of one of them.

Eventually, she hitched a ride with a vanload of the boys' friends who just happened to be going to a music festival near where Alex's estate was (she'd seen the poster on a wall near the till when she got up to refill her tea, and had kept wistfully repeating the names of the main bands until one of the boys offered to try to sneak her in along with them—once again, luck seemed to be inexplicably on her side—if she'd believed in God, she would have thought He was looking out for her). She pretended to smoke the joints offered to her and nursed a beer until they were getting close to Alex's. Then she feigned a horrible bout of car sickness, going so far as to stick her finger down her throat to throw up so they'd stop assuring her she'd feel better once they got to the concert. She apologized and had them drop her off at a farm a few miles from the concert. It was dusk. The gray sky was bruising into a dark purple. It would be dark soon. Unfortunately, this would be when anyone guarding Alex would be expecting her. But the cover of darkness was really the best chance she had.

She pulled her jacket tighter against the chill, and patted the backpack to make sure she hadn't somehow lost the phone. Then she trooped her way across the wet fields, scattering the sheep out of her way as if she crossed this field every day. A helicopter passed low overhead. She waved. It buzzed along on its way, chop-chopping through the damp air. If it was looking for her, or had recognized her, she guessed it would have circled back for another pass before calling in the reinforcements.

At the edge of Alex's estate was the ruined ring of an old fairy fort. She climbed to the top of it. Down in front of the house, there were dozens of black vehicles parked in the driveway. Groups of men were walking the perimeter and up and down the driveway, shining bright yellow flashlights into the darkness. A helicopter fluttered by. They certainly were not trying to take any precautions as far as keeping a low profile. Consequently, they either were trying to set up a trap, or the man in Paddington had called and said Veronica Stone was on her way. Maybe the police thought she'd just give up the minute she saw the amount of force blocking her from getting to Alex. They clearly hadn't read any profiles on her.

A lucky mist floated in from the moors, hanging low in the grasses and weeds. She skirted down the hillside to the ruined old stone fence. Alex had shown her a door here once. It was a secret passage into the house, used by one of the former men of the house to be able to sneak out and have his way with the local peasant girls. Alex had played knights and dragons in it as a child. Veronica crouched and looked around her. She saw no one, and heard nothing but one lonely owl.

She pulled away a wrapped pile of scrub and brush. The door was still there, unlocked. On the other side, the police might be waiting for her, but she doubted Alex would have knowingly helped them keep her out. On the rainy afternoon he had shown it to her, after they'd been caught by a thunderstorm picnicking out in one of his farthest fields, he had told her that only he and Geoffrey, and now she, knew of the passage's existence. She took a deep breath and opened the door.

Various old plastic flashlights lay piled in the entranceway, left over from Alex's childhood playtimes. There were also a couple of rusted beer cans and rain-sodden cigarettes. A rotting toy bear hung from a noose above the entrance. She tried to will her eyes farther into the darkness. All she could sense was dust and cobwebs and sodden earth. No one was waiting for her inside.

She shook several of the flashlights until one sputtered to faint life. Then she made her way down the passage. She held one arm in front of her face to knock down the immense curtains of cobwebs, using the backpack as a makeshift shield. She had to hunch her shoulders to keep from banging her head on the intermittent beams holding up the earthen roof. She couldn't see more than a foot or so in front of her. Dust and moths fluttered in the beam of her light. Still, she heard nothing.

Finally, she reached the black iron cage that blocked the tunnel from a door leading into Alex's bedroom. The lock was broken, held closed by only a frayed gold curtain tieback. She untied it and opened it slowly. Even so, to her, it seemed to scream impossibly loud. She waited for the soldiers to come bursting through the soil above her.

After waiting until she was as sure as she could be that she hadn't attracted any attention, she slipped through the bars and opened the big wooden door to the house.

"Stand where you are," said a man's voice, its English accent commanding authority.

Veronica held her hands above her head. "Geoffrey, I'm here to help." Alex's butler was standing in front of her holding a large-barreled pheasant gun. The strain of the past few weeks was evident in the old man's face. She wondered how she looked to him.

"You've tried to kill Master Alex and the American president."

"I know it looks like that—but do you really think I would? You've known me for a long time, Geoffrey."

The old butler nodded. He faltered, then pulled the gun back up. "I should turn you in to the police."

"Do I seem capable of all this?"

"Capable? Of course."

"But are you always warning Alex about me?"

Geoffrey blushed. "I don't do—"

"Don't worry. Alex tells me—I like that you look out for him. You always tell him I look at everything from the standpoint of how I can get the most personal gain."

"True."

"What on Earth do I have to gain from this?" exclaimed Veronica in fatigue and exasperation.

Geoffrey thought for a moment, then lowered the gun. Alex was lost in the sheets on the bed behind him. His pale face shown in the lamplight. The room was otherwise empty. "What are you going to do for him?"

Veronica rushed past him to the bed, slinging the backpack off her arm in one smooth motion. "Will the soldiers come in here?" she asked.

"They're not allowed into this room. Alex's family have been very strict on that, even though they're already circling over who gets the estate like a murder of old crows. No one knows of the old adultery passage except the three of us."

"That's why you were waiting for me here."

"I knew you'd be along eventually," said Geoffrey, smiling.

Veronica sat down on the edge of the bed and ran her fingers through Alex's thin hair. It was falling out in clumps. Angry pink blotches of scalp showed through like blots of strip mining on a hillside. His skin was peeling as if he'd been burned. "I'm going to need some time alone with him."

Geoffrey squared his shoulders. "I'm staying—but no one else should be in to bother us."

"Alex," she whispered in Alex's ear. She saw movement but he didn't answer. "I'm here, you're going to be all right." She kissed him gently and opened the backpack.

43

THE MEN OF Bravo Company worked around the inside of the concrete satellite bunker, cataloguing everything they found in this strange outpost in the middle of a South American jungle. They were under strict orders not to touch anything after the initial assault. The flash-bangs had only scorched some of the aluminum cabinetry. Everything else was just as they had found it, though there was nothing particularly calming in that.

The squad leader stood in the center of the bunker looking at the strangest thing they had found. It was the desiccated skeleton of a man, once with very long hair and a beard. He was dressed in polyester shirt and pants, and had a plain white lab coat dangling from his shoulders. He was spread face down on the table next to a dust-coated chessboard. He looked like he had been in the middle of a game when he died. Captured pieces stood at either end of the little table, although there was no chair for his opponent. Several cobwebbed video cameras were pointed at the game and the prone figure. The rest of the room was filled with old computers and generators. Pen ink doodles of dragons and angels danced across every surface. A giant drawing of an eyeball covered one white wall.

"So, what the hell do you think this is, sir?" asked one of the soldiers, carefully diagramming the positions of the chess pieces in his notebook. "You think this is just some kind of bat-crazy experiment or something? Should we have gas masks on, sir?"

"So you feel light-headed?"

"No, sir."

"Then you're not working hard enough. Keep drawing," said the squad leader. He picked up one of the captured chess pieces from the table. It was painted, made of light wood, with scrap felt across the bottom—a piece that looked as if it had been clipped from a child's flannel pajama. He rolled the piece across his fingers. A knight. His favorite piece on the board.

Suddenly, a loud phone rang somewhere in the bunker. All of the soldiers reached for their rifles. It rang again. The soldiers looked around. The squad leader put his finger across his lips for silence. He put down the chess piece and drew his sidearm. So far, he couldn't place where the ringing was coming from.

The surrounding computer screens and movie cameras came on with a burst of noise and light. An overhead spotlight flipped on, illuminating the chessboard. The entire bunker filled with the incredibly loud bells and noises of highly amplified phone tones. The soldiers crouched as if they could duck the sound. The squad leader thought they were sitting ducks if this was cover for some sort of attack.

One of the last computer screens turned on. He looked up at it. A beautiful, dark-haired woman who could only be Veronica Stone was staring out from the screen, holding a wide-eyed corpse, its eyes open and tearing, a silent groan emanating from its lips. Veronica's eyes practically burned with concern and determination. The squad leader thought she was staring right through him, as if she could see him through the miles, see right through him to the bottom of all he was. For all he knew, she probably could. Then the lights, cameras, and screens snapped off as quickly as they had come on.

In the deafening silence and darkness, only the last screen with Veronica and the corpse was still on. Veronica was gone. The corpse's face was already starting to flush, as if it were a flat balloon that could soon be blown up into a living, breathing man. The squad leader looked closer at the screen. Next to the rapidly improving man were two high-tech cell phones and a note written on lined yellow paper. A phone number was written across the top. Below that, all it said was, "For the Monroes—As fast as you can."

44

Alex's eyes looked up at Veronica with sheer relief. He could feel himself getting better. He didn't understand what had just happened and was still too weak to ask. She smiled down at him and gently rubbed his head. She could feel heat coming off of him again. He felt alive again. She looked up at Geoffrey who was in a total state of shock. He looked at her and smiled so broadly she thought he was going to hug her.

"He'll be okay now." She put one of the phones in an overnight bag and handed it to Geoffrey. "You must make sure this gets overnight to the president immediately." He nodded and, without asking any questions, he rushed outside to give the phone to the group of soldiers and policemen.

Alex had fallen asleep. She looked down at him and smiled. He looked like a sleeping child, no worries or cares in the world. He must sense that he's going to be okay now, she thought to herself.

"You're going to be just fine now, my love." His eyes didn't open, and she figured that now was the time for him to sleep. She knew he was going to be okay, and she had a lot of work to do. She had to get back to Boston and find out if StoneCorp had been leveled or not. She had to find out how her sister was doing, and she had to clear her name. The long fight was nowhere near over; only Alex's was over.

She stood up and opened the door to the secret escape. She knew she couldn't walk out the front door. She'd never be able to clear her name if she was captured now. As long as she knew that Alex and the president were going to be all right, the pressure of time was gone. She looked back at Alex, happy to see him looking better. Just as she was about to enter the secret escape, Geoffrey opened the door.

"Wait! Ms. Stone!" he yelled and ran over to her. "You must go quickly, they're right behind me. You don't have much time." He leaned over and gave her a slightly cold English hug. "You saved his life. In my book you are a savior."

She smiled and disappeared through the door. Geoffrey quickly moved the bookcase in front of it so he could give her time to get away.

45

Alex got off the single-car train and climbed the rest of the way into Saint Jean Pied de Port, passing through its ancient stone houses and over its rounded paving stones. The town itself looked like a fortress, surrounded by a high stone wall where Alex could imagine archers looking down on him, watching his approach, and waiting to cut him down in a rain of arrows.

The shopkeepers in the doorways watched him walk past. He had completely recovered from whatever the illness had done to him. He felt good, and the mountain air scoured through his lungs as if he'd never used them before. He'd given up smoking, and he'd started working out. He felt as if he'd been given a second chance.

He walked into the tiny café on the corner next to Saint Barnabas Cathedral. The café was empty except for a woman behind the counter resolutely stacking oranges into something resembling a tremulous pyramid. A beautiful young woman sat at one of the bar stools near the back, watching the small television above the bar. Her hair was bleached bright blonde, with red highlights strung through it. In the sunlight through the window, she looked like one of the angels from the neighboring cathedral's roof, if it had flown down and landed in the café.

He could hear the television talking about the American president's amazing recovery, and saw the president and his family waving to a crowd outside the White House.

Alex walked up to the woman and put his fingertips on her shoulder. "Hello."

"So you found me?" asked Veronica, a warm smile on her face as she looked up.

"Geoffrey gave me your note after I recovered. I want to thank you."

"For what?"

"For saving me," said Alex, slipping onto the stool next to her.

Veronica looked down at the paper she had in front of her. There was a long story on her and on StoneCorp. StoneCorp was under constant surveillance. The story talked about her involvement with Hiro and the president's attack. It went into detail about her struggle to save all their lives. The US government still wanted to talk to her, though. She felt she needed more time in hiding before she'd let them interrogate her. She needed some answers and a way to destroy the weapon she helped create.

"Look at my baby," she said flatly. "Look what I've let happen to the things I've worked so hard for. I can't even go back there. It's under lock and key."

"I know," said Alex. "There's some rumors over going into some Middle Eastern country for revenge, probably Syria. There's been some stuff on the news connecting you to

Syrian-supported insurgents in Iran. I'm guessing they'll use you as a good excuse to go and take some oil."

"Have they taken everything from StoneCorp?"

"Assets seized. Factory shut down. It looks like the government took its chance to take hold of StoneCorp's technology without having to pay for it. They're trying to use it to figure out how the bunker in South America works and how it's connected to your phones. It's all very top secret."

Veronica grimaced. "And Hiro?" she asked.

"No word—even the most basic information about him has disappeared off the Internet. And from libraries, bookstores, and newspaper files. I had some of my people look into it. It's as if he never existed at all."

Veronica nodded. "Mary."

"What?"

"Mary—they hired her company to erase all traces of Hiro. She's the only one that could have done it."

"She can't erase people's memories."

"She doesn't have to. Those who could remember him are the ones trying to make the world forget. Is anyone looking for me?"

"No. It doesn't seem so. They don't need you anymore. Either someone high up is protecting you, or they're planning to take you out quietly. We should probably go. They might have followed me here."

"I'm willing to take the chance for the next few hours. Why don't you go up to the counter and buy us a bottle of wine—we can take it up to my room. It's just down the street, a few houses away." Veronica smiled flirtatiously.

Alex grinned. He started to get up from the table. "So does this mean it's over?" he asked.

"Of course, my love—don't worry," said Veronica.

Alex smiled again and walked over to the counter. She could hear his clumsy bounce from the other side of the café.

Veronica took a crumpled piece of paper from her pocket. She smoothed it out on the table. It was covered with diagrams and strange doodles of skeletons and guns. It will be over. Just not yet, she said to herself. Then she put the slip of paper back into her pocket, patting it softly and wildly thinking about all the people that would pay for what had happened. She thought of Hiro and Sergei. She had made a brutal mistake taking on their project. She would never do that again. This time she would rebuild her empire and she would do it with the help of those she had come to trust and respect. The first step was to rebuild that weapon and then disassemble it. But maybe not before using it to her advantage. Oh yes, she thought to herself. Chapter One was over, now on to Chapter Two.

CPSIA information can be obtained at www.ICGtesting.com
Printed in the USA
LVOW070316040512

280322LV00001B/79/P